Best
{ BRITish }
Short Stories
2020

NICHOLAS ROYLE HAS published three collections of short fiction: *Mortality* (Serpent's Tail), short-listed for the inaugural Edge Hill Short Story Prize in 2007, *Ornithology* (Confingo Publishing), long-listed for the same prize in 2018, and *The Dummy & Other Uncanny Stories* (The Swan River Press). He is also the author of seven novels, most recently *First Novel* (Vintage), and a collaboration with artist David Gledhill, *In Camera* (Negative Press London). He has edited more than twenty anthologies, including nine earlier volumes of *Best British Short Stories*. Reader in Creative Writing at the Manchester Writing School at Manchester Metropolitan University and head judge of the Manchester Fiction Prize, he also runs Nightjar Press, publishing original short stories as signed, limited-edition chapbooks.

By the same author

Best
{BRITISH}
Short Stories
2020

SERIES EDITOR **NICHOLAS ROYLE**

S
SALT

CROMER

PUBLISHED BY SALT PUBLISHING 2020

2 4 6 8 10 9 7 5 3 1

Selection and introduction © Nicholas Royle, 2020
Individual contributions © the contributors, 2020

Nicholas Royle has asserted his right under the Copyright, Designs and Patents Act
1988 to be identified as the editor of this work.

First published in Great Britain in 2020 by
Salt Publishing Ltd
12 Norwich Road, Cromer, Norfolk NR27 0AX United Kingdom

www.saltpublishing.com

Salt Publishing Limited Reg. No. 5293401

A CIP catalogue record for this book is available from the British Library

ISBN 978 1 78463 235 9 (Paperback edition)
ISBN 978 1 78463 236 6 (Electronic edition)

Typeset in Neacademia by Salt Publishing

Printed and bound in Great Britain by Clays Ltd, Elcograf S.p.A

In memory of Clive Sinclair (1948–2018)

CONTENTS

NICHOLAS ROYLE

INTRODUCTION

IMAGINE IF WE had a high-profile weekly newsstand magazine, in this country, publishing a new short story every week. Americans have the *New Yorker*. Obviously we can read the *New Yorker*, we may even subscribe, but how often will we find a British author featured? Every now and then, sure, but the magazine doesn't tend to look very far beyond the upper echelons (British writers featured in the magazine last year included Hari Kunzru, Salman Rushdie, Hanif Kureishi, Pat Barker and Tessa Hadley). The *New Yorker* doesn't appear to feel any need to encourage emerging British writers – and why should it? That would be the job of a prestigious British magazine, like, say the *New Statesman*. I suppose we should be grateful that the *New Statesman* continues to publish stories at Christmas and, somewhat unpredictably, in either or both of their spring and summer specials.

The trouble with the Christmas double issue is that it carries both dates – the old year and the new. Was Kate Atkinson's story, in the 2018/19 Christmas special, published in 2018 or 2019? You might think it doesn't matter, that I should be less obsessed by dates, but you've got to have rules. Without rules you have anarchy. The 2019/20 Christmas special had a story by Lucy Ellmann. Three other stories appeared in the magazine in 2019: Daisy Johnson's *Big Brother* satire 'How to Win' in the spring special and Sarah Hall's discomfiting 'The Woman the Book Read' in the summer special. In the autumn books special, William Boyd introduced a story by Olga Nekliudova. Knowing of William Boyd's enthusiasm for metafictional trickery (remember Nat Tate?), I went online to find out a little bit more about Nekliudova and the very first link took me right back to the *New Statesman* and a section of the magazine's website devoted to the fiction it publishes, which, when I scrolled down, appeared to solve the mystery of which year its Christmas stories are published in. The Lucy Ellmann was dated 11 December 2019 and the Kate Atkinson 5 December 2018. Mystery solved. Except that a little further down I find an Ian Rankin story dated 8 January 2016. My collection of back issues includes the 2015/16 Christmas special, dated 18 December 2015 – 7 January 2016; it contains the Ian Rankin story supposedly published on 8 January 2016, so, in fact, mystery not solved, after all.

Still, I think we'd all like it if the *New Statesman* would publish more stories. One a week would be nice, please. The 2020 summer special came out while I was writing this introduction and I flicked through it looking for the expected short story. There wasn't one - or isn't one. But perhaps this is a matter for next year's introduction. Next year? Didn't I announce last year that this year would be my last, as series editor? I did. Concerned, however, that the series might be discontinued, I changed my mind.

I had already made most of my selections, for the present volume, before the arrival in the UK of Covid-19, but, crucially, what I didn't do was fetch a number of books and magazines from my office at Manchester Metropolitan University before the lockdown put them beyond reach. These were books and magazines that I would need to do as thorough a job of writing this introduction as I normally aim to do.

I did, however, have *some* of those books and magazines at home, among them *Wall: Nine Stories From Edge Hill Writers* (Edge Hill University) edited by Ailsa Cox & Billy Cowan. I loved this. The stories are good, it's attractively designed and it's short. Ultimately one story stood out. I liked how the absence of a conventional narrative in Sarah Schofield's 'Safely Gathered In' made you want to create one, or more than one, only for one eventually to emerge that was different from any of the ones you'd dreamt up.

Two more volumes of *Tales From the Shadow Booth* appeared. The editor is Dan Coxon and there's still no publisher named, but there's a website. One has to assume it publishes itself. Stand-outs (in volume three) included Richard V Hirst's 'The School Project' and Robert Shearman's 'I Say (I Say, I Say)'. Volume 4 boasts some great names, including Lucie McKnight Hardy, Gary Budden, Jane Roberts, Giselle Leeb . . . I could go on. In fact, I could just repeat the list of contents. The imprint page is dated 2018, which I assume is a mistake, unless in the world of the Shadow Booth time goes backwards. *Citizens of Nowhere* (Cinnamon Press) edited by Rowan B Fortune, an anthology of utopian stories, is distinguished by stories from Jez Noond and Diana Powell, who, in 2019, won the Chipping Norton Literary Festival short story competition with 'Whale Watching'.

I enjoyed original stories by Alicia J Rouverol, Mark Lindsey and others in issue 15 of *Route 57 Environs: Modern Natures* edited by Dan Eltringham and Vera Fibisan, part of a collaboration between the University of Sheffield and

The Hepworth Wakefield; new stories by Angela Readman and Regi Claire stood out in *Unthology 11* (Unthank Books) edited by Ashley Stokes and Tom Vowler. Threads and paths through life offered a way of connecting up the stories in *Somewhere This Way* edited by Rob Redman, the thirteenth volume in an ongoing series from the Fiction Desk. *Shallow Creek* didn't appear to have an editor credited, but it was a new venture from Storgy Books, in which the stories, by Tom Heaton, Daniel Carpenter, Aliya Whiteley, David Hartley and others, had to be set in the fictitious eponymous town.

Port, edited by MW Bewick and Ella Johnston, is a fascinating and cherishable addition to the editors' own Wivenhoe-based Dunlin Press catalogue. It features, poets, place writers and short story writers responding to the theme suggested by the title. My favourite piece was Sarah-Clare Conlon's 'The General Synopsis at Midday', about sailing to the Isle of Man. There were more boats, buoys and pontoons in Conlon's 'Warning Signs', in a flash fiction special issue of the ever-wonderful *Lighthouse* journal from Gatehouse Press. At the darker end of the spectrum, *Black Static*, from TTA Press, continues to disturb and unsettle. My thanks to editor Andy Cox and some of his contributors during 2019, including Stephen Volk, Tim Lees, Steven Sheil and David Martin, for continuing to shine their flickering torches into the darkness of the worlds both around and within us.

Cōnfingō Magazine is super-reliable. Last year's two issues included stories by David Rose, Stephen Hargadon, Justine Bothwick, Elizabeth Baines, Tom Jenks and Vesna Main. I especially liked David Rose's 'Smoke', but not quite as much as his 'Greetings From the Fat Man in Postcards' online at *Litro*. Highlight of *Structo*'s 2019, for me, was David Frankel's story,

'Shooting Season', in issue 19. The regular arrival of *Ambit* remains a cause for celebration and the fact I selected only one story from their four issues last year – Richard Lawrence Bennett's 'Energy Thieves: 5 Dialogues' from issue 235 – is a reflection of how many good new stories are being published in magazines, anthologies and collections, and online.

I very much enjoyed four debut collections: Jane Fraser's *The South Westerlies* (Salt), Jennifer Nansubuga Makumbi's *Manchester Happened* (Oneworld), Nick Holdstock's *The False River* (Unthanks Books) and *The Map of Bihar and Other Stories* (Circaidy Gregory Press) by Janet H Swinney, whose 'Washing Machine Wars' is a wryly observed tale of politely warring Turkish and Indian neighbours in suburban England and their years-long bouts of competitive cooking, gardening and household appliance acquisition. '"I don't know why they're called white people," said Aslan, one of Mrs Çelik's older boys, "because they're grey."'

From Valley Press came a science fiction anthology, the winner of last year's longest title award: *Science Fiction For Survival: An Archive For Mars, Terra Two Anthology: Volume One* edited by Liesl King and Robert Edgar. *Terra Two*, it turns out, is an online magazine hosted by York St John University. Down the A19 and right a bit, Catherine Taylor edited *The Book of Sheffield* for Comma Press's ongoing 'A City in Short Fiction' series. At least, I hope it's ongoing. There wasn't a bad story in this anthology. Leaving aside Philip Hensher's 'Visiting the Radicals', a novel extract, stories by Margaret Drabble, Geoff Nicholson, Gregory Norminton, Naomi Frisby and Tim Etchells were all strong, but there was something somehow more mysterious about Helen Mort's 'Weaning' that appealed to me. Etchells' *Endland* (And Other

Stories) took me back to his 1999 collection *Endland Stories* from Pulp Books, an imprint of Elaine Palmer's seminal small press Pulp Faction. The new volume combined reprints from the previous work with new stories.

Etchells' stories fizz with the kind of disruptive energy that animates the contents of I *Transgress*, an anthology of mostly previously unpublished work edited by Chris Kelso for Salò Press, which has also been publishing original short stories in chapbook format, which it calls, rather wonderfully, 'Flirtations'. Andrew Hook's 'The Girl With the Horizontal Walk' was one of these. Another chapbook, NJ Stallard's *The White Cat*, a beautifully crafted artefact, arrived from The Aleph, which 'designs and publishes rare and limited editions'; these are definitely worth investigating.

One of the highlights of volume 12 of *Bristol Short Story Prize Anthology* (Tangent Books) was Cherise Saywell's yearning tale of satellites, human beings and a dog, 'Fellow Travellers', while issue number 16 of *The Mechanics Institute Review* was, I think, the biggest and most handsome volume yet in that publication's history. Billing itself 'The Climate Issue', it features stories (and poems and essays) by established and emerging writers alongside MA/MFA students from Birkbeck. The project director is Julia Bell and the managing editor is Sue Tyley, who has a sizeable editorial team working with her. In this volume the editors have saved, in my opinion and talking only about the short stories, the best till last, with two very strong pieces at the back of the book, 'Gold' by Lorraine Wilson and 'This Place is No Vegas' by KM Elkes. Wilson writes beautifully about birds, and Elkes about life, death and ponds. Wilson writes about life and death as well, and bird baths, if not ponds.

Issue 11 of *The Lonely Crowd* was packed with good stories from Iain Robinson, Jo Mazelis, Jaki McKarrick, Susanna Crossman, Niall Griffiths, Gary Budden and many others. I had not previously come across *Mal*, 'a journal of sexuality and erotics'. Edited by Maria Dimitrova, its fourth issue, 'Real Girls', focuses on 'girlhood and agency'. Luke Brown's story, 'Beyond Criticism', appears alongside pieces by Natasha Stagg and Chris Kraus as well as poetry and illustrations. Simply yet beautifully designed, it is a sharp, intelligent publication. I hadn't come across *The New Issue* either, but that is because it is a brand-new publication, a subscription-only magazine from the *Big Issue*, edited by Kevin Gopal. Issue 1 featured a new story by Sarah Hall taken from her new collection *Sudden Traveller*. Another new magazine, which I discovered too late to think about picking either or both of the excellent stories by Martin MacInnes and Janice Galloway, is *Extra Teeth*, put together in Scotland by Heather Parry, Jules Danskin and Esther Clayton.

I enjoyed Michael Holloway's story, 'The Devil and My Dad', in issue 23 of *Open Pen*, edited by Sean Preston. The same writer pops up in *Still Worlds Turning: New Short Fiction*, edited by Emma Warnock for Belfast-based No Alibis Press, with an entertaining account purporting to be 'From Andy Warhol's Assistant, 1964'. It was one of the highlights for me, along with stories by Joanna Walsh, Eley Williams, Lucy Caldwell and Sam Thompson (I think I've stayed in his 'Seafront Gothic' hotel).

I read one story last year by a highly regarded author in a very prestigious magazine. In many ways it was masterful, but one thing bothered me. Point of view is handed around like cups of Earl Grey. Not a flicker of emotion was there, either, in this story of mortality. It's the sort of carefully written story that I have to force myself to finish reading. I find myself wondering what must such stories be like to write? What motivates the authors of such stories to keep going? They're very fine, but rather dull. And what about point of view? Is it all right to let it float around so much – or at all? If you write in the first person, you restrict yourself to that point of view, so why not restrict yourself in third-person narratives as well? At least within paragraphs, or sections. And yet, in at least one of the stories included in the present volume, point of view is all over the place. Maybe it bothered me, fleetingly, but there was something exciting about the story that seduced me, that made me think maybe I get too worked up about point of view.

Here's a point of view to end on. It's about the *Paris Review*'s announcement of a 'call for applications to our volunteer reader program'. The *Paris Review* went on: 'This is in anticipation of an expansion to online submissions after sixty-six years of accepting unsolicited submissions only in hardcopy manuscripts. (We will continue to receive and consider manuscripts submitted by mail to our New York office.) In this new iteration of our submission process, we hope to grow a far-reaching network of readers who will be responsible for assessing unsolicited submissions of both prose and poetry.'

Hang on there *un petit moment*. The *Paris Review* is recruiting volunteer readers to assess submissions?

It goes on: 'One of our goals is to equip readers with technical language and critical acumen (such as the composition of reader's reports) necessary for assessment of contemporary literary work. We hope that they will be able to bring these skills with them after their time as readers with *The Paris*

Review, particularly those who wish to pursue a career in publishing. Therefore, applicants at a stage where they feel they would benefit from such coaching, whether in a graduate program, recently post-grad, or interested in gaining a foothold in publishing, are strongly encouraged to apply. However, we will consider candidates at any point in their lives, in any location, so long as they are excited about the project of assessing new writing on *The Review*'s behalf.'

Alors, an exciting democratisation of the gatekeeper role at the *Paris Review*? Or they want you to go and work for them, virtually as editors, but without paying you *un sou*?

It goes on (it does go on): 'This is a volunteer position requiring *at least* 5 hours of reading time a week, which can be done remotely, with a commitment of at least six months. Hours can be completed at any time during the day and week. Interested candidates should provide a resume, cover letter, and a half-to-one-page reader's report on a piece of fiction or poetry published in a magazine or journal (not in *The Paris Review*) in the past year.'

I have probably allowed my point of view to be inferred, but I would be very interested to hear from anyone who applied, successfully or not. Lots of editors spend a lot of time 'assessing new writing' without getting paid for it, those of us who run small presses and certain little magazines. Is that the same or is it different? Is it, like the title of Stephen Thompson's story in this volume, same same different?

NICHOLAS ROYLE
Manchester
May 2020

Best
{ B R I T I S H }
Short Stories
2020

BEYOND CRITICISM

I

THE MAN ACROSS the aisle from Claire was no longer
reading poetry. He had put down the book and picked up his
phone, inserted one ear bud and turned to lean against the
window, hiding his screen from passers-by on the way to the
buffet car, but he had not thought of the way it would reflect
on to the window behind him, the girl who was sitting on a
low sofa and moving her hand between her legs in a room that
gleamed with the green light of California.

Claire had seen this sort of pornography before. In her
last days with David, when he avoided having sex with her,
she had asked him to show her what he watched when he was
alone, what it was that got him off.

But David said he didn't watch porn. Well, only very rarely.
Sometimes, obviously, but mostly out of anthropological interest. Honestly? Did she really want to see?

There would be no judgment, she insisted. This was the id.
Desire was beyond criticism.

Real girls was what David liked, women about the age of
the undergraduates she taught, when they were persuaded to
take their clothes off and masturbate on a sofa as part of a

screen audition which they hoped might win them work as a 'calendar model'. He liked to see their suspicion supplanted by arousal but never fully allayed, to watch the way the women surrendered to their own corruption, the dawning truth of their ambition, like it was, in the end, a relief.

This, she presumed, was how he saw it, though they never talked about it again after that night so she might have been putting words into his mouth. The man behind the camera in these videos liked to begin the series of crises that broke the woman's resistance by stroking her cheek before slipping a finger into her mouth to see whether or not she would suck it.

Before the man on the train had begun to watch pornography he had been reading a debut collection of poetry which Claire had been intending to buy for herself. Before he started to watch pornography on his phone she had imagined beginning a conversation with him; she had taught for six hours that day, the last of term, and the idea of reading for pleasure that afternoon, or ever again, was implausible; she wanted to talk and to drink with other bitter adults, to hear her own voice becoming improper, for hours and hours, until she was dead. Perhaps the man watching pornography had been teaching too, and what he was doing now was only a practical wind-down routine to get him back in the mood for reading poetry. To concentrate on anything these days required constant improvisation. After each orgasm he could probably read for another hour before he was tempted to look at more pornography. You could read a poetry collection in that hour. Perhaps she should be watching pornography too, her own female-friendly pornography, sensitive gangbangs, sympathetic ravagings at the hands of men dressed as soldiers, which she could monitor with her own single ear phone and ineffective discretion. Perhaps we could all court each other in this way now, revealing our trespasses in reflections which we were only pretending were accidental. This is my niche. Is it tolerable? We need never acknowledge the part of me that isn't.

He looked up at her and away as though the sun was in his eyes. Then he looked back and smiled. She was wearing a new dress and no tights; it was a hot Friday in May, and he had not been the first man to look in the direction of her legs that day. His bag was on the seat next to him, artfully obscuring his crotch. The girl on the screen stood to turn away from the camera, and pull down her—

'Is it good?' she asked him, surprising them both.

It was good. The man flinched backwards.

'The collection,' she said. 'I've been meaning to buy a copy.'

He had turned his screen off immediately and was blinking at her. 'Yes, it is,' he said.

'You didn't look like you lasted long before you put it down.'

The man gripped his bag and pulled it further over onto his lap. 'Oh, you know. Social media. Twitter. I'm one of the great distracted morons of the present.'

His smile was actually rather nice. You couldn't write off a man for looking at pornography: not unless pornography had completely turned you off from being heterosexual. You couldn't write off a man just for enjoying the degradation of women.

'You too?' she said. 'I seem to have forgotten how to read today.'

He put his bag on the floor and turned his knee to point to her.

3

She said, 'I suppose I should just download some pornography and have done with it.'

'Ha ha!' And then he said 'Ha ha!' again. He had scruffy hair and a big beard, was only a few years younger than her.

'Do you know any good sites?' she asked.

He did his best to put his smile back on. 'I mean, I don't know what you're into.'

She had kept her promise and tried not to judge David on what it was that turned him on, though it was difficult from then on not to think about the extent to which the other image he presented to the world was fraudulent, this man who was always judging other men, the sensitive NGO executive who had worn with complicated irony a 'This Is What a Feminist Looks Like' T-shirt on a stag do, who had read Irigaray and Butler, who had 'done the work', who cooked and cleaned, more than she did, and who liked to see women in their late teens as they were groomed by devious predators.

And then why shouldn't a man unzip his principles then zip them straight back up again? Surely that was what the zip was invented for, to have one's trousers on and off at the same time? Claire had tried to convince herself that the videos were probably staged in any case. That's how she had watched the videos, with David that night and afterwards one time on her own: forensically, analytically. The women were too pretty. Too pliable. But the optimistic tattoos some of them possessed – the cursive profundities so difficult to read, along one side of the ribs or underneath a breast, the cute little animals' faces, was that a *squirrel*? – they felt like the pointless blemish, the detail for the sake of detail, which conferred the presence of the real. She didn't think the pornographers had read Barthes. And the actors were very good if they were only acting pensively.

To try to neutralise the mood that watching these videos with David had established, Claire had acted out a role herself that night. She played the corruptee, going to her bedroom to get changed and coming back in an old tartan mini skirt she had kept for emergencies from her dressing-up days as an undergraduate. She was a sexy student who had been missing his classes. David had tried to get into it, tried to spank her, but he was too embarrassed. The id made its prompts and so did his knowledge of workplace harassment. He was worried he was failing another test.

Claire looked back up at the man on the train. 'I'm into, er, never mind,' she said.

He smiled, put his phone in his pocket and picked up his collection again. 'Thanks for reminding me I was enjoying reading this before I got stuck on Twitter.'

'You're welcome,' she said, and she waited to see if he would become distracted by Twitter again.

2

Before David she was meeting Patrick in a club in Soho, one of the famous ones, which his work paid for, he said, when he suggested meeting there, as though he had forgotten that the last time they met there he had told her that he'd been given a free membership for being interesting. Could that be right? Patrick was only averagely interesting, after all. Perhaps he had been deemed more interesting once but had to pay now that whatever metrics they used had ascertained that he, like everyone else she knew, had become less interesting. Perhaps being averagely interesting was more than average these days, and the median was now soporific. Her mother would have had a saying refuting this sort of despair. Life's as interesting as you make it. Only boring people get bored. But her mother's second stroke had stopped her from witnessing the news coverage of the Brexit negotiations, or seeing the way that her mother's feminist heroes were being vilified. Her mother had breathed oxygen in the days before the world had divided itself into so many incompatible good-and-evils.

Anyway, she had no issue with Patrick paying for a private members' club with his own money, if he wanted to, though it was funny to remember that their friendship had been formed while fleeing the police during a protest about globalised capitalism. It was the G8 summit in Birmingham and they were reclaiming the streets. As the techno lashed and the police closed in, they had bought speed pills from a dreadlocked hippy, swallowing them in spite of their mutual distaste when the hippy produced them by reaching down inside the crotch of his cargo shorts. After the police charged, and they ran, they found themselves kissing each other in New Street station, and when they got back to Oxford they stayed up having sex until daylight, their first and only time together. It had been the first time either of them had sex on drugs; they'd been amazed at how good they were at it; they were like professionals, they could have gone on for days. That morning they had taken their first-year exam paper and she had got a first and he a 2.1, after which they didn't speak for the rest of the summer, and after which Patrick lost all interest in political protest and illegal drugs for the rest of his degree.

She had thought about bringing drugs into her relationship with David when their sex life had become so moribund.

But by that time she was trying to conceive, and what might drugs do to a foetus? Perhaps the risks would have been worth the opportunity cost, adding to the once-or-twice-a-month vaguely around ovulation, which David often contrived to leave the country for. They were not making the required effort, though she was trying to. She suspected she knew what David was doing when he retreated upstairs. She sometimes turned off the music she was listening to and listened hard for very small screams of sexual delight. She had wanted him to bring whatever he did up there into the light so they could look at it together. To stop wasting his orgasms and bring them to her. He could degrade her if he had to, if male desire could only be roleplayed now that its evil had been universally agreed upon, if it could only be defused by exaggeration, by consensual pantomine, fetish parade. He could wear a black cloak and fangs and whip her if he had to. Did he have to? She feared he had been draining himself in the study not from desire but from cunning, a desktop curator of a low potency that was neither no potency nor enough to make a baby. His libido kept cool by a fan whirring in the inside of a computer tower.

Patrick was sitting in a corner of the upstairs bar with a glass of beer in front of him. He was looking at it with great concentration, and though his face was still as unwrinkled and boyish as it had been when she met him, the expression he was pulling would begin to put some dints in it soon. When he stood to greet her he went to kiss her on both cheeks but she held on after the first kiss and felt his restraint relax as she hugged him.

'Oh, Claire,' he said. 'Thanks for that. It's nice to see a friend who's not repulsed by me.'

7

Which she was only a little repulsed by. He asked what she'd like to drink and she ordered a glass of wine – 'No,' he said, 'let's have a bottle.'

She cast her eyes around for celebrities as she sat down – it was that sort of place. She didn't recognise anyone, though she was out of touch and a lot of the old ones were probably ankle-tagged and under house arrest by now.

'How are you? Where are we with everything?' she asked Patrick, but he didn't want to talk about that yet.

'It taints everything. I want to know how you are first. What are you doing in town? You're not here just to see David, are you?'

Patrick and David had never liked each other. Patrick knew David judged him: the centrist who lacked faith in Corbyn-era Labour politics, who argued during dinner one night that the diversity initiatives installed at his workplace were super-ficial and weren't making things any fairer. 'Are you an actual racist or just being provocative?' David had asked him, before Patrick put his coat on and walked out of the restaurant. Claire had stood up for the complexity of his argument when they got home and David had lectured her on how two pri-vately educated people could never understand the ways that structural oppression worked. 'What does that twat know about the working class?' he asked, before stomping up to the study and banging the door shut behind him. Earlier that morning, when they had been lying in bed together, Claire's app had pinged to tell her she was ovulating. 'Tonight,' he said, leaping up. 'I'm going to be late for work if I don't move now.' And then dinner with Patrick and the argument. The convenient moral outrage. She waited ten minutes then crept down the corridor. Behind the closed door she could hear the sound of a woman crying out in pain, and she listened to that noise for a few seconds before she burst into the room. He had his headphones on and was watching—

'What's that?' she said.

'What are you doing?' he said, startled.

'What are you doing? Are you into women in head scarves?'

'What?' he said, looking back to the screen.

'What are you watching?'

'It's a documentary about the occupation of the West Bank!'

He was thinking of such different things to her. What did it mean that at that moment she would have preferred him to be watching porn for men who were turned on by women in hijabs? Anything to show that living with her hadn't put him off sex for ever. Anything to taint one of his good causes and bring him down to her level, the baby-hungry function she hated becoming, the bourgeois woman willing to let her mind and principles be rotted by her hormones.

'I'm not just here to see David,' she told Patrick. 'I'm staying with my sister, taking my nieces to the theatre to-morrow, just going to wind down and walk around, see some exhibitions.'

'Good. I was worried you might be considering getting back with him.'

'Maybe I should. I haven't found anyone else.'

'You can't have been looking hard enough. Any single man would be mad not to want you.'

He was not convincingly smooth. What she had liked most about him when they made friends was his abrasive-ness, his willingness to argue against the consensus. But this was not a quality which would serve him well in his current predicament. Nor would any other qualities he possessed or didn't.

'Are you serious?' she said. 'I have my eye trained on every eligible model. It gets me into situations.'

She told him the story about the man on the train and how she had surprised him.

'No!' Patrick kept saying. 'That's brilliant. Well done, you.'

She waited to see if he would offer her the opinion that he *didn't really like porn*. Casually, as an afterthought. As men had offered to her before. Sitting back in their chairs and looking her in the eye with an unnatural amount of care.

'Do you watch porn on trains?'

'No, I do not. I'd be worried about my data plan. Look, do you really have to meet David later? Blow him off and hang out with me.'

'That sounds obscene.'

'I suppose I should feel lucky you haven't reported me to the sex police.'

'"He said, bitterly."'

'I am bitter!' he said.

'I know you are,' she said. 'I know.'

3

It was nine when she met David; she was half an hour late; each time she refused to acquit Patrick without charge another argument sparked and needed to be stamped out. He was prepared to forego his complete innocence in the abstract but not on a single specific instance of wrongdoing. Despite the rhetoric she kept hearing from men that they 'had to learn from women', most still had the idea that they had to be innocent to be loveable. Impeccable. When it was the contortions they made to convince everyone that they were blemishless that made them most ugly.

David, always frugal, had suggested a Pizza Express on the South Bank. *It's fine*, he texted, when she told him she was late but on the way. *I've got a book*, and she could picture it, something published by Verso that he would tell her about. Full of underlinings and annotations. What was happening to her to make her understand David's intelligence so negatively? That he read philosophy purposefully enough to summarise and argue with it and apply it to public policy should have been a seductive thing about him, so why had she once dreamed of him ejaculating dusty pencil shavings over a white conference table?

As Pizza Expresses went, David had picked a nice one; it looked out on the Thames, on the bankside tinselled with fairy lights. Perhaps, she thought, he had chosen the place to be romantic. She worried that the reason he annoyed her so much was because she still wanted something from him, still believed he was reformable. They were both thirty-eight years old and knew they could live together in something like peace; they had done so for four years in her long breaks from teaching, in amiable semi-seclusion, on a sofa together with their books or in their separate working spaces. But what had seemed civilised then was no longer the type of peace she wanted; she was ready to sacrifice peace, even though she loved the peace she no longer wanted. How unfair that he had only ever had to acquiesce to her suggestion that they tried for a baby, that it was he who had forced her to bring it up, and that the first thing he had suggested when she admitted that their relationship was floundering was that perhaps this was because it was too soon for them to have a baby. She had been thirty-five then and it was not too soon for anything.

He was sitting upstairs at a little table by the window, tapping a pencil against the book he had open. And he looked just the same as she remembered him, his hair at the longer end of the length he let it get to, his beard a bit thicker than it had been, but still tidy, and his face had not cracked up, she saw no great scars left by her absence, just the slight crows' feet and wrinkled brow that all sentient people their age had. He was a good-looking man, another unfairness. She watched him read something that disturbed him and he squeezed his brows together, scribbled something down. And then he smiled and let out a little laugh, and she remembered his sense of humour, the pithy accuracy with which he put down their shared enemies, and how she had loved him because of who he was, and not in spite of it. Even without a baby they might have been happy.

She was swilling that thought around her mouth, looking for the note of poison in it, when he looked up and saw her. His smile dropped for a second before he put it back on. That was understandable. She had probably not been smiling herself before he noticed her. But she smiled now, and he stood up and came out in front of the table and hugged her, and it felt natural to press their bodies against each other.

'Hey, how are you? You look great,' he said.

'I'm good,' she said. 'You look great too.'

'Stop being polite. You really do look great. Like a French actress. I don't remember that dress.'

'I only bought it yesterday.'

'I should be honoured you're wearing it first for me.'

'I'm not wearing it for you.'

His face fell. 'Of course, of course, how silly of me to say that. I don't mean to imply—'

'Calm down, David. I'm teasing you. Sort of. Let's sit down. I'm sorry I'm late.'

'Yes. Patrick's having an emergency?'

'Yes, a little bit.'

'What is it?'

'Oh, let's not waste our evening talking about that.'

'He's not?'

'What?'

'Well, all this Me Too stuff. I wouldn't put it past him.'

'Let's not start on Patrick. You've always hated him.'

'Hate's a strong word. I just think he's an arrogant, Eton-educated twat.'

'But for you *twat* would always follow the words "Eton-educated".'

'With good reason. Have you been watching the news? I suppose I might give George Orwell a break.'

'You must remember Patrick didn't enrol himself there.'

'Must I? Who says I must?'

'Anyway,' she lied, 'it's nothing like that.'

When the waiter came, David showed him a voucher he had downloaded to his phone, two for one pizzas, which the waiter said he would take later, and then David ordered the cheapest bottle of red without consulting her beyond the colour, as though there was nothing to consult, which was something else she liked about him, his common-sense stinginess.

She refilled her glass when he was half through his and topped up his as an afterthought. They had navigated past Patrick's danger to women, and now David was talking to her earnestly about the work his NGO was doing, and about his new promotion to head of strategy, and why was it, she wondered, that she had lied to David about the circumstances of Patrick's current crisis?

'So,' he said, eventually, 'what about you? Any news? Are you seeing anyone?'

There had been a Victorian a year ago. A Romantic the year before. They gave her injured looks when they passed her on the corridor. And there was a lesbian colleague she wondered about sometimes.

'Do you fancy her?' he asked.

'Look at your eyes light up. No, not really. I think she's attractive. I like her company. I wonder how she feels about me sometimes. But, anyway, I haven't given up on the conventions of a heterosexual life yet. On motherhood.'

He looked away and changed the subject. 'You don't mind Pizza Express, do you? I don't eat out that much these days. I didn't know where to suggest.'

'It's fine,' she said. 'You picked a nice one.'

They looked out at the Thames together. The tourists walking past made her think of the city breaks they had taken together to coastal cities, the waterside restaurants, the swimming, the reading, the galleries.

'I seem to remember the Tate Modern's open late on a Friday,' she said.

'We could be two tourists sightseeing.'

They watched the river, thinking what she thought were the same thoughts. The waiter showed a couple of young men to the table next to theirs.

'So,' she said. 'It sounds like you're not dating if you're never in restaurants.'

'Well, yeah, my Tinder days are over, anyway.'

'You were on Tinder?'

'Aren't you?'

'No. Can you be on Tinder at our age?'

'Of course. Though maybe it's different for a man. Women probably enter an older age-range than men do with women.'

'Women probably do. Men probably do. Which did you do, David?'

'You know. A couple of years above. A few years below.'

'A couple and a few.'

'Well, anyway. I didn't like the thing. It felt artificial. The conversations could be hard work.'

'Hard to find women who cared about changing the world?'

'Don't be sarcastic. It was hard to find women who were curious about the world, who thought about it much at all. I certainly never met anyone like you.'

'I'm sorry. I didn't mean to sound sarcastic.'

'Don't become cynical.'

She smiled. 'The world offers provocation.'

'I can't argue with that.'

'These dates you went on. Did they never lead to sex?'

'They sometimes led to sex.'

'Despite the conversation.'

'In spite of the conversation.'

She realised she wanted him to tell her about them. Perhaps somewhere private. 'One-night stands?'

'Er, yeah. Sometimes two- or three-night.'

'Sounds fun. And being single doesn't tempt you back there?'

He looked down. 'Ah, well.'

'Oh?'

'I've sort of been seeing someone.'

She had been curling her hair with her right hand and she gently returned it to rest on the table. 'Oh. Good. For you.'

'Yeah, thanks.'

'Who is she?'

'Someone I met during the council elections. We ended up door-knocking together.'

'Right.' She pictured the sort of shouty Corbynite she saw on Twitter. Down with capitalism. Good and evil. The right opinions, those which she shared, theoretically: David would get bored of her. 'What's she called?'

'Isla.'

Which ruined the image. Now she was thinking of the Australian actor, those dark eyes and long red hair, a woman anyone would want to . . .

'Is she . . . Australian?'

'British.'

'I see. I was thinking of Isla Fisher.'

'Oh, no. She's Ailah. A-i-l-a-h.'

'I see. Interesting spelling.'

'Yeah.'

'Is that . . . Scottish?'

'It's a Pakistani name, I guess.'

'Ah. It's a Pakistani name. Of course.'

'*Of course* it's a Pakistani name?'

'Tell me about her. Tell me about Ailah.'

'If you change your tone I will.'

She took a breath. 'I'm sorry if I seem combative, David. I don't mean to be. I'm interested though. Who's Ailah?'

'Like I said, I met her doorknocking. She's a party member, an activist.'

'Is she our age?'

'Yeah, a bit younger.'

'Right.' She wasn't going to ask.

But he couldn't resist. 'She's not far off thirty.'

'Not far *off*?'

He had not been drinking but now obscured his face with his wine glass and poured some more for both of them when he put it down. Not *far off*. He hadn't even been able to say *nearly*. Was he really bragging to her?

'And what does she do?'

'She's a social worker.'

'A Muslim social worker.'

'What does that *tone* mean? What is wrong with that?'

'Everything is *right* with that. Who doesn't love a social worker?'

'I doubt you know any.'

'As close friends? You're right. It's my failing. I'll go and find a social worker to marry straight away.'

'Oh, come on.'

'Does she wear the hijab?' she asked.

'What has that got to do with anything?'

'Nothing. I'm just curious. It just helps me imagine what kind of Muslim she is, what kind of woman she is.'

'Oh, really? A head scarf would tell you what kind of *woman* she is?'

'Does she wear the hijab?'

'None of your business.'

'Are you going to convert?'

'Listen to yourself. I'm an *atheist*. Anyway, none of your business.'

'This is so typical of you. Everything's an authenticity

17

contest. Well, congratulations. You're at the centre of things now. It's a good job you got away from me before I forced you to make me pregnant. Imagine, I could have given birth to someone as boring as us.'

The two men on the table next to them were glancing over at them without moving their heads.

He reached over the table and touched her hand. 'I really am sorry that didn't work out. I know how hard it was for you.' He was speaking as if to a difficult child on public transport.

'I knew what you were doing up there, you know,' she said, 'when you were in the study.'

'I'm sorry?'

'Tunnelling away. Scraping out your escape route. Exhaust yourself on porn, then you can redeem yourself with a member of the historically oppressed, someone who can prove your credentials, cast my apathy into the starkest light.'

'Oh, Claire, come *on*.'

'Does she wear a hijab?'

'You're obsessed! No, she doesn't. And the idea that I'm with her out of some kind of virtue signalling is so fucking offensive. I'm with her because she's not jaded, she's not bitter, she believes in things, she's not defeated.'

'How old exactly is she?'

'I don't have to answer your interrogation.'

'How old is she?'

'You want to know? She's twenty-seven.'

'Well, of course she's not jaded! Of course she's not defeated! She hasn't *been* defeated yet. She hasn't wasted enough time with sanctimonious hypocrites like you.'

David stood up. He was gripping the edge of the table

and enunciating carefully. 'There were things that frustrated me about you when we were together, but I never realised how fucking reactionary you were. You sound like a fucking Islamophobe, do you know? No wonder you and your racist mate Patrick get on so well. I thought it was the decent thing to tell you in person about Ailah, sensitively, but I should have known better.'

And then he left. The two men next to her didn't know where to look but the rest of the room was looking straight at her.

She looked out the window and saw David striding down the South Bank. He had left no money to pay the bill. She couldn't stand to be there a second longer, but she had no cash to leave on the table, and so she sat and waited for a waiter to come near. The waiters had seen what had happened and were steering clear, out of fear or misguided kindness.

She caught the eye of the two men next to her. One of them smiled at her sympathetically.

'That man,' she said to him. 'Who called me Islamophobic. I used to live with him. I caught him once. Watching videos . . . Of Muslim women.'

'That's awful,' said the man. His partner nodded. 'Awful. Are you all right, love?'

'I'm not racist,' she said. But if you ever had to say that, then you *were* racist - everyone knew that. The whole restaurant knew what she was.

4

She paid for the pizzas which they hadn't eaten and took possession of them in two pizza boxes so she could at least give them away to someone who needed them. She was far too angry to eat now. David had taken his voucher with him when he left so she had been charged for both pizzas. He was the type of man who would have suspended hostilities to send her a screenshot of the voucher, if she had asked, but she was not the type of woman to ask.

Now she balanced the pizza boxes across one arm and wheeled her suitcase out to the lip of the Thames, breathing in and out, wishing she had a cigarette. When she reached the South Bank Centre, by the skate park, the top box slipped off the bottom box and landed flat on the floor upside down. She swore the correct amount for the situation. People looked at her and walked past.

A boy skated up as she struggled to put down the other box; he got off his board in a fluid movement, picked up the box and flipped it quickly upright. He was smooth-faced and as pretty as a whippet, his hair long and curly underneath a baseball cap.

He smiled. 'That smells good.'

'Thank you. Please have it. I don't want it. I thought I'd give them to a homeless person, but I expect homeless people are probably too drunk and high by now to eat pizza. My god. That's an awful thing to say. I'm worried I don't realise how much of an awful person I've become. You don't have a cigarette, do you? I'll swap you a pizza for a cigarette.'

He reached into his jeans and pulled out a packet of rolling tobacco. 'I bet you're not an awful person. You do sound like you need a cigarette though. Shall I roll it for you?'

'Please. That was an outburst.' She took a deep breath and made herself smile.

'Are you all right?'

'Oh, no. Getting there. Who knows?'

He rolled the cigarette in a matter of seconds, offered it to her and lit it for her when she put it in her mouth. He looked at her without any challenge, just curiosity.

She took a long pull, watching the skaters roll down ramps and jump up to skid across rails. 'Seriously, take the pizza, give it to your mates. I'll give money to the homeless people instead. I'm going to sit here for a bit and smoke and watch. You're all really good, aren't you?'

'They're *all right*,' he said. 'They're *OK*,' and he gestured towards them with his head. 'Why don't you come over and share it with us?'

So she did. The boys were gentlemanly.

'Why do you have all this pizza, miss?' asked one of them. She told them.

'And he just left you there?'

'Yeah.'

'What a total jerk.'

'Thank you. Do you think everyone there thought I was a racist?'

'You're too nice looking to be a racist.' That was her boy.

'I think there are many beautiful racists, actually.'

'Maybe in photos. But when they move, they move racistly. You can see it.'

'I bet he moves racistly, miss. We can spot a racist a mile off.'

'Call me Claire. How do racists move?'

'They scuttle. Like crabs. Not like us, miss. You never saw a racist who knew how to skate.'

They were a mix of ages, these boys, but the youngest was probably at least seventeen, and her boy might be twenty-three, twenty-four. The 'miss' they used was cheeky, flirty rather than serious.

Once the pizza was gone her boy offered her another cigarette. He took his hat off and shook his hair out, rolled the cigarette and handed it to her.

'You've been very kind,' she said. 'But I'm in your way.'

He lit the cigarette for her. 'You're not in the way.'

'I am. You get on with it. I'm going to smoke this over there and watch for a bit. Then I'm heading off. Thank you. You've made me much calmer.'

'No worries, miss. It was good pizza.'

She walked back to the railing by the Thames and leaned against it, watching her boy as he rolled down a slope, flipped his board up so he turned and rode its edge along a platform. As she smoked she caught his eye after every trick he made. He was good, though his movements on the board, all of the boys' movements, were not graceful. The way they contorted their bodies before landing, the balancing act so strenuous and fragile, the tiny distances their boards jumped that took so much effort to recover from. Reckless boys, so clamouring – she wanted to see them scrape against the concrete, get to their knees and pick themselves up. She could help. Her boy kept looking at her after each stunt he pulled. Every squeak and scuff. Perhaps, if he came over again, she would ask him if he wanted to come for a drink, she would take him for a bottle of champagne in one of the theatre bars. Could she do what they did, risk that leap, should she lean over and whisper something in his ear to make him lose his balance? Could she ever land that trick herself?

IRENOSEN OKOJIE

NUDIBRANCH

Nudibranch: soft-bodied, marine gastropod molluscs which shed their shells after their larval stage. They are noted for their often extraordinary colours and striking forms.

When the goddess Kiru emerges from the shoreline on the small Island of St Simeran, the third hand in her stomach lining contracts, steering her towards the sounds of the eunuchs surrounding a large fire on the beach, shrouded in an orange glow from the flames. The eunuchs are hollering, mating calls that are like war cries. Privates exposed, they stand in a loose circle rushing back towards the fire, beating their chests while the carrier pigeons fluttering above shed feathers on their bare skin. Kiru waits patiently on the side-lines. Her third hand drops soft-bodied, lightning-coloured seeds in the space between their heartbeats. It is Haribas, the festival of love for eunuchs. Every five years, eunuchs gather to celebrate, maybe find someone special, slits from their lost or dysfunctional penises tumbling in the dark corners of the heavens. Kiru steadies her breathing, watching. Salt water in her mouth leaves a tangy taste. Pressed against the night, she has already changed its shape into a mountain face that travels when white water lapping its lines evaporates. Fragmented moonlight gives proceedings an ethereal appearance. Mist curls and uncurls to reveal things seductively, slowly. Squashed Guinness cans sink into the sand. A gentle breeze passing through makes them hollow, unexpected instruments punctuating the main event. There are jagged mountains in the distance with handfuls of uranium inside, rumbling quietly. A bloodstained scroll is planted in the sand before Kiru at an angle. Huts dotted around the island on stilts have orbs of orange light piercing through tiny holes. Slick, moist fossils languish amidst stones, in moss-carpeted pockets, on cool rocks that anchor the flailing hands of a dawn. The eunuchs have clouds in their mouths; their motions are erratic, as though they'll fall into the fire one by one backwards. Then soften each other's injuries with white puffs of breath. They are burning the clothes they arrived in. The sound of fire races to meet bright molluscs in a space that expands and shrinks as things unfold. The carrier pigeons squawk, producing a din that sounds like black rain falling at an angle on the heads of stillborns, like a crow beak tapping against the entrance of Kiru's cold womb, like the screeching from going blind temporarily travelling through a tortoise shell in the sky, then falling into the water with shell markings that cause flurries, breaches and an undulating silence. They mimic the sound of a lung sinking, chasing an echo thinking it can catch it.

The mating cries of the eunuchs rise, travelling across the island to soft-bodied women emerging through the soil, the whites in their eye sockets morphing into irises of every hue. Mist bleeds red at the edges, seeping into a rough-hewn mountain that will use a sarong as a bandage over its mouth at some point.

The soft-bodied women uproot from all corners of the island bearing drunken tongues from wine spilled in the island's earth for seven days before proceedings. They rush towards the mating cries, nipples puckered, mouths softened, momentarily curbed by night dew. They are of the earth. Kiru has an advantage, being of the water. She bends down to lick blood off the scroll, blows her breath inside it to see how the cream-coloured paper will interpret it. Small orange blobs shaped like tiny micro-organisms shimmer on the scroll. She smiles; she has come to fall in love.

For now Kiru
Is a woman
From Algeria
With dark hair

swishing down her back and an easy, charming smile. She is wearing a black bikini. The blue shift over it is damp at the bottom, occasionally clinging to her thighs, bearing small trails of sand.

After the burning ceremony, she picks up Matthew, a scientist from a makeshift bar on the beach; light off the huts casts a warm glow on their skin. The soft-bodied women pair off with men who are still high from their ritual. There is alcohol flowing, a social lubricant that makes any gathering less awkward. Kiru assesses these women clinically, knowing their flaws will rise to the surface of clear water before breaking through. She listens for it. Matthew is talkative, eager. They laugh, carrying their drinks to the back end of the beach, deep into the belly of trees and land that feels joyously remote. There is the occasional rare white orchid and empty bottles of alcohol containing formations of past nights. Music from a stage at the far end of the beach filters through. Gulping rum, they are joined by iguanas eating sap from the pale trees that makes them dazed, and one-eyed water crickets from a tale man forgot to include in the Bible.

I'm so happy I burned the clothes I arrived in! Matthew flicks a petal from his Hawaiian-patterned shorts. Oh yes! It's liberating, as if a shackle's been broken. There is something in the air here. I feel like another version of myself. And the women fuck!

We can do anything here.

You are like Einstein, Kiru offers, pulling him closer. Like his equation of general relativity, mutating in the fabric of space and time.

Yes! he says, a look of wonder in his eyes at her, the surroundings, the possibilities.

I am $Gpv = 8\,\pi\,G\,(\mathbf{Tuv} + \mathbf{p\,n\,g\,v\,v})$.

He knocks back his drink. Matthew considers himself a eunuch because of his impotency. She tells him about the shape and girth of an invisible penis he will gain by the time the night is over.

Do you know what betrayal tastes like? she asks.

There is a burden to carrying salty alphabets on my tongue.

Matthew blinks up at her, heady, tipsy, a little confused.

Three hours pass. Kiru becomes annoyed. She cannot imagine Matthew reaching for the sound of bones tumbling in water, succumbing to being realigned in the frothing white, stark against it, brightly lit, and carrying mouthfuls of seaweed with stories of their own to tell. She realises she cannot love him. His receding hairline elicits sympathy, not attraction. His snaggle-toothed breathy revelations about science had begun to grate. He would yammer on endlessly until she strangled him on the shoreline.

Catching him unaware, she sticks her fingers into his chest, melting flesh. The charred scent rising up to their nostrils as a pattern of smoke unwinds from his chest, shaped like small nudibranch. She reaches through bone, a blueprint at birth washed away by the pumping of blood. Her fingers reach further in, finding his misshapen heart. She runs a finger over the muscle, over the pumping rhythm she has already caught with the damp folds of her vagina. He is hypnotised by the gleam in her eyes, the baring of her teeth, the lightning-blue lines of light running beneath her skin as though she is a circuit.

Her fingers grab his heart, pulling it right out. A sucking sound ensues, followed by a vacuum.

He makes an aaargh noise. It is surprise. It is relief. It is tender.

A carrier pigeon hovers above, shedding a feather that tumbles into the vacuum in his chest, skimming the last conversation he had with an air stewardess once on an easyJet flight about the weight of atoms. The feather tumbling in the dark will change colour once it hits the bottom. The carrier pigeon will report this to others in its flock.

Kiru finds a quiet spot to eat his heart, beneath a tree oozing sap, enjoying the shelter under its drooping, white, palm-like leaves. She is ravenous. His heart tastes of cigarettes, red wine, tiny bits of aluminium, of small murmurs machines hadn't detected yet. She polishes it off in four bites, licking her fingers clean. Then, she stands beneath the ghostly tree holding her arms up to the light; she sheds her skin.

Now she is
Afro-haired
Long-limbed
And brown-skinned

with the pretty face of a young woman in Cuba who runs a stall making small art pieces from food, who has a beauty mark on her face that changes position slightly depending on the humidity.

She finds Patrice smashing a lobster's head on a rock. He has an elaborate, cartoon-like moustache which tickles her funny bone, and a Romanian accent.

Are you enjoying the festival? Kiru asks.

Oh, yes! Very much. It's nice to be around other men like me.

You mean other eunuchs?

Well . . . you know, men who understand. I've been celibate for five years. Now I want to break that vow.

I am understanding. I understand that people who die through sudden accidents don't know they're lucky because it's quick. I understand when you destroy something you give it the opportunity to be born again.

I'll take your word for it! What an unusual creature you are. He is drawn by the smoothness of her skin, the beauty spot he cannot take his eyes off for some reason.

I can re-enact one of your strongest memories. Would you like to see?

Surely there's only one answer to that! He is smiling. His mind is distracted by the lobster dangling from his fingers, dripping rivulets of water onto his feet. Badly injured, the lobster is attempting to escape to the second shoreline the carrier pigeons have drawn with their beaks.

Kiru re-enacts his most indelible teenage memory: when he rescues a boy from a house fire. It was terrifying, exciting. He was driven by instinct, recklessness, adrenalin. He watches open-mouthed, astounded that she knows this. Her blue shift rides up her thighs a little as she performs.

Later, she discovers that Patrice's wife died five years before. Of course he is saddened by his loss. She is sad about this unfortunate turn of events.

She cannot compete with his dead wife or the memories she left behind that float and duck between his organs. She wants to leave a bite mark on his collarbone that he will stroke even after they've faded. She wants to breathe against the pulse in his neck as though she can tame its movements with her breaths.

I'll build a new penis for you from a current, she says. Not leave you with the old one that still carries the touch of your wife's fingertips.

He laughs uncomfortably, replying, When I was a teenager I used to dream of Pam Grier sitting on the edge of my bed holding a rocket.

She smiles at this. It is a sincere curving of her plump lips, which are intoxicating to him. Kiru wants to apologise for the things she cannot tell him.

If only you could hit your head on rocks below shimmering surfaces of water and not be fazed by the impact or your blood momentarily blinding fish.

If only you were how I imagined you to be.

What do I do with the disappointment of this? With the gap in between?

What do I store there for cold, isolating winters you will not be a part of?

She eats half of Patrice's heart in the early hours of the morning when the island is still asleep. She dumps the other half in the waters of the blue sea for a whale that has recently given birth in the Pacific, longing for the call of its young. She recalls the gathering of carrier pigeons swallowing patterns of nudibranch-shaped smoke from Patrice's chest, the shed feather turning to gold in the darkened vacuum of his chest.

Small, golden triangles rise to the surface of Kiru's skin. She glows in the hazy grey light of dawn, watching mist softening the lines of mountains for what the day will bring. The island's creatures create a gentle din to run her fingers over.

A tear runs down Kiru's cheek. She is lonely. She wants to fill the ache that grows inside her, that isn't knowable no matter which corner of herself she reaches it from, no matter whose footsteps she temporarily borrows to do so. It is vast. And she is like a small chess queen loose in the sky, clutching at shapes, at possibilities which amount to nothing as she opens her hand on the crash down.

After she sheds her skin, she watches it in the water. It is like a diving suit with a face, carried away by ripples.

She does not know what it is like to have female friends. She spends two to three hours interacting with the soft-bodied women who speak as if words are foreign objects in their mouths, whose lungs she can hear shrinking while the iguanas crawl around the island without heads that have vanished.

Late in the afternoon Kiru rests in one of several boats

moored on the island. She thinks of the stray items the soft-bodied women have begun to stash away: two fire extinguishers, a telescope, a high wooden chair with a dirty velvet seat, three propellers, and two cable cars. She panics with her eyes closed, as she is prone to doing occasionally. She is tired from the energy she expends prowling the island. Her tiredness results in strange visions that carve a path through the day. She dreams of a catastrophic darkness where everything falls away one by one, orbiting in a black star-studded distance above the earth with warped frequencies that result in it all falling down again in the wrong place: with the sea now a glimmering sky, the sky a weightless, cloud-filled ground, rock faces hiding in caves, mountains made of the island's creatures leaking tree sap, trees uprooted in panicked flight, alcohol bottles filled with new weather shot through with spots of ice, eunuchs emerging from a fire charred, offering to hide bits of their lives in shed skin. When light from the black star-studded space above the earth threatens to split her head in two, Kiru sees herself sitting on top of the mountain of island creatures eating fossils one by one, but she knows this will not do. She clambers out of the boat.

By the time she finds Ray from Madagascar fixing one leg of the stage at the far end of the beach, Kiru is

A curvy Mediterranean
Beauty with a
Boyishly short
Pixie cut.

Amber nudibranch from the telescope lens have made their way to them but Ray has not spotted this. He is wiry, handsome, a little sweaty from his efforts. He has a brutish slash of a mouth. As if things had accidents there. Other men pass to wander the island's pathways, mountains and peaks. Some emerge from the beach huts with daylight waning in their eyes. By now the soft-bodied women, her competitors, are gasping for air between conversations, grabbing bits of sand that slide through their fingers.

Can I help you? Kiru tugs down her shift, watching Ray's head.

No, thanks. Don't move, though, he instructs. Somehow you standing there is making this task more bearable.

Why are you fixing the stage?

He chuckles, throws her a bemused look. Because if I don't, some musicians among us might get injured.

You cannot fix all the world's stages. What do they do when you are not there to help? Injury is part of living.

This is true but I can't just leave it knowing people could get hurt. Besides, I have a soft spot for musicians. I think I may have been one in a past life.

What are you in this life? She kneels then, sinking into the sand, shallow pockets to catch odd bits of conversation.

The stage is even again. He dusts his hands on his backside. I'm a fisherman.

Something in her turns cold. A thin film of frost finds its way into her insides.

She sees herself dangling from a hook in the ceiling of his shop, bright purple. He is surprised that she has adjusted to the air of the shop despite the hook inside her trying to catch things that take on different forms. Despite the hunger she will spread to other creatures, who do not know what it means to truly be insatiable, dissatisfied. She knows to listen to her visions when they come. Her eyes are patient, understanding. He feels compelled to say, I don't know what instrument I played in a past life.

I can tell you, she says. She stands. Tiny spots of blood on her shift have dried to a barely noticeable decoration. She begins to make the noise of an instrument that feels familiar, that sounds eerily accurate, like a horn maybe, yet he cannot place it.

They hang around the stage area into the evening, watching a series of performances and fireworks exploding in the sky she imagines assembling into bright lava-filled tongues. Later, they go for a walk.

Tell me how you became a eunuch. She encourages, touching his arm.

Overhead, the carrier pigeons drop blank scrolls in different parts of the island.

I had testicular cancer.

I'm sorry for your cancer.

Don't be, he says. We killed it.

They hold hands. Intermittently, he tries to guess which instrument she mimicked.

He is unsuccessful.

On her walk back through the trees, the gauzy light, and beneath the knowing bold sky, Kiru eats Ray's heart naked, mouth smudged red. How could she place her heart, her future, in the hands of a man who didn't even know what instrument he was destined to play? His heart tastes like a small night tucked in the plain sight of a morning, like standing on a brink with your arms outstretched, like eating a new kind of fruit that bleeds. She notices the soft-bodied women are now in the white trees shrieking.

Over the next four days of Haribas, Kiru eats seven more hearts. By the time she heads back to the shoreline on the last day to sleep in white waters, she is now

> A *little girl*
> *Sporting pigtails, pregnant*
> *From eating the hearts*
> *Of ten men.*

She hopes to fall in love one day. For now, she hollers, a call that signifies the end of a mating season for her. A hallowed echo the mountains and mist recognise but sends panic into the crevices of an island rupturing; clusters of uranium erupt, rooftops of huts catch fire; life rafts made from felled trees dot the shoreline, waiting for something dark and sly to hatch on them; moored boats hold the soft-bodied women from the earth, only able to breathe for four days before running out of their allocated air. But the eunuchs are not dead. They are trapped on the island, dazed, meandering around without hearts wondering why the musical instruments buck in the water, why the carrier pigeons are now one-winged and blind, circling scrolls with guidance for the next festival. Kiru leaves St Simeran in this state.

> *It is*
> *An alchemy*
> *A purging*

A *morning sitting on*
Its backside
A *thing of wonder fluttering*
In the periphery of
A *god's vision.*

THE PHONE CALL

THE PHONE RANG. I'll go, he said. Normally he left the phone to her but they were cross so perhaps he wanted to put himself even more in the right. She remained at the table. This keeps happening lately, she thought. Oh well, what if it does? He came back: It's for you. – Who is it? – He shrugged: Some man. By the time *she* came back he had cleared the table, washed the dishes and was watering the beans – *his* beans – at the far end of the garden. She stood in the conservatory, observing him and trying to make sense of the phone call. A long summer evening, birdsong, everything in the garden doing nicely. But she could tell, or thought she could, that he was watering the beans much as she supposed he had washed the dishes: to be indisputably in the right. She could almost hear the voice in his head, the aggrieved tone. Not really pitying him, nor herself either for that matter, but because she did not want it to go on till bedtime, she walked down the garden and stood by the beans that had grown high and were crimsonly in flower. She smelled the wet earth. He turned and came back from the water butt with another full can. That's good, she said. He said nothing, but he did nod his head, and she saw that the job, which he loved, was softening him. When he had emptied the can, he said, One more.

She waited, watching him, thinking about the phone call.
Over his shoulder, as he finished the row, he asked, Who was
it then? Some man, she answered. He said he'd met me twenty
years ago, on that course I went on. The husband put down
the empty can and looked at her, mildly enough. What course
would that be? – The course you gave me for my birthday, the
poetry course in the Lake District. You said I'd been rather
down in the dumps and a course writing poetry in the Lake
District might buck me up. All my friends said what a nice
present it was. – Oh, that course, the husband said. And the
man who just phoned was on it with you, was he? – Well he
says he was, but I can't for the life of me remember him. I said
I could, but that was a fib. – But he remembered you all right,
enough to phone you up after twenty years. – To be absolutely
honest, I'm not even sure he did remember me, not me myself,
if you know what I mean. He said he did, but I'm not so sure.

The husband turned away to put the can back by the water
butt where it belonged. She watched, wondering more about
the man who had phoned than about her husband and his
questions. Did he have a name, this man? he asked, returning. Yes, he did, she answered. He said he was called Alan
Egglestone. But I honestly don't remember anyone of that
name on the course. I remember who the tutors were, and
two or three of the other students, but I don't remember an
Alan Egglestone. Then the husband said, Well it was a long
phone call with a man you can't remember. You must have
discovered you had something in common, to go on so long.
Yes, she answered, I'm very sorry I left you with the washing-
up. I couldn't see a way of ending it any sooner. I didn't have
the heart to interrupt him. Now the husband looked at her
as though, for some while, he had not been seeing her for

what she really was. Don't look at me like that, Jack, she said. I'm not looking at you like that, he replied. I just don't know what you could find to talk about with a complete stranger for so long. Perhaps you've been on his mind for twenty years. Perhaps he's been writing you poems for twenty years. I very much doubt it, she answered, beginning to feel tired, and not just of the conversation about a phone call, but, as happened now and then, of everything. Jack must have seen this. It was pretty obvious. Nobody else of his aquaintance lost heart quite so suddenly, quite so visibly, as his wife. I'm not getting at you, Chris, he said. You don't have to tell me anything you don't want to. I was only wondering what this Mr Egglestone had to say to you that took so long.

With the index finger of her left hand Christine pulled down and let go, again and again, her lower lip. She did this when she was nervous or puzzled or both together. It was a bad habit, annoying to other people, and she had often been scolded for it by her mother as a little girl. He told me he's got leukaemia, she said. He said he's probably only got three weeks to live. And she looked at Jack as though he might know what to make of it. But Jack shook his head: Don't give me that. You don't phone a complete stranger to tell her you'll be dead in three weeks. I never said he was a complete stranger, she answered. I said I couldn't remember him. And if he's a stranger to me, he says I'm not to him. He says we were on that poetry course together in the Lake District. And I'm in his address book. – You're in his address book? – Well there's nothing very odd about that. Why shouldn't people on a course swap addresses at the end of it if they feel it has been a special time? The fact that I can't remember him is neither here nor there really. And, let's be clear about this, it's not just me he's phoning, he's phoning everyone in his address book, he told me that at once. So he's into the w's, said Jack. Not far to go. No, he's nowhere near the w's, Christine answered. He's only in the b's. - So why, may I ask, did he phone you? - Because on the course I used my maiden name. I don't mean I told people I wasn't married. I used my maiden name because I thought that's the name I'll use if I ever get anything published. You never told me that, said Jack. Didn't I? she answered. I'm sure I did. But it's no odds whether I did or I didn't. You didn't, said Jack. And he gave her another look and went very deliberately back into the house.

Christine stayed in the garden. It was pleasant out there, quite like the country really, for a suburban place. Foxes came with their cubs in the summer early mornings and you heard them, the dog and the vixen, barking and screaming in the winter nights. And owls too sometimes, in the hospital's big trees. She stayed out, fingering her lip. She stayed until around her shoulders she felt chilly.

Indoors, Jack was watching the news. There had been another massacre. I think I'll go to bed, Christine said. He switched the television off. I'm sorry for this Mr Egglestone, he said, of course I am. But I don't see why he has to tell everyone in his address book that he's going to die. Aren't his family and a few close friends enough? And how many strangers does he have to phone a day, I wonder. He'll hardly get through them, will he, if he's only got three weeks. In the Wakelin household, Christine had become the authority on the dying Egglestone. He does have a family, she said. Three girls, to be exact. But his wife left him and took them with her when they were still at school. She said he was selfish, apparently. So he hardly ever sees his family, and he hasn't

39

told them what his condition is. And perhaps there aren't all that many people in his address book, perhaps half of them are crossed out dead, they are in ours, and perhaps it's the old address book that his wife left behind when she cleared out and she started another for her new life and most of the addresses in the old one, the one he's working his way through now, were her side of the family and her friends anyway, they are in ours, you must admit, there'd be nobody alive in ours if I waited for contributions from you. But how should I know? I've never met the man or if I have I can't remember what he looks like or anything about him. He told me he'd just been told he'd got three weeks to live and he was going through his address book in alphabetical order and he'd reached the b's and come to me. Now can we leave it at that?

In bed Christine reflected that you shouldn't let the sun go down on your wrath because one of you might be taken by death in the night and forgiveness be prevented. But it wasn't wrath, she decided, and really they had nothing to forgive. Anyway, Jack was already asleep. Christine lay awake trying hard to remember anything whatsoever about Alan Egglestone but nothing came back to her. Instead, with sudden emotion, she remembered somebody else on that poetry course in the Lake District, Steve somebody-or-other, quite a young man, a good deal younger than her at least, which he hadn't seemed to mind but had suggested they bunk off for a walk together one afternoon when there were no workshops and everyone was supposed to be getting on with their own poems quietly. He knew the way up from the old coffin road to Alcock Tarn and beyond into the dale that was known as Michael's Dale after Wordsworth's poem about an old man who was building a sheepfold up there but his son had gone to the bad and broken his old father's heart so some days he climbed into the dale and just sat still by the work in progress 'and never lifted up a single stone'. Tears came into Christine's eyes on that line of the famous poem, the poor father, the poor disappointing son, and the young man called Steve who had obviously found her attractive enough to suggest a walk with him to places she would never have gone to on her own.

Next morning Jack got the breakfast as he always did. Nothing much wrong then, Christine thought, and quickly googled Alan Egglestone, to see whether he had become known in the passing years, but nothing came up that could possibly have anything whatsoever to do with him.

After breakfast, in fact just as she was leaving home to do her morning in Oxfam, she told Jack that Google know nothing at all about Alan Egglestone. So it was a waste of money on him as well, said Jack. Christine saw that Jack knew at once that he should not have said such a thing. But she left the house with only a curt goodbye before he could apologise. On the street, walking quickly, she reflected that you should no more leave the house wrathful than you should turn aside to sleep wrathful because you might go under a bus and the wrong that needed righting would remain a wrong for ever. Then quite deliberately in the back of the shop with the other Tuesday Ladies sorting out the tons of stuff families send to Oxfam or Help the Aged when a loved one dies, she thought about Steve and Alcock Tarn and the steep climb beyond into Michael's Dale. It was early June and the shallows all around the banks of the tarn were entirely black and seething with quite big tadpoles and the word 'selvaged' had come back to her out of one of the poems Hardy wrote for his wife when she died and his dead love for her revived, the white-selvaged sea, the black-selvaged tarn. Steve said that in their density but every single one of them distinct, every one of them in the mass a separate possibility of further life, each driven separately into the next stage of its life, they resembled sperm, the selvage of the tarn was spermy. And she had thought that not in the least indecent or embarrassing. Her word and his were such as might occur to you if you suddenly saw something in a new light. And when they began the climb into Michael's Dale, out of the rock face there a rowan jutted, jutted out and at once rose up, out of rock, out of very little sustenance, out and at once upwards, as it desired to, and flowered densely, creamily, in its own peculiar scent, upwards into the air, out and up over nothing, over thin air, over a sheer fall, upwards. Steve insisted that before they began the climb itself, into the dale, they should get as close as possible to where the tree started horizontally out of the ferny rock and as soon as it could aimed for the sky. He took her hand and helped her, it was almost like rock-climbing, and when they got to the place itself, the very place of the tree's emergence out of the hill, he concentrated so hard on the sight, on the thing, on the exact nature of the phenomenon, she felt, in a nice way, quite forgotten, nice because she had the double pleasure of contemplating him, his self-and-her forgetting intense attention, and the rowan tree itself by which he was so rapt.

Back home, Jack had laid the table for lunch, which he never did. He looked very hang-dog and said at once, I'm sorry, Chris, I shouldn't have said what I said. I know very well your course wasn't a waste of money, you enjoyed it, didn't you, and that's all that matters. Yes, I did enjoy it, she replied, and it did me good. All my women friends noticed the change in me. I was well for nearly two years afterwards, if you remember. Jack cheered up. Now what are we going to do about this poor bugger Egglestone? he asked. Anything or nothing? Nothing, said Christine. What *can* we do? Nothing. – I mean, he didn't say he'd phone you again, to let you know how he was getting on? And you didn't say you'd phone him? No, said Christine. No he didn't and no I didn't.

So Jack and Christine Wakelin continued their own slower courses towards their separate ends. And the phone call meanwhile continued to work in them, separately. Christine had heard Alan Egglestone's voice and could not get it out of her head. Indeed, day by day it became more present there, more insistent. Helplessly she listened to its aftertones of terror and desperation. She recalled how little she had spoken, how he had scarcely given her chance to speak, and what could she have said anyway of any use or comfort? What did he want, except not to die? Did phoning alphabetically through the address book help him in the least? All she heard now was a man talking on his own to a person who did not remember him. She pitied him, but the dominant feeling in her on his account was horror. And she saw Jack watching her. She understood, and it sickened her, that they had Alan Egglestone in common. In bed or at meals or standing side by side doing the washing-up, one or other of them without preamble, as though it were the only possible subject of reflection or conversation, might wonder aloud about him, posing a question, rhetorically, not really expecting an answer. Or from Jack or from Christine came a speculation. Perhaps, said Jack, he was hoping for a miracle. That would be quite understandable. Say there are fifty people in his address book, well perhaps one of them had heard of somebody who stopped a leukaemia dead in its tracks, halted it, by some miraculous means, or held it up for a while at least and won the dying person an extra five years, or a year, even six months? You may be right, said Christine. Though he didn't ask me did I know any such person. She saw this made Jack wonder again why Alan Egglestone had phoned her at all. Then a day or two later, quite suddenly, she said, It struck me he was maybe going through in that methodical fashion to check there was nobody in the book he owed an apology to or who owed him an apology and he phoned to say there wasn't much time left for making amends. At that, visibly, Jack's suspicions really did return: Did he ask you that? – No, he didn't. But it has occurred to me. And later that same day, actually interrupting Jack who was talking about something else, she said, It's very wrong of him not to tell his wife and children about his condition. He must want them to feel bad when they find out he's dead. But nobody should be vindictive when they're near the end. Phone him and tell him, said Jack rather crossly. – I don't know his number. – There's ways of finding out. – I don't want to find out. I don't want to speak to him again. I don't want to hear his voice. I hear it anyway, Jack, all the time. I don't want him adding to it in the flesh.

Once or twice Jack said outright that her Mr Egglestone was a bloody nuisance. He'd no business phoning people up like that and spoiling their lives just because he was nearing the end of his. Everybody has to die, said Jack. Why is he so special? And he looked with even greater suspicion at Christine, so that she knew he believed there were things she hadn't told him about the damned poetry course. And in town one day, trailing along with her while she did the shopping, he asked in a false-casual sort of way whether she still had anything from that course, any old letters, poems, photographs, any souvenirs at all that might help her, and him too for that matter, understand why Mr Egglestone had phoned her to tell her he was dying. No, she replied, putting the liver and bacon in her bag, if you really want to know, I threw everything in the bin one morning about two years after it when I started to feel bad again. Everything I owned about that week – it was all in a folder with a ribbon round it – I threw the whole lot in the bin, I watched through the window till the bin men had reached next-door-but-three, then I went out and threw my folder in the bin so they would certainly take it and I couldn't change my mind. That's what I did with my souvenirs of the poetry course. You never told me that, said Jack. No, I never told you that, said Christine.

Day by day Christine saw Jack looking more worriedly at her. I know what he's thinking, she said to herself. Then three weeks after the phone call, to the day, another beautiful evening, down by the beans, he was watering them and she was standing oddly to one side, half watching, half not, and fingering her lower lip in the way he didn't like but had got used to over the years, he set down the empty can and said, Chris, you're not going funny on me again, are you?

VASHTI

I MET JOHN at the dance summer school. He was standing at the lower set of doors towards the bottom of the hall, half-in, half-out, as if he was hoping to be missed. Cherri was sitting on the empty stage. The other girls had left half an hour ago. When she saw her father, Cherri picked up her yellow rucksack and walked towards us, her chunky pink trainers squeaking on the old lino. The building had once been a theatre and now served as a community centre. As she walked across the hall, I turned to him. Mr Smithley, I said, unable to finish my sentence. I wanted to say that he should have been there earlier. It did something to a child, always waiting for their parents. But he smiled, as though he had been expecting me, not the other way around. I fingered my pendant, readjusted my neckline. I could not tell what he wanted exactly: men were often baffled by my fantastical appearance in a banal environment.

He peered at the name badge pinned on my dress. Vashti, he said. Call me John. He held out his hand and, after a second, I had to withdraw mine because it started burning. So, he said, looking around me but not focusing on anything. What will my daughter learn in the next few months? Barbara's Premier Touring Dancing School Makes Winners in the Essex Region, he read aloud from the promo poster tacked on the wall. Cherri waited, rubbing her itchy-looking ankles together. She looked nothing like John, with her red skin and fuzzy blonde hair. He frowned at her, like she was a fossil in a museum or something else that had once been interesting. The girls learn to dance and sing, I replied. And even if they don't go on to a career, they leave with our ethos to guide them through life. What's the *ethos?* he asked, baring small white teeth. Confidence, composure and commitment, I said. His confrontational manner implied great self-assurance or deep insecurity. I could not yet tell them apart.

Have you had a good time? he asked Cherri. I pretended to inspect my clipboard. Her bobbled ponytail bounced up and down in my peripheral vision. I'd noticed her straight away, with her white eczema gloves and thick glasses. She stood not so far from the other girls that it looked odd, but not so close that it was obvious they were ignoring her. During the breaks, she sat on the stage, looking at her flip phone. None of the other girls had phones. It gave her an air of privilege, along with her expensive professional dance clothes. But the clothes didn't quite fit, or match, in the same way that her skewed pigtails seemed to have been done absent-mindedly.

Before she could say anything, I put my hand on her shoulder. Cherri is a promising student, I said. I could feel her squinting up at me. John rubbed his neck, in the same way that she did. Well, I told you, he said. Didn't I say so? For a few seconds we were all connected, with his hand on her other shoulder, Cherri in the middle.

Over the following weeks, I introduced the girls to aspects of my spiritual practice. I drew them into a circle, made them link arms. Shut your eyes, I said. Visualising helps you achieve

your innermost desires. I examined each face like a tarot card.
There are no longer many respectable jobs where women get
paid to dance *semi-adequately* – time runs out quickly! I said.
Where do you want to be when you're eleven? Think, think!
Sometimes a girl whispered, I just want my mum and dad
to enjoy it. Is that all? I asked, trying not to look disappointed. Come up with better answers during break. I set
the alarm clock on the empty stage, watched them clump into
their corners. The hall began to smell of carbonated drinks
and beefy crisps, which I had long come to associate with
summer afternoons.

My interest in Cherri had grown, but she was suspicious
of attention. She had not made any friends since the summer
school started. Even the shy, quiet pupils who were drawn
to each other didn't speak to Cherri. Her self-styled outfits
suggested neither parental devotion nor a compensatory bur-
geoning teenage sophistication. I was not one of those teach-
ers who oversaw the classroom like an indifferent god. I had
derived most of my teaching skills from a self-parenting book.
When I looked at a troubled, lonely child, I assumed they
had a hidden talent, that they were waiting to be called, just
as dancing had called to me. I would like to see *you* dance, I
said to Cherri, whenever she stood apart, shuffling her feet. I
emphasised *you*. Once, she looked at me blankly. I *am* dancing,
she had replied.

I had divided the girls into houses named after inspi-
rational cultural icons. Cherri was in Britney House with
Taylor, Manda and Emily, three girls who had been the town's
carnival princesses in successive years. They wore matching
dolphin charms which they liked to raise in the air and jangle
at the same time. You should be in a different group, I heard

Taylor telling Cherri and two other girls, twins with chunky glasses. She made circles around her eyes with her fingers. Taylor was ten, but looked thirteen. She wore belly tops and liked to beat her round, rubbery-looking stomach for her friends' amusement.

In the third week, each house performed a short sequence that they had devised themselves. Cherri ran on after Taylor and Manda, the pigtails she was too old for beating on either side. She moved like someone in the late stages of needing to pee, flexing her lower half urgently, bent over, her legs stiff as a column. She was unable to keep up with the others, so she had started improvising. The rest of the class were laughing. She carried on, without looking at them. When the twins ran on, Cherri slowed down, her limbs heavy, her face occupied.

I came up behind Cherri while the other girls were changing. Her back twitched but she didn't turn around. She was sitting on her own, already dressed, her rucksack next to her. It was tough today, wasn't it? I said. She didn't reply. I sat down. It took me years to get where I am. And I'm not even qualified yet! Would speaking to your father help? We could all get together, talk about your *confidence*. She shrugged. You could try. She said it in a disembodied way, like a ventriloquist's dummy, repeating it with an exaggerated slump of her shoulders.

I had often seen Mr Smithley - or John, as he said to call him - waiting in his car for Cherri. He had never looked across to see me staring. But calling would feel like we were carrying on a conversation, because he had been on my mind since I had first spoken to him, his smile with its even white incisors, and the way my hand burned. After class, I scrolled through the emergency contacts list on my phone. My heart beat faster. My nerves were unexpected. I had to swallow several times for fear that I would run out of air when he answered.

The ringing stopped. John, he said, as though he was going to be the subject of the conversation. It's Vashti, Cherri's teacher? Don't worry, nothing has happened. I feel we need to talk about Cherri's confidence. Obstinance, he said. Confidence, I repeated. Maybe her mum would want to come along. She died when Cherri was five. I'm so sorry. Is there anyone she might have for feminine guidance? I waited, cupping my mouth. Fiona, my wife. Of four years. But let's say there are many ways in which a marriage can be over. It's hard to be on your own, I said, before he had to explain further. You're very supportive, Vashti. Sometimes the most potentially able students are the least self-assured, I replied. He murmured yes, maybe we could talk about that over dinner. I laughed, because I didn't want him to think that I was naive. It would be deeply unprofessional of me, I said, thinking of how I had never been so compromised as to say those words before and how I might never be again.

The walls of Bonita's were mounted with muddy macros of flowers. Candles in dimpled red jars glowed on every table. The mid-tempo music was evocative of beaches and tropical weather, even though all I could see out of the big windows was the movement of the empty escalators. I was in Lakeside Thurrock, a giant shopping centre off the motorway. On the phone, John had said he liked its atmosphere – and that it was nice to get out of Wakesea for the evening. But he looked flustered when he came in, despite being early. The wet wrinkled half-moons of his underarms slid into view as he took off his unscuffed leather jacket. He sat down and looked around. I like to see what the big boys are doing, he said. Who are the big boys? I asked. The big boys of franchising. I'm in the franchising business, he said. Anyway, tell me about yourself.

The room went dark, light, dark as the candles flickered. I felt as though we were in a play and had to perform ourselves. Everything looked like a prop. I became nervous, the way I always did when anyone asked me to talk about my life. I had established facts about myself – I was once a dancer, now a modern jazz instructor for children. I was nearly twenty-seven. He slapped the table, so the cutlery jumped. I thought about being an actor when I was your age. He said your age dismissively, as if he had beaten me to my age in a race. I can do great impressions, he said. I don't watch television or the news, I said. You won't know who I'm impersonating then, he said, raising his eyebrows.

I might go back to dancing, I said. He examined the bowl of guacamole near my plate. You've been at the school a long time, he said. Have you heard of YouTube? I asked him, my mind racing. I didn't know anything about YouTube but it sounded impressive, like I was thinking big. We could film the girls dancing. Cultivate them as personalities. I just need to convince Barbara. The Tube, it's on the computer, isn't it? I'm not a computer guy, he said. Anyway, I can't really leave her, I said. She's given me a lot of opportunities. She built the dance school from the ground up. I recited what I had written on the funding application earlier that year: Barbara's is the most successful touring dance school in the eastern region.

I'm fascinated by *you*, he said. It was hard to explain to a self-made businessman that some of us got satisfaction from being needed in ways that didn't always confer authority. If everyone put themselves first, we'd be doomed. What do *you* want? he asked. It was the way he said *you*, as though I had never thought about myself before.

We stood in the car park facing each other. What's going on? I asked, because I had been telling myself not to ask. He moved forward, so I had to stare up at him. You intrigue me, he said. It seemed a strange thing to say after I had told him about myself. He wanted to pretend that he didn't know what was happening between us. I knew that meant we would see each other again. But the only way I could be sure of what he was thinking was to make him think the same as me. I grabbed his neck, drew him closer. He began kissing back after a few seconds. Hoo, he said afterwards, I wasn't expecting that. He looked at me sideways. It reminded me of how I had been told to look at goats in the petting zoo when I was younger, but I think he was trying to show me that he was shy or that it was his best angle.

Barbara seemed to know that something had changed. She called me to her office for a catch-up session. While I had never purposely kept anything from Barbara, I thought it best not to tell her about John. It was nice not to share something with my boss, as though I had a lurid piece of gossip about myself. He had called me the previous night. He spoke on the phone with a different voice and I pretended not to know him as he told me his sexual fantasies.

During summer, Barbara and I relocated the school to various coastal towns in Essex. The rest of the year, we had a small studio in Colchester. Barbara drove back every night, and because I still hadn't learnt to drive, I rented a place in whatever town we were staying in and sublet the little flat I had in Colchester. But her office felt the same wherever we went. The scent of clary sage which she pumped into the air every few hours to relieve her tension. The blinds always down.

Have you heard of YouTube, Barbara? Pardon? she said, adjusting her glasses and then the golden orb she wore around her neck. Whenever I suggested anything new to do with the business, she became tired or her hearing went, so that it was embarrassing to repeat myself. Nothing, I replied. I've seen you moping, Vee. I'm not going to be around for ever, she said, again. The first time, I'd thought she had cancer or some other terminal illness, but she had been saying it for a year now.

You have to *empower* yourself. She reached for the clary sage. Long walks, flower-arranging, learning Italian, weight-lifting, decoupage, kick-boxing – pick one, she said, when I asked her how. Empowerment sounded lonely. She was trying to hand me my freedom in the way that people do – teasingly, haltingly. But I was afraid, so I said I was happy.

John and I went to another restaurant in the shopping centre. I called our dates parents' evenings and he thought it was because of his age, not because he was a parent. At the res-taurant, he made notes, asking me to rate it on a five-point scale for service, presentation and ambience. I kept thinking of what Barbara had said, about empowering myself. Pasta kept falling out of my mouth, like I couldn't concentrate on doing two things at once: eating and looking normal. What's wrong? he asked. We both watched my unchewed gnocchi land back onto the plate. My jaw snapped the empty air. Work,

I said. Afterwards, we drove back to Wakesea, the water flat and black below us, the town's outline sawtoothing the sky.

White lozenges of motorway signs dissolved into the dark and we were finally in the town, winding past the tiny houses. He put the radio on, a song that had been playing from every car and shop all summer. The chorus went *carry on having fun, fun, fun/never stop being young.* This is such an odd place for a lone woman to move to, he said. He said 'lone woman' in a quavering voice like someone might say 'lone killer'. I've always wanted to move around for my work, I said. But it probably wouldn't have happened if Barbara hadn't called the day after the psychic. I stopped speaking, changed the radio station. What psychic? He glanced at me, and then looked away swiftly, as if he was worried I would answer. I shook my head. Nothing. My road came into view. It was always quiet, as though the other residents had fled.

I lived in a rented house at the end of the terrace. John peered out at its lit windows. He didn't turn the engine off. Why are the lights on? I do it to put off the burglars, I replied. I've told you that. He had never come into my house before. I asked him nervously whether he was going to get out. He leaned over and kissed me, mouth pursed. And then he moved back and stared ahead, seemingly waiting for me to leave. Well, I'll hear from you soon, I said. I got out and slammed the door. The night air was cold coming in from the sea. It tapped my chest and my bare arms. I searched for my key, hoping it wouldn't take so long that it looked like I was waiting for him, but also that I wouldn't find it so quickly that I would disappear into the house and he would forget about me, about us.

The car idled outside as I stood in the hallway and stared

into the mirror. My make-up had run. I looked like a child's drawing of a dangerous stranger. Lipstick bleed, mascara pitted around my eyes. Was that why he hadn't come in? No one withheld for that long. When I went into the kitchen, the floor was covered in slugs. They must have come in when it rained. But it was now so hot again that they had dried up. I didn't have any cutlery, or anything sharp, apart from a nail file that I had left on the counter. I knelt down on the floor and scraped up one greying slug with the file and threw it into the bin. Then I walked back into the living room to draw the curtains. The halogen bulb made the fat pink roses on them swim. I switched it off and lifted a curtain. John was watching me from the car, his face grainy in the darkness. I imagined him as a strange man compelled by my every move. I walked to the door slowly and waited for him to knock.

At the end of each class, the girls practised their routine for the show. There were two weeks left before the finale. The better dancers had solos, the less good ones were part of the general chorus. Cherri danced by herself in a corner of the room. She had not come to resemble John, but sometimes I could see him crouched behind her eyes, watching me. It made me want to reach an uncomplicated part of him. Cherri, shouldn't you be over there? I pointed to the other back row dancers who were watching us. I realised that the abrupt movements that she was making were part of a sequence that she had devised herself.

You said that you wanted to see me dance, she said. Cherri had not yet learnt how to synchronise her arms and legs. She could still only move one set of limbs at a time. My self-parenting guide had taught me that handling such moments wrongly could be permanently damaging, that my words could one day pound in her head like blood. You have to practise a lot to do a solo, I said. People have expectations, not just me but all the people who will watch you. I know, she said, as if that was unimportant. We could dance together after class. Just you and me, I said.

She peered down at her new-looking trainers. The soles lit up and were inappropriate for dancing. I can do it myself, she said. But you can help if you want. Will your dad come to the finale? I asked, after a few seconds, as if it was an afterthought. She nodded. We could work on a dance that will impress him, I said. She looked up sharply. I don't want to impress him, she said, I just don't want to be in the back row.

Have you been with an older man before me? John asked a few days later. I said yes. He looked disappointed. I picked up the oil bottle from the side of the bed and put it into the cupboard, which was mostly empty, apart from a few toys I had bought in anticipation of tonight. He lay on the bedsheets, his head behind his hands, his body stiff, like he was imitating someone relaxing. This house is so unlived in, he said. What's your house like? He didn't answer. Will you put pictures up if you stay? he asked. He kept looking around at the bare walls. No, I don't think so, I said. I hadn't noticed before that they had nothing on them. I lay down next to him and put my head on his chest. Staring up at the ceiling, I noticed for the first time that someone had traced a smiley face with the gloss paint. Terrible things happened to you once, he said. Before we met, he added. I didn't know how he knew, but it made me think that we could connect. When people shared their most awful and life-changing experiences, they were more likely to fall in love. It wasn't just a coincidence Barbara found me when she did, I said.

I thought about it every day but when I told it, gaps inserted themselves. The order became confused. I left home and moved to a bedsit in London where I spent every night circling job adverts in *Loot*. I stopped dancing because classes were too expensive. Something had to change but I didn't know who could change it, I told John. And then a business card came through the letterbox. It was from a real psychic called Nebula. I called and made an appointment. I went to Nebula's place in Camden. She stood in the hallway, vest top sliding down her shoulders, cargo pants falling off her skinny hips. She led me through beaded curtains that kept on swinging and knocking against each other as we walked down another corridor. There were laminated pictures of ethereal, pastel women on the walls. She took me into a small, dark room with a white plastic table and two chairs, which looked like garden furniture.

Nebula sat me down, drew my arms into the centre. She closed her eyes, squeezed my fingers. We held hands until the table started shaking and she began digging her nails into my skin. The whites of her eyes became so big it was like they'd been boiled. You're cursed, she said. I need £50 to lift the curse. That was the exact amount that I had saved from my dole for next month's rent. I don't have £50, I said. She sighed, got up and switched the light on. Started opening one cupboard after the other, leaving them ajar. We were in a kitchen but there was no food anywhere or anything that might be useful: no plates, no cups, just a polystyrene container with dried noodles hanging from its lip. When she turned to me, she had an armful of green candles. She bundled them towards me: Take these, burn as many as you can, she said.

I went back to my bedsit with the candles in a carrier bag. I drank three cups of lumpy instant coffee and lit each candle, watching until they burnt to nubs. I fell asleep before the last one. The next morning Barbara called me on my phone and said that she had a job for me. I had applied for so many that I didn't know who she was or what she was talking about, but I said I'd take it.

I didn't tell John about the fire. When I stopped talking, he was sitting upright, staring at the door. It was past midnight. You should speak to someone, he said. About what? I asked. The curse, he said. By someone, he meant a professional. Not him. After a few minutes, he got up and started looking for his trousers. I need eight hours of sleep every night, he said. I always need eight hours, whatever happens. He laid out his trousers on the bed before going to the bathroom, clutching his white pants in his fist. His peeing was loud, as if he were pouring water out of a bucket into the toilet. It went on for ages. He came back into the room and sat down next to me. His underwear sagged below his rounded stomach. I wanted to reach out and stroke the soft hairs tufting in the dough. There's no such thing as a psychic, he said. Just charlatans. I know, I replied. I wondered what it would be like to be Cherri, and whether he patted her head in the same way.

John stopped pretending to be a stranger. He said that he wanted to see me in person only, me as me. In the meantime, Barbara was away and I was in charge of the school. I had never been in charge, not in seven years of assisting her. I paid the rent on the hall, I checked in with parents, I updated our website. My anxieties were being stealthily replaced by new ones, like when people's homes get made over on weeknight television by well-meaning friends and neighbours. What if I stayed in one place? What if I pursued my own dream of dancing in front of adults?

There was a week left before the finale. I went to the little room at the back of the building where I liked to get ready after class. It had been a dressing room when the building was a theatre. Everything was stripped out but a small table and a mirror with lightbulbs around it, the kind you imagine an actress would use in a melodrama. There were framed posters on the wall for amateur performances of *Grease* and *West Side Story*. Boxes of abandoned props stacked against the walls. I felt the emptiness of the whole place behind the door, as though I might step out into nothing. I started taking my day make-up off, putting my night make-up on. I was seeing John that evening. There was a knock, as I began swiping my cheeks.

I had watched the last girl leaving, waited for the clang of the front entrance shutting behind her. There should have been no one left. Cherri's snot-bubble voice came through the door: are you there? Can I come in? I thought you'd gone, I said. I opened the door. She stood, coat draped over one arm, milky thumbprints on her glasses. Dad says he's going to be late, she said. She wriggled onto a patchy velvet stool in the corner. We had never been alone together for any length of time since the first day of the summer school.

In the mirror, I watched her twist around and look at the boxes. Are you getting dressed for something? You look so beautiful, she said, digging her fingers under a glove. I like to be ready for anything, I replied. I didn't want her to think that she had to wear make-up to look beautiful. But it was important to be prepared. Beauty on the inside is fine, but it's not going to last for ever, I said. The world can make you feel terrible about yourself. I glued on my lashes. Can I ask you questions? she said. I made a noise that could not have been construed as either yes or no, in an attempt to politely deter her. I had been careful not to pay too much obvious attention to Cherri, but I had not thought that she was paying attention to me.

Do you have secret children, Vashti? Where would I keep them? I said. I believe that it's immoral to do anything but adopt. She opened her mouth, and kept it open, staring blankly at me. When I started to explain, she laughed. The game was to say things that shocked her. Vashti, do you have a secret husband? Because you're old. Not old like my step-mum Fiona. Or like my mum was. But *oldish*. My lash glue was starting to drip onto my cheeks. There were no windows in the room, no air. I pulled the lashes off. It's the twenty-first century and you will no longer learn anything meaningful by asking women these questions, I said. If you want to know someone, in a deep and substantial way, you ask them things like – do you make your bed every day? Do you read your horoscopes every day? Do you *believe* in them? I paused for breath. Did you practise psychokinesis as a child? My voice started to shake. Write those down, I told her.

I don't know what psychokeenis is, she said. Psycho-kee-nee-ses, I said. It's the power of moving things with your mind. That's not real, she said. Is your father on his way? I asked. The glue was webbing my fingers together, I was starting to feel hot. Her phone buzzed. She shouted: He's here! and threw up a little fist in the air.

I'll come with you. I'm old enough to go on my own, she said. You don't know who's out there, I said. I hiked up my thin tights, arched into my heels. Cherri rolled her gloves back up. We left the dressing room. She put her hand in mine. Outside, the air was shimmering, the horizon smeary like a dirty window. In the distance, I could see John leaning against his car. His hair was pouffed out and he wasn't wearing his leather jacket, just a suit jacket like most businessmen his age.

John looked up as I smiled at him. He grimaced but maybe he was just tired from franchising all day. He waved weakly, glanced at Cherri before getting back into the driver's seat. There's your dad, I said. She scanned the road, finally noticing the car. How did you know which one it is? I just guessed, I replied. Aren't you going to say hello? she asked. I should return to the school, I said, knowing that it would be wrong to go any further.

John called me that night, after our date. When the phone rang, I thought it was coming from outside of the house. My mobile never rang unexpectedly. The dialling code was for a landline. John had always rung from his mobile, sometimes withholding his number to make it suspenseful. But I knew it was him each time because I only heard from him in the middle of the night. I can't keep doing this, he said, when I picked up. I stared at the smiley face on the ceiling. I tried to focus, remembering the advice in the self-parenting book about grounding panicked children. I hadn't yet asked him any questions when he started speaking again. You have expectations of me that you're unwilling to admit, he said. What if I did, I said, even though I hadn't expected him to fulfil any.

I can't fulfil them, he said, as if reading my mind. I had *low* expectations, I clarified. That's passive-aggressive, Jackie, he said. Who's Jackie? I asked. He coughed loudly, cutting off my question. Stop contacting me, he said. His throat caught, so I had to bring the phone right up to my burning ear to hear him. It was a mistake and you took advantage of my vulnerability. Before I could reply, I heard a woman whisper loudly in the background: put the phone down, John. You've told her now.

I didn't switch my mobile off for the rest of the night. Its red death signal started blinking in my peripheral vision. That was not the end of it. I would not allow someone to be so cowardly. I grabbed the bed sheet which had been crumpled in the corner since John's last visit. He had slapped vanilla oil on my body and made minute adjustments to it as we had sex. My limbs had been cold, oil had stained the Egyptian cotton. I dragged the sheet to the kitchen like a dirty wedding train and stuffed it in the washing machine. A greasy trail glittered in the semi-darkness. On the counter were some half-empty beer cans from when John had last been around. I opened the back door. It had rained; the smell of meaty wet earth dizzied me. I emptied the rain out of the bowl I kept on the step and poured in the dregs to stop the slugs coming in, but it was too late.

Barbara called me for a meeting when she came back. The blinds in her office were down again, the lamps were on, the room smelled of clary sage. I was trapped in her sunglasses like a slow-moving target. She said that she had important news for me: she wasn't ready to retire yet. It wasn't for her, slowly losing all her functions like an outmoded piece of technology. I'm going to look into YouTube, though I'm unconvinced. It'll never catch on, she said. She sniffed, took a deep breath. But the good news is that I want you to take over the day-to-day running of the school.

She leaned forward so we were only a few inches apart. I could see reflections of myself everywhere: her glasses, the golden orb that she had around her neck. If you want to, of course, she said. I knew she was waiting for my answer. I didn't tell her that I had imagined myself somewhere else next year. The image – a big city nowhere near a sea, a waiting audience – wouldn't disappear. I hadn't even visualised it. It was as instantly familiar as an advert. She moved back, put her fingers on the orb and made me disappear. Don't be afraid of change, she said. There's only so many fires that one person can accidentally start.

John texted me before the class that day: *I wd like to c u. Things bad. But that not why. Come to beach cafe with C.* He always used text speak, even though I replied in full sentences. I wanted to weep. Something was pressing against the inside of my chest, a balloon swollen with water. I walked around the hall, watching the girls as they rehearsed for the finale. They were singing the song they had chosen for the dance: *fun fun fun fun.* A spitty croon through a girl's new teeth – was anything as sweet? It was the last time that I would see them dancing before the show. Time goes quickly! I said. Practise! In the corner, I could see Cherri dancing as if someone invisible was trying to push her over. She was practising her solo, the one that I said I'd help her with.

I remembered the bits about consistency in the self-parenting book, how important it was to treat the child of a man who had humiliated me like any other. Be the most consistent person in your life, the book said. Can I copy you? I asked Cherri. If I learn your dance, you can see how it looks. And then you can change it if it's not working. She nodded. I began moving, imitating her steps, fluidly bringing them together. That's not right, she said, staring at my feet. You're making it *different*. I stopped. She looked embarrassed, as if I were the one who couldn't dance.

Can I ask you a question? No one was nearby. Do you know anyone called Jackie? Or maybe Jacqueline? Cherri's pigtails flapped as she slowed down. How do you know about Jackie? she replied. I don't know her. Who is she? I asked. Cherri wobbled on one foot, shielded her face. I gestured for her to put her arms down. Her face was redder than usual. Jackie was a bird who used to sit outside my window, she said. Not a real one – well, she was *sort of* – she was my 'imaginary friend'. Cherri did quote marks in the air. She had big purple feathers and made loud noises in the middle of the night. She couldn't fly, like a dodo or an ostrich, she said. Cherri carried on speaking but I couldn't hear her any more. Was I a private joke between them, the father and daughter unit? I wanted to vomit, but I pinched my neck instead to retain my composure.

Later, I saw Taylor approaching Cherri. I watched them from the back of the class. Cherri looked at Taylor suspiciously. They had not spoken to each other – as far as I had seen – since I first placed them in Britney House together. Taylor rarely spoke to anyone but her friends. She liked to jangle in unison at the other girls. She liked to intimidate them with her height and comedy stomach beating. I could always intervene if anything happened between them. Or I could just watch. Who was I to think that Cherri needed my help in every situation?

I began circling. I stopped near them, looked into the middle distance. If you point your toes when you do the step, it's easier, I heard Taylor saying. Do this - she started spinning - and keep it pointed. She danced out Cherri's steps, her eyes trained on Cherri to make sure she was watching. When Taylor stopped, Cherri copied her, moving faster with confidence. She finished more quickly than she expected, looking surprised when she neatly rounded off the sequence. Taylor beat her stomach: You can do it! she said. Cherri stared, before beating back: Yes, I can!

I reread John's text as Cherri and I left for the beach. I can't believe you're coming too! she kept saying, as we walked down the deserted road. I thought of Jackie the bird, flapping hopelessly at the window. The flat glaze of oil on the bed sheet. John was sitting outside the only cafe on the stretch that led to the pier, where all the daytrippers and carers gathered. His suit was rumpled and he was spooning ice cream from a bowl. He hadn't noticed us coming. We had never seen each other in stark daylight.

He nodded at me, before turning to Cherri, who was now standing at the table looking at the dessert. He took a five pound note out of his wallet and handed it to her. Take this, he said. Get what you want. Apart from the ice-cream. He stuck his arms out, puffed his cheeks and moved from side to side like an inflatable mascot in a storm. If you want to eat something fatty you have to pay for it yourself, Cherri said in a robotic voice. Exactly, he said. She grabbed the five pounds and went into the cafe, stamping her feet on the concrete.

After the door closed behind Cherri, John turned to me, focused on the empty bowl. I'm sorry about the Jackie thing, he said. Why did you call me Jackie? I asked. Fiona found the restaurant receipts and the extra phone, she made me call her – you, he said. I couldn't tell her it was Cherri's teacher. Not a one-off. As for Jackie – I can't remember where the name came from. He looked down, fiddled with the spoon. My feelings had been hurt, I told myself. And then she left, he said. She cut her hair a few weeks earlier. It was like this. He made a box-like shape around his head. Very neat, very sensible, he said sadly. She made me call you and she bloody left anyway. And took the car. I had to walk all the way down here. His shoulders fell, dried sweat flaked off his forehead.

Cherri came out of the cafe, carrying a can of Fanta. I'm going to the beach, she said. She dropped the change on the table. We watched her cross the empty road and disappear down the steps. No one came to that stretch of the beach: it was too far from the pier, and most people in Wakesea were old or had mobility problems. We could see Cherri walking near the groynes, stopping to look across at us, small as we were. She'll be fine, he said. We used to come to this beach a lot when she was little, with her mum. He looked up at the sky, as if she were hovering above us.

I know you're disgusted, he said, after a few seconds of respectful silence. You hate me, don't you? I don't *hate* you, I began. You *should* hate me, he said. Are you going to stay? He asked, after I didn't reply. As in, are you going to stay after the school ends? I thought of Barbara, of all the coastal towns ahead, of an audience waiting in a darkened room. Without wanting to, I caught his eyes brightening, even though he didn't know what I was undecided about.

Tinny, familiar music rose from the beach. It was the finale song: *never stop being young/fun fun fun!* In its pauses, we heard a phlegmy cough turning into laughter. We both looked towards the sea, the sand. There was no one there, no sign of Cherri. John got up, brushed down his ill-fitting suit. I followed him across the road, stopped with him at the ramp that led to the beach. Below, there was no sign of recent occupation, apart from a jagged red bucket that was half-buried in pebbles. Cherri, he shouted over the music. The ramp was covered in a lurid green slime. He turned to look for another way down. The laughter broke out again. We both leant over the iron railing. In a recess only visible when we craned forward was a balding man sitting on a crate. Lined neatly next to him was a portable radio, a thin blue carrier bag and a pair of old brown shoes. He was rocking back and forth with laughter. If his hands hadn't been wrapped around his knees, he would have fallen headfirst into the sand. In front of him was a small pink cowboy hat I recognised from the school's prop box. Cherri came out from the recess, wearing her finale costume, her other dress sticking out from underneath it, so she looked twice her normal size.

The man began to clap. She started dancing, hesitating between each step. John reached over the railings, yelled her name. The music was too loud. He stuck a foot onto the mossy ramp. He would have to go further down to the other set of steps in order to get Cherri, or risk sliding down the slope and injuring himself. He would have to leave her there with the man, just for a minute or two. He couldn't decide. I shouted her name. She went on dancing, grimacing and mouthing numbers to herself. It was the first time I had seen her whole solo, its steps in sequence. She moved without pause. She twirled, both of her dresses flying up and exposing her red thighs.

She stopped and punched her gloved arms in the air, one after the other. Jumping back, she stumbled and recovered with a big smile. She was sure of herself. I had never known her to be so confident, so composed. The old man threw some coins into the hat; they glinted in the sun. Cherri, what are you doing? John shouted as the finale song segued into a tune I hadn't heard before. Cherri looked around and up. The old man walked past her quickly, carrier bag dangling from his wrist, shoes held to his chest. She saw her father, waved. He didn't wave back, just stood there, his hand on his chest, breathing heavily. Her gaze went from him to me, and back again. She ran to the hat, picked it up carefully, stared back up at us. Look! she shouted. Can you see me? I'm here! I'm here!

ENERGY THIEVES: FIVE DIALOGUES

I. HOW TO INCREASE ATTRACTIVENESS

'MY THEORY IS that most people are energy thieves and will gravitate towards those persons who have the most energy. So if we take the example of a large number of people being in a room for a party or a get-together or a conference or whatever, and of their gravitating towards someone, as far as anyone does gravitate anywhere, then they will always gravitate to the most energetic person there, because that person will make them feel good, or will make them laugh, or will give out something that will make them feel fortunate to be there. It's a matter of physical and mental energy. Same difference.'

'Yes.'

'For as long as there is an excess of energy and plenty to go around, there is a good chance that you will get some for yourself. An anecdote, an opinion you can use, a joke perhaps, or some information, a story, a lead, a job, a reference, an amusing insight . . . and thereby a feeling of renewal or liveliness or pleasure. Just something, anyway, that will make you feel better than you did before.'

'Yes.'

'I mean, no one drifts towards the worried-looking guy with a headache in the corner of the room who wishes he wasn't there. That is because it is physical and mental energy that we seek.'

'Yes.'

'And just as unluckiness and unhappiness in others can be seen as infections to be avoided by sensible and self-centred people, similarly laziness and tiredness in others can make us feel as though they might be catching, too, so we want to get away from people exhibiting them. Quickly, in fact, since we can all be prey to such feelings.'

'Yes.'

'But the reverse, that is, to be full of energy and ambition, is inspiring for others. It is difficult to have great ideas and transmit them while suffering from idleness and fatigue, but it is easy and possible when one is full of sparkle and zest. And so we look out for the lively ones.'

'Yes.'

'With energy you get to express yourself and win over others who will love you both for your ideas and for the enthusiasm with which you transmit them.'

'Yes.'

'Therefore to be more attractive, have more physical energy.'

'Yes.'

2. HOW TO DISPEL WORRY

'People often say that when their doctor gives them a diagnosis for a disease that will cause their death they suddenly feel much calmer. They have been told they have six months to live or something similar and it is only then that they can relax and enjoy life. You must have heard of that?'

'I have. It happens frequently to those sort of people to whom it happens.'

'And then they report some greater wisdom that comes from knowing that they are going to die. That is: knowing what is finally and truly important, enjoying the good things in life, and laughing off the bad things.'

'Yes, they do indeed say those things that they say.'

'But I have a theory that turns that on its head.'

'Ah.'

'Which is that they don't appreciate those things that they say they do – families and sunsets and such like. At least, not exactly in the manner purported.'

'Oh.'

'But simply that they have no worries, which liberates them to enjoy everything all the time. No worries, except one. Only the big one. Having only one worry in the whole world reduces and ultimately annuls all the other worries which they might have. Indeed all the other worries seem no longer to count as worries at all, so great is the main worry. And so the death-marked person realises of a sudden, "Oh, I am not worried any more, how odd. Apart from *that*, of course."'

'So it is the number of worries, rather than the severity of them, that comprises the debilitating strain of worry?'

'Indeed. The more the worse and the fewer the better, regardless of size. By surrendering the sum total of all worries to one giant worry, one finds that the rest of life is worry-free. Hence the enjoyment of sunsets and love of family life.'

'So death cures worry?'

'Yes. To avoid worrying, contemplate your own death and nothing else.'

'Ah.'

3. HOW TO CONSIDER YOUTH

'I have noticed that people will say, "Oh, well, you are young," to a young person who, whilst they will be accepting of the fact that they are younger than the old and decrepit fossil who is calling them young, will nonetheless not be accepting of the fact that they themselves are young.'

'Yeah, how come?'

'Because the younger person will be the oldest they have ever been. And he or she will be conscious that they are one year older than they were the previous year, and that the tally is always rising. A 25-year-old, for example, who appears a mere child to a 50- or 60-year-old, and to whom the latter will feel impelled to issue a constant reminder of the former's youth, is nonetheless older than a 21-year-old.'

'Yeah.'

'And owing to youth's fickleness, the 21-year-old is also considerably younger-feeling than the 25-year-old and will be keen to remind them of their age difference.'

'OK, yeah.'

'But in turn the 21-year-old is a fair bit older than an 18-year-old who will consider the 21-year-old to be old and wise, even. And maddeningly an 18-year-old will feel adult responsibility and decision-making falling upon his shoulders and will himself look back on being 15 or 16 as being young and easy.'

'Years counting for more when you are young because as a fraction of your total life they are big, innit?'

'Indeed so. Similarly, a 15-year-old will look back on being eight as some magic time, never to be recaptured. Likewise an eight-year-old will look back on being five as a perfect childhood bubble.'

'Numbers confuse us, too, though, yeah?'

'Yes, we are entranced by numbers and their supposed significance. A person reaching 30 will feel they have become old partly because the number seems offensively aged to them.'

'Yeah.'

'Yet it is just the turn of a digit. Likewise 40, 50, 60. It hurts a person to reach these supposed "milestones" because they feel that they must be old to have reached them. But if 30 is old, then what is 60?'

'Yeah, and what is 60 if you are 90?'

'Young by comparison, dear boy. In experience turning 60 must necessarily come with the feeling of "old", but in fact the key word is, and can only be, "older".'

'Yeah, that's it.'

'And that applies whether at 18 or 30 or 50 or 65. Also at 76 or 89 or 91 or 111 . . .'

'Yeah, true.'

'To wit, one is never young.'

4. HOW TO COMBAT AGEING

'Common sense might have it that a person upset by turning 40 should spend more time with 60-year-olds.'

'How so?'

'Because by doing this he will feel young again, much

73

younger than the 60-year-olds he now surrounds himself with and who keep telling him how young he is. They will flatter his ego and give him the sense that time is on his side once more.'

'Indeed so.'

'Similarly, anyone downcast by turning 60 should spend time with 80-year-olds, and those disheartened by turning 80 should immediately hang out with 100-year-olds. Likewise, 100-year-olds should speed into the company of any 120-year-olds still living. In such a way all those depressed by the ageing process will find new vim and vigour by associating with people older than them, who in turn will envy them their comparative youth, and remark upon it, and indeed at the mere hint or suggestion of the word "youth", the downhearted person will come back to life again. But it is not so.'

'How so is it not so?'

'Because it is homogeneity which assures us vim and vigour, and not difference; it is homogeneity which emboldens us, more so than associating with those for whom we feel pity, or hope to use to get one over on for our own benefit and in such an unsightly way.'

'How so is it unsightly if we get a little fillip from the misfortunes, I mean, the ageing, of others?'

'Oh, but it is. Consider this: the entry of a group of six-foot men into a room immediately fills all who observe them with pleasure at their six-footedness. The inclusion of a five-foot-ten or below man amongst them spoils the impression. Similarly, a group of blondes is all the more lovely if they are indeed wholly and completely a group of blondes and there isn't a non-blonde amongst them.'

'Blondes are just so.'

'In any social gathering one might expect to find several blondes. They should immediately form friendships and spend time together and people will observe them and feel happiness at their blondeness because nature loves homogeneity and a wholesome homogenous impression gives joy to those outside the group whether they care to admit it or not.'

'Fantastic, so.'

'At the same time, and to get to the real heart of the matter, spending time with others of the same ilk will encourage a person to match them or go beyond them and see what is possible for themselves. The "if they can do it, so can I" approach. Thus normalising their own experience of being six foot or 40 years old or blonde. Those people who are tall will maintain posture and dress appropriately in the company of similarly tall people. Those persons reaching 40 years old will share advice and wisdom appropriate for their age range and no other. And blondes will maintain their hair colour and discuss fashion advice and act in ways suitable to blonde-haired people by hanging out with their blonde friends in a blonde cohort.'

'So brilliant.'

5. HOW TO VALIDATE GROUPTHINK

'People tend to think that groupthink is a universally bad thing and that we perpetually need new voices and new attitudes to stop it from happening.'

'What's that? You've bought a new hat or something? Let me turn this thing on.'

'They suppose that groupthink is a negative concept that describes what happens when humans form a group and think for the purposes of that group and in the manner of that group.'

'Yes, it certainly looks like a man.'

'But there is no alternative. Either one comes in and changes the group to make everyone think like you—'

'And I like you!'

'—or you surrender to the group and change yourself to suit it.'

'Never surrender!'

'But a group would never get anything done if everyone actually thought differently, because then there would be no consensus.'

'No? There's one every ten years, I think.'

'So by reaching an accord—'

'Yes, lovely plane, they should never have discontinued it.'

'—with regularity, you get a thinking style and a way of doing things, and even a way of behaving and speaking, that is distinctive and unanimous. And hence companies and organisations tend towards a united state.'

'Have you? You know, I've never been.'

'But it's nothing to be frightened of. It's completely natural.'

'Really? It looks more like a wig to me.'

'And so we shouldn't rail against the human condition when these things are inherent.'

'No, not a thing, old chap.'

HALLOWEEN

IT IS A gaudy display, something I might expect to see in the window of our local high street bakery, a family business seemingly unmoved by the spirit of regeneration in this area. But they look pretty: rows of biscuits shaped as witches, skeletons and pumpkins, painted with thick icing swirls and laid out on an enormous foil party tray covered with orange tissue paper. The doorbell rings. 'Go on then,' I say to Jamie, smiling but not able to look him directly in the eyes.

The smell of baking fills the kitchen, softening for once its steely decor. In the early stages of Jamie's illness, the sharp lines of our new flat had provided a certain comfort. They had prompted me to clean more often than I would normally, which helped counter my belief that an unpleasant odour now flowed through our lives like a contaminated river. I would continue cleaning until I felt I was stemming its course. Still, I imagined I carried the odour on me, out into the world. Some days I was sick with worry that I must fill other spaces with it: the open-plan office, friends' houses, darkened cinemas, even pristine white gallery spaces that you would hope might be a refuge.

But the flat today smells only of the sweet sting of sugar and when I walk through into the living room, I find that the smell has pervaded there too, making our structured sofa appear more comfortable than it is and warming the pale wood floors. It nestles among the books that line one entire wall, creating a friendlier communion between Jamie's graphic novels and engineering manuals at one end and my photography books and contemporary fiction at the other, usually so awkwardly separated. And when I move into the bedroom to change out of my work clothes, experiencing, as always, an extra flutter of apprehension here, I discover that it has even settled between the plaintive sheets of our bed. I study the untidy folds on Jamie's side, the impression of his body where he must have rested earlier, leading his life as he does now in small, broken periods of time. My side is carefully smoothed and tucked in to disguise my nocturnal torments. But it is here that I lie each night unable to quiet my mind while beside me Jamie falls in and out of his drugged half-life. A nebulous form lies between us – a spectral lover, rejected but undiminished. Everything had taken on its pallor. For a long time, I will lie awake, slowly tracing the cottony contours of my body until the blood thumping in my ears finally, exhausted, falls away.

Back in the kitchen, Jamie winks at me as he returns with the tray, a good number of the biscuits now missing. I pick up a piece of broken witch biscuit. It tastes good. 'They loved them,' he tells me. 'They kept saying "Aw thanks, mate".' He imitates their callow talk. I nod, smiling with my eyes and pressing my fingers to my mouth, making exaggerated little chewing movements as if I want to clear my mouth quickly in order to respond to him. But it is an elaborated pause. I have no idea what to say, no immediate way to comprehend this unexpected turn.

I eat a skeleton biscuit, surprised by how much I enjoy its soft icing and buttery snap. Food for the two of us lately is no longer associated with pleasure. It is presented always as a remedy of some kind, our diets determined by the ebb and flow of Jamie's optimism. He will spend hours in the kitchen, with me quiet but encouraging at his side: he has read that a high-potassium, low-sodium diet may cure advanced cancer, or he has allowed himself to believe a newspaper report that a woman in Japan prolonged her husband's life through a *shokuyo* lifestyle that involves eating mostly natural grains and plants, and so we sit night after night faced not with what we desired but with the indigestible truth. Meanwhile, I have gained an extra layer of fat that I can feel now pushing at my waistband. Curiously, I am expanding at the same rate he is diminishing. I reach for another biscuit, and while Jamie rearranges the tray, I move behind him and stroke the back of his neck, plant a kiss there, in that place I love. He has been ill for so long I have started to forget about his soft places, to measure him instead in tablets and needles, and by that particular look he has when he thinks I am not looking, when he stares at the wall and allows his eyes to focus finally on the future.

I will see that look again about a week later when winter has fully set in and I return from work to an unheated flat. I will find him sitting in our bruised leather armchair, where he likes to relax, looking at the wall. Only this time I will notice that he does not blink. I will wait for a while, thinking that maybe it is not necessary to blink, that I am sure I have read an article about someone who underwent cosmetic surgery on their eyes which left them unable to blink. The trouble is I cannot remember if they were blinded by the procedure that left them permanently wide-eyed, or even if it is possible to continue living in that state. Jamie will go on not blinking for a while longer, but I will not want to disturb him in case I distract him just as he is about to blink. I will stand there for a long time not wanting to disturb him.

The doorbell rings for a second time and Jamie picks up the tray. Big laughs this time from the doorstep. Recognising the voice of a neighbour, I decide to join them. The cold hits me as I descend the stairs, so that when I reach the door, I put my arms tight around Jamie's thin waist and press myself to him. Linda, who lives two doors down, is mid-sentence and does not acknowledge my appearance. Her full attention is on Jamie, making sure he is OK, smiling and acting up to lift his spirits in a way that would usually irritate me. My role is so all-consuming that the passing concern of others can feel like an encroachment, or in my more vulnerable moments, a criticism, as if I am not trying hard enough. But tonight, I let Linda's words wash over me. I even allow myself to enjoy the determinedly buoyant talk. I hold Jamie close, combining our warmth against the cold, and I look over his shoulder at the tray, letting the bright colours and sweet smell take me away to simpler times, times I wonder if I will ever experience again, like trips as a kid to the bakery round the corner after swimming with my dad on a Saturday morning to buy split jam doughnuts as a treat, synthetic cream running down my chin.

'Come in, Linda,' I find myself saying. 'I'll make some tea.' It will be the first time anyone on the street has crossed our threshold and tonight it feels like a space that would be welcoming. But Linda refuses, fusses about getting her dinner ready, though she carries on talking. I sense myself drifting from the talk but try not to stray too far, thinking about the day after we moved in when Linda came to introduce herself. She brought a pot of winter-flowering pansies, which I have placed here on the front step. It isn't a flower I like, and the pot is not to my taste either, so I am proud that I have kept it here and taken care of it. I notice Linda's eyes flick to it several times during the conversation.

I have tried other ways to assuage all our fears, taking Linda a cutting from a plant she had admired in our front garden and promising to contribute an honesty book stall for a charity event at the community hall. But I do not know what Linda really thinks of us, a young couple whose lives started far from here, and who have moved in with no connection to this place, except that the house prices match our circumstances. Talking to Jamie now, Linda may well be thinking of the old man who used to live in our flat, wondering what we have done with the bench he used to sit on at the front of the house or why we did not bother to trim the hedge as neatly as he had. Like other recent newcomers to the street, Jamie and I remain apart, essentially a self-contained unit, despite everyone's efforts. How self-contained will I be without him?

A few moments later, walking back up the stairs ahead of him, I have the sense of reaching the summit of something, a giddy satisfied feeling. While wanting to cling on to this sensation, I find I cannot help myself. As Jamie sets down the half-empty tray in the kitchen and turns to face me, I look back at him and I reach behind his head for that soft place again, knowing that with this simple caress I will once again lose my grip.

IN THE MOUNTAINS

EVERY DAY SHE walked alone on the slopes beyond the guesthouse or sat for hours on the crumbling red ochre, drawing the mountains encircling the valley. Her pencil traced ridges, followed fissures and ruptures and the sudden bursts of green thrusting thickly up along seams of hidden water. She peered down at the clusters of the houses nestled in hollows, searching their rootedness for a sign. She longed for a sign to show her the way, now that she had run away to Spain, to this endless sunlit stillness: a new calm, a new perfection. At the guesthouse, Beatriz, the owner, told her about a market the next day in the village. Anya went alone, through olive groves and a carpark, the cars seemingly abandoned before an opening to a narrow shaded street: the entrance to the labyrinth. Its walls were formed of the bodies of houses joined together as one heavy mass, chalk-white with lime. The windows were shuttered, the balconies empty. Ancient chestnut doors hid lives within, and disused chambers.

At the centre of the labyrinth was a small round plaza with a single silver birch tree and a tiled *fuente*, water splashing from three spouts into a stone trough. Sellers had set up tables of herbs, oils, soaps, incense, olive wood sculptures, red wine, rough brown bread and cakes with wet dark berries and plums glistening inside. Anya wandered through the bodies and voices and sat at the edge to draw. She saw Beatriz in the crowd, kissing everyone who came to greet her. Beatriz, who had lived in Madrid before, had spoken of her friends from the village, who, like her, had come to the mountains to make new lives. Some had succeeded while others had been overcome by the force of that clear pure stillness: a promise, a void, a magical mirror, mesmerising and luring the unsuspecting into delusion, stilling thought, dulling desire.

An old man in a corduroy blazer came past and stopped, leaning on his walking stick, to look down at her drawing.

'Long ago, I used to come here to draw,' he said. 'In those days there were no roads, only tracks.'

'You live here?'

'For forty years. If you come to my house I'll show you my watercolours of the village – it was very different then. People still kept animals on the ground floor. You should have seen the flies!' He chuckled.

She didn't know what to say. She often didn't. She never knew what to speak of when talking with strangers.

'Well, see you,' he said, and went slowly up a slope past the fuente.

She returned to her drawing, but the old man had disrupted her. He had sounded English, a foreigner in the strange village that he had claimed for himself. Why had he stopped to talk with her? In England she never sketched outside; she never wanted to. Now she kept wanting to draw, everywhere she went.

'Have you seen the cacti?' The old man was back, holding out a gnarled cactus leaf covered with white encrustations. 'It's the cochineal bug. All the cactii in the village are infested.'

She had seen them on her walks, the big-lobed cactii with their broken limbs, rotting and weakened by the life gathered on them.

'You can make dye with it,' the old man said. 'It's what they used to make the red coats of the British army. And you can paint with it, but you'll need to stop the colour fading: maybe vinegar or salt – you should try it. I have a lot of cactii in my garden, if you want to experiment.'

'Maybe,' she murmured, trying not to encourage the man.

Why did he keep coming to her? He clutched his stick as he leaned down to place the leaf beside her, then staggered up past the fuente again.

'I see you've met David,' Beatriz said, coming over. 'He's a famous artist in Spain.'

'He's invited me to his house to look at paintings.'

'He must have liked your drawings.' Beatriz studied Anya's sketchbook. 'You're good! You should go. He loves to teach. I can see the two of you becoming good friends!'

But Beatriz didn't know about Anya. Anya was not good at making friends. In the office her manager had told her to get better at teamwork, but Anya hadn't known how. She had trusted no one at the office, feeling their pity and disdain of her, a certain wariness around her, that she had been glad to leave behind.

'Go and see David,' Beatriz urged.

'Is it safe to go alone?'

'Safe? Ah, don't worry, it's nothing like that, he really will just talk about painting – you won't be able to stop him! Tell me a time and I'll come and rescue you!'

'There's no need.'

She wasn't going. Of her family, it was her brother who

made friends easily. He was the generous one, her mother said. He was open-hearted and kind; Anya was hostile, her heart was hard and closed and secretive.

Musicians arrived in the plaza: a man and woman with matching golden dreadlocks began to drum. People gathered around them. Another man came pulling a *cajón* on a rickety trolley and joined them, sitting crouched over the mellow-gold wooden box, his fingers rippling a shuddering rising rhythm with the drums. The drumming rose up above the voices and the splashing of the fuente; it throbbed against the ring of stone houses around the plaza and reached up to the empty blue sky. People started dancing. The drumming was in Anya, it throbbed in her eyes, her ears. She couldn't draw any more, she couldn't breathe. She reached for the labyrinth, entering its shade and sudden cool. It curved into quiet, into a tunnel with ragged wooden roof beams and peeling blue walls. She walked towards sunlight at the far end. Stone steps climbed to a cactus, half in bloom half dying, by a gatepost.

'Oh, so you came,' said the old painter and opened the gate to let her in.

The painter's house was built into the rock. The beams of the ceiling were whole chestnut trunks. The walls were painted with ochre from the mountains and hung with Berber rugs. In the kitchen he poured beer into glasses and they sat at the table before a deep hooded fireplace and he showed her his paintings: exquisite, detailed and full of a delicate precise admiration for the place he had discovered and loved. A younger man, tanned and smoking a spliff, came through from an inner room.

'My son, Hector,' the old painter said.

A young woman with long black hair followed.

'This is Maria, his girlfriend.'

They both came over and kissed Anya, greeting her without hesitation, as if they were friends.

'Would you like to stay for lunch?' Hector asked.

'Oh, no, it's okay.'

'It's just some vegetables and couscous,' Maria added.

'No, I have to be going.' Anya headed quickly for the door.

It felt unsafe to stay inside their open-hearted ease for she knew she would be revealed to them.

'Let me give you some cochineal,' the old painter said, coming with her.

From the dying cactus he scraped the soft clinging white-ness with a knife, and smeared it into a plastic bag.

'It's the females that make the dye; they never leave the plant, they just stay there laying eggs until the whole plant dies. They're reddest when they've had their young.'

She took the bag.

'How long are you staying?' he asked.

'I don't know.'

'The house next door belongs to a friend, he rents it cheap if you stay a few months – you could stay and keep drawing.'

Surely something so unexpected yet longed for could not really happen? Surely it would prove a trap, a mistake?

'That house used to be the old bread oven in the village,' the painter said. 'A part of the oven is still there.'

She gazed up at the square stone house up on the rock, shaded by a giant fig tree.

'Could I look inside?'

'Of course, go in, the guests left earlier.'

Downstairs, in the kitchen, was the raised stone ledge of

the old oven, where village loaves would have risen inside a circle of fire. A ladder went up from it to a bedroom with a desk by a window and a view through the branches of the fig tree to the mountains slumbering in the sun, majestic and indifferent to the flickering of life in the hearts of people.

When Anya went outside the painter was tending to a geranium. A furry grey cat curled on a stone seat, purring.

'Bye,' Anya called to the painter.

'Let me know how you get on with the cochineal, I'd like to see the results,' he said.

He really did want to know – she saw his eagerness and the curiosity that had once brought him along mule tracks for miles over the mountains to the village that was his now. She felt awkward not kissing him goodbye like a local. And she didn't want to leave him, but she hurried back to the silence of the tunnel.

The drumming in the plaza had stopped. There was a smell of garlic and frying onions. A man stirred stew in a pot hung over a fire. A woman in a polka-dot apron laid tables outside a house. Beatriz sat with a group at a table, laughing with a man. Anya didn't know how to join them. She stayed in the plaza watching the people still strolling around the stalls. Three figures stepped out from the crowd, the principals in an opera, about to begin their song: two women and a small girl in a blue dress. The child's pale-brown hair fluttered against her cheek as she stood dreamy and musing. The woman holding her hand, the mother perhaps, asked a question, but the child didn't answer, still caught in dreams. The woman asked louder but the child still didn't hear. The woman's voice grew sharp, then a slap cracked the air as she struck the child's arm. As always there was no warning, no time to prepare. The child's mouth fell open, her shock turning to shame and the horror of betrayal. Anya felt it rush back to her from a secret place of her own, deep within her.

The child started to cry, wails of misery writhing out through the voices and laughter. People turned startled. The mother looked harassed and pulled the child by the wrist to go over and join the other woman at a stall. The two women stood looking over amulets and belts and earrings of dull gold, curled into ancient coils. Behind them the child cried alone, her arms wrapped around her, two tiny probing fingers stroking where she had been struck. Her eyes were fixed on the back of the mother, disbelief dark and puzzling in the child's gaze. Anya knew her question, knew the terror of the answer that might come. An elderly woman paused to stroke the girl's hair. The mother spun round and the old woman drew back and hobbled away.

Inside Anya was a wavering trail of pencil lines: one line for each slap, a stroke of her own drawn inside her wardrobe, a secret snaking growth in the darkness. Her tally, her score, a belt of nails to tighten around her; she had worn it for the longest time. Now it was broken, falling open to reveal her naked; unheld she spilled from its grip, formless, unsheathed. She ran into the labyrinth's silence searching for the way out, but the alley swirled her deeper in. A vine-shaded street unfurled down to a dark still stream, a stone slab, a bridge to cross over into a courtyard overlooked by the terraces of houses. A dog barked down at her from behind an iron railing. She turned into a passageway filled with sun. Outside a blue-painted doorway a snake lay on a step. Startled, it slid swiftly on, silver and olive-green, a line of black diamonds rippling on ahead of her and up around the stone bulges of a wall before disappearing into a hole in a rock.

Around the rock was a garden with great bushes of lavender, rosemary, marigolds, marijuana and a small square chapel with a bell-tower shaped like a minaret. Anya entered the chapel's deep chill silence and sank onto a pew, covering her face with her hands as tears ran out from her darkness and the hard stone heart breaking open within. The door banged behind her. She wiped her eyes at once and sat up straighter, but the figures running down the aisle didn't look at her. A man sat down at a piano. A woman cradled a violin and brought up a bow and the violin's call soared into the emptiness. The piano eased in, dancing warm and golden, their song rising up to the saints in red gilded alcoves and marble angels reaching down their translucent pale hands to Anya. There was always someone reaching out, there was always the new and golden. It would lead her through the labyrinth to its end, to her new beginning.

When she left the chapel, the bag of cochineal had burst in her hands. Her tears had dissolved the frail white sheaths to a fierce new redness. She crushed the women and mothers, staining the walls of the labyrinth as she found her way back to the old painter and the ancient furnace next door, ready to take her place.

THE GIRL WITH THE HORIZONTAL WALK

The heart weighs 300 grams. The tricuspid valve measures 10 cm, the pulmonary valve 6.5 cm, mitral valve 9.5 cm and aortic valve 7 cm in circumference.

Nicholas Arden looked over the newspaper at his wife, Ellen, buttering his toast at the opposite end of the breakfast table.

'How hard can it be, honey?'

'You haven't read the script. I'll need to dumb down.'

'I always said you were too intellectual.'

Ellen slid the toast across the table, catching the bottom of the paper. The ink was freshly printed and she imagined some of it colouring the butter. Ellen wondered how much it would take to poison someone. Not that she wanted to poison *Nick*. But she was easily preoccupied.

'I need an angle,' she said. 'I don't want to be led by the studio on this one.'

'Then put your foot down. Both of them, if you have to.'

She waggled the butter knife. 'Don't get smart, wise guy.'

'I'm trying to catch you up.'

It was a diamond-bright spring morning. They sat on the

terrace extending from their white-painted house under clear blue light. Beneath them, the swimming pool caught ripples off the sky. Somewhere in the house their two children were getting ready for school. Ellen loved them, but she was thankful of the maid. There was only so much noise she could take.

Nick folded the paper, wrung out one end with a rueful expression.

'Go on,' he said. 'You're burning to tell.'

Ellen brushed a toast crumb away from the corner of her mouth with her right-hand pinky.

'I play a photographer, Marilyn Monroe. I get to go platinum. Preferably a wig. Marilyn doesn't take great pictures, but she's always in the right place at the right time. Plus she's pretty – we know how many doors that opens, front and back. She carves out a career for herself, *Life*, *Movieland*, *Modern Screen*, all those covers. She gets invited to all the right parties, then some of the wrong ones. So there's then a photo of the president, in flagrante. Before you know it, she's killed.'

'Sounds meaty to me.'

'That's just the half of it. There's more. But the dialogue, Nick. It's so corny. I don't know why they've written her this way. It lessens the role.'

'How?'

Ellen stood. She ran a hand through her brunette hair, placed another on her hip, pouted: 'When you see some people you say, "Gee!" When you see other people you say, "Ugh!"'

'I get it. But she's right.'

'*She* doesn't exist. That's Schulman.'

'The guy with the belly?'

'That's the one.'

'And does she talk like that?'

'Like what?'

'In the breathy guttural way you delivered that line.'

Ellen sat. 'She's such an actress, but she isn't one, you know what I mean? That's how I intend to play her.'

'You're an actress playing a photographer as an actress? That doesn't sound like acting to me, honey.'

Ellen shrugged. 'It's all in the method, Nick. All in the method.'

The right lung weighs 465 grams and the left 420 grams. Both lungs are moderately congested with some edema.

She swept onto the lot in her pink Lincoln Capri. A few heads went up. She was running late but they'd factored that in, shooting scenes around her. She twitched her nose, sinuses blocked and hurting. Seeds pollinated the surrounding air. She waved to Cukor then ran to her trailer. Baker was there. She held up a flesh-coloured bodystocking.

'Have you seen this?'

Ellen shook her head. 'What is it, a fishing net?'

'It is if you're the fish. It's for the pool scene.'

Ellen laughed. 'I am *not* wearing that.'

Cukor entered the trailer: 'My way or the highway, Ellen.'

She kissed his cheek. 'Is that why you wanted me in the picture?'

He shrugged. 'It's a closed set. Only the necessary crew.'

'How necessary?'

'It's a pivotal scene. Entrapment. Monroe has the pictures and she wants something from Kennedy. When he arrives she's swimming nude. You don't want to swim nude, do you, Ellen? I know you crave authenticity.'

'I don't remember this scene in the script.'

'Schulman's rewriting daily.'

'One hand on the table, one under it.'

Cukor barked a laugh. 'C'mon, Ellen. This picture will make you.'

'*The Girl With The Horizontal Walk*? I'm already made, thank you. Now I'll be typecast.'

Cukor touched her arm. 'It is what it is.' He put one foot on the trailer step. 'They've agreed the wig,' he said. 'It's in the box. On set in an hour.'

Ellen watched the door close. She turned to Baker. 'Some day we'll have equal rights.'

Baker nodded. She walked over to the box, sucked open the lid. 'Here's the wig.'

'Here's the role.' Ellen took the platinum curls and turned them around in her hands, her fingers becoming entangled in the fabric. 'Looks authentic, at least.'

Baker nodded, gestured to the chair by the mirror. 'Are you ready for your transformation?'

Ellen sat. She closed her eyes, searched for the character. Monroe was there somewhere. It was like peeling an onion. You had to discard the layers until all that was left was raw. Baker elongated her eyelashes, red-lipped her pout, stuck on a beauty spot big enough for a picnic, pinned back her hair and then *pinned* the wig into it. When Ellen emerged from the trailer she *was* the photographer, Monroe, a Konica Autoreflex T SLR 35mm camera dangling off its strap on one finger, white jacket, white blouse, white skirt, white heels. She walked the way they wanted her to, right across the lot. Cukor nodded approvingly, standing to one side as she approached the set. She didn't understand his expression, til he yelled *Cut!* and turning she saw the camera rolling behind her.

'Cukor. I feel violated. I want to be an artist not an aphrodisiac.'

'Enough of that. We making a movie or not?'

The liver weighs 1890 grams. The surface is dark brown and smooth.

Light dappled her body as she turned and twisted under the water. She was embraced. She swam to the bottom, touched it with an outstretched finger, then rose upwards, eyes open. Her breasts were in sway with the motion, the water adding fluidity to their movements, something which rarely happened when wearing underwear. She could see Kennedy standing poolside, his left hand holding his right wrist. Breaking the surface she scattered droplets on his black brogues.

'Hey,' she breathed.

'Miss Monroe.' He bent and gripped her extended right wrist, effortlessly hauled her up, residual water stripped from her body as she left the pool, as though she were sloughing a layer.

She stood exposed in the moonlight. She didn't want him to take her, and he had to know that, even though she seemed there for the taking. A couple of inches separated them. She watched him unmoving until goosebumps bumped her dry. Eventually he stood aside and let her pass, handing her a towel which barely covered what he'd seen.

'I thought you might have sent someone.'

His jaw was so chiselled he might have auditioned for Mount Rushmore. 'I wouldn't miss this for the world.'

She walked into the house. Wondered where his body-guards were. 'Something to drink?'

Kennedy nodded. Watched her pour a couple of fingers of bourbon. 'Nothing for yourself?'

'Maybe when we're done.'

'Will we *ever* be done?'

'You'll have it all. The prints, the negatives. I never intended to take those photos. I stumbled into that room.'

Kennedy downed the whiskey. 'You stumble into blackmail, too?'

Monroe sat down, crossed her legs. 'There's a story,' she said. 'There's a pretty girl on the train, not a beauty, but still something to look at. A guy boards and sits opposite. He's not good-looking either, but he's not bad. After a while he leans over, and says, *I hope you don't mind me saying this, but would you sleep with me for a thousand bucks.* The girl does mind, but she doesn't say anything because the offer has caught her attention. There's something she's wanted to buy, for some time now, a pipedream. And he's polite, not a bruiser. So she says, *yes.*' Kennedy watched Monroe's eyes dart around the room. She continued: 'So the guy leans back, crosses one leg over the other. *How about for twenty?* The girl almost shouts, *Twenty! What kind of girl do you think I am?* And the man, Mr President, the man says, *We've already established what kind of girl you are. Now we're just haggling the price.*'

Kennedy eased himself onto the opposite sofa. He placed his empty glass on a wooden side table with an audible knock.

'What security do you have that I won't kill you?'

She laughed. 'I've paid the huntsman.'

Outside, dark fell in a torrent, a molasses-thick night. All the lights of Hollywood couldn't penetrate the gloom.

The spleen weighs 190 grams. The surface is dark red and smooth.

'Keep the wig on.'

'Oh Nick.'

'Just keep it on.'

'Hey, you're hurting.'

'Ssh.'

'Don't *ssh* me!'

'Sorry, losing concentration.'

Ellen put her legs over his shoulders. 'Fuck her then. Fuck Marilyn.'

Nick slid his cock in and out of her cunt. There was something universal in her expression. She was his wife and yet she wasn't his wife.

Ellen did the voice: 'I think sexuality is only attractive when it's natural and spontaneous.'

'Is that from the script?'

'There's always a script.' Ellen put a finger in her mouth and bit. She knew it looked seductive, but it was to keep her from laughing. There was something ridiculous in Nick's ritual determination, something animalistic. She normally loved sex, but getting in Monroe's head had proved anathema. Her character was all about insinuation, but never the act. It was Ellen who had convinced Cukor that simmering heat was better than fire. The script had Kennedy and Monroe making love, but Ellen suggested it should be the mental emasculation of the president which would lead to Monroe's death. Not that it was a death, for she had indeed paid the huntsman.

Nick climaxed and fell on top of her. She tucked her legs around his back, then changed her mind and scissored off him at the onset of cramp. Rolling onto her front she reached out to the side table for a cigarette. 'Want one?'

Nick lay on his back beside her. 'Let's share. You can take that wig off now.'

'Maybe I'll wear it a while. Freak the kids.'

'No. Take it off.'

Ellen pouted. 'What is it now?'

Nick dragged on the cigarette. 'There should always be some distance between fantasy and reality. How's the movie going?'

Ellen sighed. 'The movie doesn't go anywhere, that implies linear motion. We film it in pieces, you know this. Monroe's dead, but then she's already come back, and sometime after she'll also be dead again.'

'You never told me what happens after she's killed.'

'I was saving some surprises for the premiere.'

Nick handed her the cigarette, blew smoke to one side. 'Just tell me, Ellen.'

She turned onto her back, pulled the sheet over her body. 'The president believes Monroe's dead but just like Snow White she's escaped into the forest. She dyes her hair brunette, changes into a plain brown wool suit, spends some time in the Pacific. She could spend all her days there, if she wanted. But she misses the glamour. So she comes back, calls herself Ingrid Tic, gives herself an accent. Fools everyone.'

'Except the president?'

'Except the president.'

Nick leant on his side. 'But what was her story? Where was she *supposed* to have gone?'

'Purgatory or hell. There was a drug overdose. She's supposed to be dead, remember.'

'So who *was* dead?'

Ellen furrowed her brow. 'The script doesn't make that clear. But when we're filming it's actually Baker.'

'Baker? Your make-up girl?'

'She's a ringer, don't you think? They wanted someone who looked like me – like Monroe – but for it not to be me. There has to be a disconnect with the audience, a nudge that maybe Monroe wasn't killed, until it's clear that she's back. So they used Baker. She was right there, after all.'

'Baker . . .' Nick mused. 'I guess Baker would do it. Did she wear the wig?'

He yelped as Ellen's elbow dug his ribs.

The brain weighs 1440 grams.

Ingrid Tic knew her way around a camera and a party. She held the viewfinder to her right eye, smiling as she mingled. Everyone wanted to be photographed, their eyes drawn to the lens. So much so that all anyone saw of Ingrid was her upper body and no one paid attention to her walk.

She was a redhead. She had regained the position she had previously held. She'd been reading. *The Last Temptation of Christ*. Chekhov plays. *The Ballad of the Sad Café*. *The Brothers Karamazov*. She had four hundred and thirty books in her library. And for her current role, *The Actor Prepares* by Konstantin Stanislavsky and *To the Actor* by a different Chekhov. On her night table was *Captain Newman, M.D.* by Leo Calvin Rosten. She was making good progress.

Kennedy was there. It had been just over a year. She couldn't resist.

'Mr President!'

Snap.

98

One of the bodyguards came over, checked her pass. Grunted.

'Oh I know,' she said, 'you cannot be too careful.'

She later realised she had caught his eye.

Everything, including the film in the camera, was loaded. Ingrid followed her way to the bathroom. A girl on her hands and knees was heaving bile into a toilet bowl. Ingrid urinated quickly in the adjacent stall, rinsed her hands, and checked the mirror. There was no question as to who was staring back. It proved that people only saw what they wanted to see. Was hair colour really that important? Of course, they believed she was dead. Maybe that was the difference. You couldn't expect a person to see someone who was no longer there.

Another girl entered, humming a tune from *Ladies of the Chorus*. That musical must be a decade old. The girl lipsticked her mouth, sang *ev'ry body needs a da-da-daddy*.

Ingrid thought: *sometimes they don't don't don't*.

She watched the girl make-up. The girl glanced at the camera slung around Ingrid's shoulder, then at the girl in the cubicle. Smiled. 'Say,' she said. 'You look familiar. Are you the actress, Ellen Arden?'

Ingrid shook her head. She felt strangely dislocated.

She stumbled out of the bathroom and straight into the arms of Cukor.

Cut! he yelled. *What were you doing in there?*

She looked back.

'I was trying,' she said. 'I was trying to be sick.'

The kidneys together weigh 350 grams.

'You've lost more than 25 pounds, I've never seen you so thin.'

She poured herself coffee. They could hear mourning doves from the terrace. She glanced down, saw the maid opening the car for the children. 'It's the role, Nick. I'm doing it for the role.'

'I went down to the lot yesterday. Spoke to Cukor. He says you're not putting the hours in.'

She raised her eyebrows, her anger: 'Why would *you* talk to Cukor?'

He sighed. 'I've seen the rushes. I've seen you. You're not well. You look like a photographer playing an actress as a photographer.'

'Being smart doesn't suit you.'

Nick shook his head. 'Truth is, I'm caught between Ellen and Monroe.'

'I'm Ingrid, Nick. *Ingrid.*'

'Are you kidding me? You can't pull this off. Something's got to give.'

She looked out from the terrace. In the distance, the Santa Monica mountains. She took another sip of coffee, then turned a semi-circle taking in their apartment's wooden backdrop, the props, the cameras, Cukor, the facsimile.

She held up her hand.

'Can we do this again? One more take? And the script. The script is Goddamn awful.'

. . . Monroe wasn't killed. So they used Baker . . .

Cukor spoke to Schulman: 'Is this a work of fiction or isn't it?'

Schulman shuffled his notes, a pencil behind his ear. 'I'm struggling to remember.'

'Just write it like it is. We're never going to finish this picture. We're ten days behind schedule as it is.'

Cukor looked out through his office window. Baker was leaning against the side of Arden's trailer, cigarette nonchalant. Arden had yet to arrive. Some mornings she was heavy-lidded. *Who said nights were for sleep?* When she did arrive, Baker spent so long preparing her for the set she might have been embalming a corpse. Cukor stroked his chin. Baker had played a good corpse. But there was more to an understudy than a physical resemblance. Not that Baker *was* an understudy. He wondered if she could be.

'Let me take a look at that script.'

Schulman handed it over. Watched as Cukor flicked.

It made no sense. Arden was Monroe was Ingrid. Schulman had scored through and rewritten the names so many times that in some places only a hole remained. Baker was written in the margins.

Cukor rubbed his eyes. 'What do you think to Baker?'

'Baker? She's plain, stutters sometimes, is overall drab. What are you thinking about Baker?'

'Could we transform her into Monroe?'

Schulman shook his head. 'You could never transform her into Monroe. You couldn't even transform her into Ellen.'

'*Ellen.* That's what I meant.'

Cukor watched as Ellen's pink Lincoln Capri swept onto the lot. She saw him at the window and waved before disappearing into her trailer. Cukor looked at Schulman. 'You see that?'

'See what?'

'Ellen just arrived as Monroe.'

'So what's she doing now? Transforming back into Baker?'

'Not *Baker*, Schulman. *Ellen.*'

Cukor threw the script to the floor. He left the office and walked across the lot. There was no time for sentimentality.

He swung open the door of the trailer. Ellen was surrounded by the cast and crew. Baker held a sheet cake depicting a naked Ellen. *Happy Birthday (Suit)*. Ellen looked Cukor in the eye and smiled. She was undeniably perfect.

In that glance Cukor might have thought *he* was the president.

'8 mg of chloral hydrate, 4.5 mg of Nembutal.'

There was a hard pain in her stomach. She looked at her hand holding the Bakelite phone which would soon go out of production. She could barely contain herself.

I'm fired? But I've destroyed the negatives.

'The appendix is absent. The gallbladder has been removed.'

Nick!

He looked over the top of his newspaper. The table was set with breakfast things. Fresh coffee. She could smell fresh coffee. Butter was melting into toast.

I paid the huntsman.

'I'm a role,' he said. 'Haven't you read the script?'

But she had *been reading. Chekhov, Conrad, Joyce. There were four hundred and thirty books in her library.*

'The temporal muscles are intact.'

She squeezed her eyes shut. She would count her true friends and everything would be all right. She would count to ten.

One.

'The urinary bladder contains approximately 150 cc of clear straw-coloured fluid.'

Two.

'The stomach is almost completely empty.'

Three.

'No residue of the pills is noted.'

She swung her head around. She'd lost count. Those damn pills. They were supposed to be her salvation.

'No evidence of trauma.'

No evidence of trauma! Who said that? Who's there?

Thomas Noguchi, Deputy Medical Examiner, looked up from Monroe's body.

'Did you just hear something?'

The man who wasn't Kennedy shook his head.

SHE SAID HE SAID

SUSHILA WAS WALKING in the park when she saw Mateo and his male assistant sitting on a bench. As she approached them, she noticed Mateo was dishevelled in his black suit; in fact, he was very drunk, which was unusual for him at that time of day, late afternoon. She greeted him, kissing him on both cheeks, and he asked if she would sleep with him. Why hadn't they slept together? he went on. They could do it right now, at his place, if she had time. He had always found her sexy but had been too nervous to mention it.

They had known each other for at least eighteen years but he had never spoken to her in this way. She was surprised and tried to seem amused. She had always liked him. Clever, witty, Mateo worked with her husband, Len. His wife, Marcie, was a confidante. They had all gone to the coast together.

The next morning, she saw Mateo again, in the supermarket. Not with his assistant, and not drunk, he came right over and repeated his remarks in almost in the same words, adding that Sushila had been with Len for a long time and surely she was bored with him. Women liked variety, he said, and he was offering some. They should get together, even if it was only once; nothing more need be said.

Sushila kept her temper. She told Mateo that she would

never sleep with him. Not in a thousand and one lifetimes. Not ever. If this was his idea of seduction she wouldn't be surprised if he were still a virgin.

Right away she called Len and reported what Mateo had said on both occasions. Len was pale and agitated when he got home. He asked Sushila if she was OK, then texted Mateo to say he wanted to meet. Mateo responded. He was headed out of town. But he hoped that Len had some new artwork to show him. Could he bring it by next week? Len had been drawing so well recently; his work had reached a new level.

Mateo was surprised when Len arrived empty-handed. Where were the new drawings? Four days had passed, and Len was now calm. He had discussed the matter with Sushila and could levelly report to Mateo what he had heard about his behaviour, first when drunk in the park, and then when sober, in the supermarket.

Mateo apologised without reservation and asked Len to forgive him. But Len said that he didn't think he was ready to. Forgiving, or even forgetting, wasn't the point. He didn't understand why Mateo – whom Len thought he knew – had behaved in this way. Mateo said that he had no idea either but that it would be best if they put it behind them. Len asked Mateo why he had repeated the offer to Sushila when he was sober and smart enough to know better, and Mateo said that he hadn't wanted Sushila to think that he wasn't serious, that she wasn't really desired.

Len thanked Mateo for his consideration. After their meeting he walked around the park for a long time, unable to put the conversation out of his mind. Silence breeds poison, he thought, and what had happened pressed on him more and more, until an idea occurred. He would discuss it with

Mateo's wife, Marcie. She and Mateo were still married but no longer together, living next door to each other as friends. Marcie had been seriously ill recently, but Len was keen to know what she made of it all, whether she found her husband's seduction attempts ugly, crazy, or something else. Maybe he was having a breakdown? Or was he just an imbecile and Len had failed to notice?

So Len went to see Marcie, who was convalescing in bed. Knowing she had grown tired of Mateo's antics with other women when they were together, he felt it wasn't wrong to tell her what Mateo had said to Sushila. Marcie knew Mateo; she might be objective.

Having relayed the story, he added that, during their conversations about it Sushila had revealed new facts to him, that he had been unaware of, which no one had told him. It turned out that in the past two years, Mateo had approached other female friends in a similarly crude way. Susan, for instance, had mentioned her experience with Mateo to Sushila, and Zora also. Maybe there were others. Had Marcie also heard about his behaviour?

Len wanted to emphasise that, as Marcie knew, Sushila was kind, protective and certainly no hysteric. It wouldn't be like her to make too much of the exchanges in the park and the supermarket. But she had been humiliated and demeaned by the encounters. What did she, Marcie, think of it all?

Although she listened, Marcie barely said anything; she didn't even move her head in an affirmative or negative direction. Her self-control was remarkable. Usually, when faced with a gap or silence in conversation, people babble. Not Marcie. When at last Len suggested that Mateo seek therapy and the source of his discontent – this was, these days, the generally accepted panacea for wrongdoing – Marcie said that Mateo had been in therapy for *twenty years*. Evidently these things took time, Len said. 'They can do,' Marcie murmured.

When Len went home and told Sushila that he had gone to Marcie's place, she was angry with him. He wasn't her representative. Why hadn't he discussed the plan with her first? She was the one it had happened to. It wasn't even his story. What did he think he was doing?

Len said that there had been nothing light or flirty about Mateo's approach, as far as he understood it. Mateo had insulted *him* as a human being too; he was entitled to take offence and seek an explanation, if not revenge. It wasn't often, he said, that you experienced deliberately inflicted cruelty. And from a friend! His view of Mateo – one of his oldest friends and someone whose advice he had always trusted – had changed for good. The insult was now general. It didn't belong to anyone and it could happen again. Women were at risk. Len would hate himself if he didn't speak out.

Sushila told Len that he was becoming fixated. It had been a lapse. Women had to put up with this kind of thing all the time. Not that she wasn't touched or impressed by Len's concern. But she didn't think Mateo would do it again; he was mortified by what he had said; his regret was genuine and his behaviour had obviously been self-destructive. Len said that self-destructive things were what people most enjoyed doing. Sushila agreed, adding that Mateo resembled a gambler who repeatedly risked his own security. She herself liked rock climbing, which at times put her life in danger. But Marcie would have a word with Mateo. Marcie was the only one who could get through to him. In the future Mateo would hesitate, if only for Marcie's sake.

Len doubted that. And he didn't understand how Marcie could just sit there, putting up with the embarrassment. But Sushila said, please, he knew Marcie was ill. It might be a good idea for him to apologise to her for intruding like that. Was he prepared to do that?

Before he could begin to consider this, Sushila went further. She wanted to speak frankly now. Len could be a little conventional, if not earnest at times, in his ideas about love. He could? he enquired. How was that? Well, Marcie was celibate and Mateo, they were coming to understand, might be a serial abuser. Otherwise they could be the model contemporary couple. Despite everything, they were genuine companions with an unbreakable link that he, Len, couldn't grasp. No one had loved Marcie as Mateo had, and Marcie was devoted to Mateo. Even if he did something crazy now and then, which we all did at times, she stood by him. You had to respect that.

Len mocked the idea of a passionless passion. It didn't make sense and was probably why Mateo was frustrated. Assaulting women made him feel potent.

Sushila said she didn't think that was it. But, with regard to Marcie, she wanted to add that often we love others because of their weakness. And if we were able to keep all the crazy people from being crazy, well, who would want to live in that dull, bureaucratic world?

They had grown tired of discussing it, there was nothing to add, and the topic seemed to have been dropped from their lives, when, a week later, an invitation arrived. Mateo's birthday was the following week and they were invited to the celebration. Sushila went into town and spent an afternoon looking for a present. She asked Len to promise not to say anything. A party wasn't the time or place. Len vowed to keep his mouth shut, adding that he would sulk a little and maintain his distance, so that friends knew the incident had registered but wasn't killing him any more.

However, once they got to the party Mateo, or at least a man who resembled him, approached Len immediately. Mateo had shaved his beard, cropped his hair, and seemed to have coloured it. Before Len could discover if this was a disguise, Mateo put his arm around Len's shoulder and pressed his mouth to his ear. He wanted to have a word with him, over there, in a corner of the room. Would Len follow him, please?

Len had told the story to many people, Mateo said. Someone in Mateo's office had even mentioned it. Now exaggerated rumours were spreading. But hadn't Len accepted his apology and agreed to end the matter? 'Do you want to stab me in the heart and make my wife weep all night?' Mateo said. 'She did that, OK? She cried after you walked right into her home and bullied her. And my assistant, standing over there, saw what happened in the park. He admits it was messy, but no more than that.'

Len pushed him away. 'Don't fucking stand so close to me,' he said. 'You don't know what you're saying. You're actually a savage. What about Susan, Zora and all the other women?'

Mateo replied that everyone knew seduction was difficult these days. In these impossible times, courtship rituals were being corrected. In the chaos, those seeking love would make missteps; there would be misunderstandings, dark before light. Anger was an ever-present possibility. But it was essential that people try to connect, if only for a few hours, that they never give up on their need for contact. Otherwise, we would become a society of strangers. No one would meet or touch. Nothing would happen. And who would want that? Of course, Len was known in their circle to have issues with inhibition. If there was an opportunity to be missed, he'd miss it for sure. Didn't he dream repeatedly that he'd gone to the airport and all the planes had left – at least that was what he had memorably told everyone at supper one night. He was a born misser.

Len told Sushila he had to go out for some air, but once he was outside he didn't want to go back. He felt as if he didn't quite recognise anything any more. The world was stupid, and there was no way around that. He started to walk quickly away but knew that however far he went, he'd have to come back to this place – if he could find it.

SARAH SCHOFIELD

SAFELY GATHERED IN

Thank you for choosing SelfStore4U! Please rest assured – your belongings will be safe within our temperature-controlled and fully monitored units. We pride ourselves on wall-to-wall security. Whatever your reason for requiring self storage we've got it covered – be it house renovations, de-cluttering, or simply to stow your skiing or fishing equipment. Are you moving back home because of break-ups, work commitments or financial problems? Rather than sell all your possessions, and have to start over again, you can store your items with us at SelfStore4U.

We adhere to the highest self-storage standards to provide you with a permanent convenient off-site storage solution.

UNIT 244

  1 Khyam six-man tent
  1 Eurohike pop-up tent. Unicorn design
  1 Vango inflatable sofa. Minus pump
  2 folding camp chairs w/ wine holder
  2 children's camping chairs. Unicorn design
  1 inflatable kayak. 1 oar
  1 gas cooker w/ integrated grill

1 gas bottle

1 Go Outdoors camping box cont. kitchen supplies (spec. 4 plates, 4 bowls, 4 mugs, camping pan set) . . .

This is containerised storage. This is your affordable and safe long- or short-term solution. This is the fix for residential and commercial customers alike. We are just a phone call away. Boxes? Parcel tape? Acid-free tissue paper? All your wants can be supplied.

UNIT 173

12 Tesco Bag for Life cont. asstd. VHS and DVDs. *Friends* box sets, multiple copies *Disney Princess* and *Davina Super Body Workout*

1 IKEA bag cont. small stuffed toy animals

3 IKEA bags cont. medium stuffed toy animals

9 Really Useful storage boxes cont. asstd. *Lancashire Life* and various weekend supplements

1 hanging rail cont. duffel coats (size L), anoraks (size L-XXL, various autumnal shades), leather jackets (black, size L-XXL)

1 green wheelie bin cont. asstd. computers, laptops and electronic components

7 Aldi wheeled shopping baskets cont. leads and chargers

9 broken Dyson Vacuums. Models DC07 x 2, DC14, DC15, DC17 x 3, DC18 x 2

Nail cuttings in a Duerr's fine-cut marmalade jar

We are the answer to all your storage needs. With 24-hour onsite security and CCTV monitoring across our premises, you

will have peace of mind that your goods are in safe hands. Free from sorrow, free from hidden service charges.

Please note that we cannot accept flammable, perishable, live or illegal goods.

UNIT 97

1 Persian rug, circa 1890. Rolled

1 Edwardian dining table and ten upholstered chairs

1 portrait, oil on canvas. Woman w/ auburn hair and amber beads

9 pairs damask curtains. Plum w/ gold-trim tassels

1 four-poster bed. Oak, late Victorian

1 roll top mahogany bureau with inlaid leather gold leaf detail. Secret drawer

1 set of *National Geographic*. Ed. April 1950 – December 1991

1 Tupperware box cont. hair and dust – labelled 'Sweepings'

2 picnic baskets cont. asstd. silver-plate items . . .

Read our great customer reviews! Find us on Trust Pilot.
Our customers come back time and again. Each walled-off pod is your own private world. We are only here to help you to fulfil your storage needs. We care about you. We see how fearful you are of forgetting.

Late payment fees apply. Responsibility for insuring possessions remains with the customer.

UNIT 87

122 cans Tesco Value baked beans
122 tins John West tuna chunks
122 tins Princes corned beef
12 bags Aldi Family bag penne pasta
12 bags Aldi Family bag quick-cook rice
12 boxes Tesco Value Paracetamol
12 boxes Tesco Value Multivitamin
12 bottles Pouilly-Fumé 2017 Ladoucette
12 bottles Rioja Reserva Viña Ardanza 2009 La Rioja Alta
12 bottles Châteauneuf-du-Pape Prestige Des Princes 2016
24 bottles Laurent-Perrier 2008 Champagne
1 Multitool w/ bottle opener
1 axe . . .

In our fully air-conditioned units, your possessions there, for ever purified. We are a hive, honeycombed cells holding your collective dust. Each one sings sad lullabies that map your route back.

UNIT 77

9 Staples file storage boxes cont. foolscap suspension files
1 five-drawer filing cabinet. Red w/ sticking bottom drawer
6 reams of Staples economy-quality computer paper
2 office chairs. Charcoal grey
1 box of flyers. 'Freedom Financial Solutions – We'll make
  your money work for you' . . .

We know your possessions are important to you . . .

We hear you, valued customer. The corrugated door rolling open is a sigh. You pause, before your footsteps crunch over the unit floor. Come to our own temple. Come.

UNIT 323

1 Berketex gown 'Rosetta' on cream satinette hanger. Size
   14 w/ tags
1 pair white diamante studded slingbacks size 6 w/ labels
14 ornamental birdcages
3 gold-effect flower pedestals
150 satin-look polyester dusky pink chair covers (packs of
   10. Sealed.) . . .

Each unit is a harvest and a grave. Wheat and tares together sown. All is safely gathered in, ere the winter sales begin.

UNIT 322

1 metal rack storage system cont. asstd. vintage board games,
   jigsaw puzzles of world landmarks and countryside
   scenes and a Chemcraft chemistry set circa 1950
1 bisque porcelain doll – name tag 'Elise' – w/ real blonde
   hair, wax arms and legs
3 medium boxes cont. Dinky toys. Varied condition
   1935–1976
1 fruit crate cont. Gainsborough pink rose-pattern tea set.
   Missing sugar bowl
1 Willow Pattern serving platter. Circa 1980
1 tissue-wrapped monkey with cymbals. Batteries missing
1 Sotheby's auction catalogue . . .

And this is where it will begin. In UNIT 322. You have no way of knowing. How can you? About the chemicals in the Chemcraft set. Their shelf life. Their instability. The vial within the box that has, over the years, been eroding to become hair thin, until it will finally crack. The solution will bleed from it and react instantly, flickering a livid blue flame. How fragile it all is, really, when you think about it.

The flame will shiver through the tinder-like chemistry box and caress the corner of the auction catalogue. It is all so dry. We pride ourselves on our anti-damp technology! See how the pages will arch and splay, touching onto the tips of Elise's real hair, licking across her fine features, the glaze crackling. See how her hands will melt to flippers. It will drip drip onto the Dinky cars like fat oily rain as the heat rises and the leaden chassis will soften and soon they will run and form mercurial pools on the Willow Pattern platter. Flames will dance across this, hungry for the synthetic furred monkey, where the heat will spread through the mechanism, setting spasms in the springs and he will bang his cymbals frantically.

The heat will lean whispering against the unit walls, and the laced hem of the bridal gown in UNIT 323 will warm and soften. The bodice will crackle to life, beads popping, the plastic boning melting. The flame will flit up the polyester lining and char the garter suspended secretly from the hanger . . .

IN UNIT 77

Flyers will burst from their box and spin to the ground like blackening sycamore seeds . . .

In UNIT 87

Bottles and tins will explode, Rioja mulled to volcanic anger hitting the ceiling, baked beans firing a tattoo against the corrugated walls . . .

In UNIT 97

The mahogany bureau will creak, the joints warping. A secret drawer will spring open and a small twist of paper will burst out. A photo? A love letter? A threat? A promise? It will be sucked up by the heat haze and disintegrate into skin-thin fragments . . .

In UNIT 173

Leather coats will raise their leather arms in the blast of the fire. The duffels will dance and pop their collars. And finally the sprinkler will start, the fine mist vaporising. And, of course, it will be far too late.

In UNIT 244

The sprinkler system will shower the unicorn chairs that have sprung from their bags into angular forms. The gas bottle will bulge. It will vibrate and the valve will hiss. The gauge arrow will melt in the moment immediately before the explosion.

And so later . . . much later . . . what do you think they will do?
  Well, you have no way to tell.
  But you secretly hope that they will come with their fine

sieves, soft brushes and sifting trays to salvage fragments from between the ghosts of buckled corrugated walls. That they will catalogue the remnants and display them on soft velvet cushions behind glass in the city centre museum. Come see, thankful people, Come! Scraps of smutted lace, a tattered label clinging to a curved shard of wine bottle, the charred bones of a folding chair, one warped miniature cymbal . . . Sticky-fingered children will glance at them on their way to the gift shop, where they will pester their parents for erasers and pencils and snow globes decorated with the SelfStore4U logo. And nostalgic, misty-eyed parents will dig out their wallets.

BELLY

VANESSA COULDN'T BELIEVE her luck when Reggie asked her out. *I'll treat you to a Nando's*, he said.

He drove her to the West End in a silver Volkswagen Golf GTi. Vanessa didn't dare ask where he'd got it. They abandoned the car down a side street off Charing Cross Road and ran laughing towards Trafalgar Square.

Reggie scrambled up the nearest stone plinth, pulling Vanessa up behind him until they were sitting opposite each other on one of the monumental bronze lions. Vanessa watched Reggie pull a spliff out of his pocket. He lit it, took a drag, and passed it to her. She inhaled and then breathed out as slowly and as nonchalantly as she could. She didn't want to cough in case Reggie laughed at her. The air around them was herby, sickly sweet.

We should get married, Reggie said.

You'd have to ask me first, said Vanessa.

How many kids should we have?

Two. A girl and a boy.

In Nando's, Reggie told Vanessa all about himself and Vanessa listened, nodded and smiled. The taste of peri-peri chicken, greasy fries, and the fizz of ice-cold Coke in her mouth was bliss. Reggie realised he'd forgotten his wallet at home so Vanessa paid.

They caught the N29 bus home, and when they got off at the last stop Reggie said, *I'll call you*. And Vanessa thought but did not say, *You haven't got my number*.

Two weeks later, Vanessa was out shopping with her mum when she noticed a boy and girl walking down the opposite side of the High Street. Vanessa couldn't help but notice the way the girl's belly strained against her T-shirt, protruding so much that she thought it might burst through the fabric, exposing its thin skin and thready veins to the world. The boy held the girl's hand tightly. He was almost pulling her along.

Vanessa's mum asked, *Who are you staring at?* And Vanessa replied, *No-one*.

THE FURTHER DARK

YOU'VE BEEN LOOKING at the email for hours and hours, the same email. Or have hours joined together to create a day and in turn days added one after another to make a week, a fortnight, a month? You find it scary to think that. So look away from the screen. Turn your head and gaze around the room. Get up out of your chair. Tell yourself to get up. OK, flatten your feet on the floor under your desk. Feel the pressure in your arches, every wriggle of your toes. Concentrate and the rest will follow. Or don't think at all and your muscles will act instinctively. Part of a chain reaction. Or perhaps not. Keep still, keep still, don't move. You're fuddled. Keep repeating yourself, it's funny how quickly it all becomes true. Stay still. Concentrate.

If you start at the beginning, surely you'll make sense of this. You will work out what is happening. You will work out why you feel this way. You can remember when the first email came. You were having coffee with . . . Maria? Somewhere down the road. Somewhere no more than one hundred steps from here. You're faint and exhausted. Sweating. You don't believe the clock in the bottom corner of your computer screen. But this is your room, your familiar room, you know everything in it, all your trinkets and non-precious objects, it's your room, you're repeating yourself now. Isn't that meant to be comforting, isn't that a way of reinforcing your sense of self in your surroundings if you just go on repeating this really isn't, this really isn't good for you. Keep saying it anyway. This is your room.

Are you hungry? You have food in the kitchen but you would have to stand up to access it and this you can't seem to do even if you are telling yourself this is what you want. You can't remember when you last ate. So you must be hungry. Repeat to yourself. You are going to eat right now. Order a pizza with free home delivery. You will choose the toppings you like: cracked pepper, artichoke, caramelised onion? At least you recognise their names though you can't for the life of you remember how they taste. Why not include a half-price fizzy drink with your order? You will open the door when you hear the bell. But that means standing up, moving about, taking steps. Your life is right here on the screen in front of you . . . you can't see anything else that's why you can't turn round you look at your fingers resting on the keyboard, awaiting instructions; delete or open? It's too hard a choice, too hard too hard too hard you repeat you repeat you repeat . . .

You received the email yesterday or could it have been last week? In your inbox on your screen you really need to focus. You click. You open. That part is easy. You see a blank. A blank is what you're looking at a blank is what you've been trying to get your head round staring at the screen hypnotised by next to nothing this is what you keep coming back to this is why you can't leave it because even though you can't see anything anything anything you keep repeating to yourself you know there must be something there because why would someone be sending you a blank email. Repeatedly. Over and over again. The same email. Blank.

You remember contacting Maria about this when it started and Charles and your online crony redFox rich in stoner wisdom and @id.iot, no that's wrong, it's @id.iot who is contacting you. The blank emails are from @id.iot. Unknown person. How much sense does that make you think and suddenly it makes perfect sense. Blank blank blank blank blank. *They're not blank!* Maria says this to you, on one of them there's a button you can press to make them stop. This is what I've heard anyway, she says, and yeah I know that goes against everything you've ever had dinged in your head that you mustn't click on any links cos they'll take you to the bad place all your files corrupted your identity stolen proper rinsed and all those things you *meant* to clear from your cache sent to your mumdad wifehusband boygirlfriend workmateboss & anyone at all you've ever wanted to impress literally the end of your fucking world . . . But I still can't see any button, you reply, there is no button. It has to be right there mate open it with a different browser. Or copy the whole damned thing into a program that shows you hiddentext . . .

But nothing is revealed nothing is ever revealed, no hidden words, no symbols, or magic buttons, and you try the same technique on each and every new email as it arrives nothing nothing nothing. Try another trick. Search for message, sender *@id.iot*, select all and then delete the whole damned lot. Gone! For a split second. Who was that old king trying to hold back the tide, Canute or Knut, they changed the spelling? And then refresh. Here they come, spewing forth cascading the deluge descends and whoosh! Your inbox chokes up with the same empty messages, and your actual emails – the ones from your friends your real friends your friends and colleagues – are submerged and lost under the pressure of incoming incoming incoming. Isolation cocoon bloody mental lockdown! Think: this is spam with no purpose apart from to really mess with your head. Don't take it personally. @id.iot is not about you. You are not special chosen. This is spam nothing else. Tell yourself this over and over. You random victim, one of very many nice kind. I like you! Send bitcoin now and I treat you good. Boom Boom. Special investment. One weird tip. Delete as inappropriate. You are not being punished. But no, no, no. If only. Instead: blank, blank, blank, no message, not a sales pitch. Nothing. Keep deleting.

A fly crawls across the screen. What is it connecting with? Perhaps the demon familiar of @id.iot. Idiosyncratic. Private. Private. Private. Private. Open each new message one after another, without sleep, into the night the day the. This is your work now you're not even *angry* any more. No movements but for the repeated tapping of your fingers on the keys, and the emails continue to arrive courtesy of an algorithm you try to tell yourself this in a bid to take back some control all blank blank blank, blink blank blank, blink blank, BLANK and on and on and on and you open each in turn trying to keep up with the flow and you gaze at each in turn, empty screen, six seconds each which is a LONG time more than enough to absorb its absence of meaning, click blink click blink click blink blank and on to the next next next next blank next. You are entranced. Your mind the same now, no content, your mind as blank as the screen and imagination fails imagine imagine *that* as your body slows down, weakens, becomes heavy like too much gravity pressing down. Concentrate! Put every last single pitiful scrap of effort in that one tiny movement, your index finger pressing over and over and over endlessly again as the hours pass, the seconds, the days, the weeks and then you see the content at last that single line of text against the white space, the one email you've been waiting for

press here to stop all this

and you jam and hold your finger down on the keyboard waiting wanting hoping for what? Think think think think blink. What DO you want? To be taken away somewhere new where something good or bad would be a change a release an escape from torment but the web is not a web it's nothing but a sticky mess and now you're stuck, trapped in your own wherever dark, and into your head pops that line from Ovid: *She rose up from the ghosts of the recently dead, walking slowly because of her wound.* Right? Where the snake bit her and poisoned her stone cold no pulse no breath, so how come bloody Eurydice gets another chance at life, but you but you why not you, or you might put it this way: I have risen from the ghosts of the living dead, holding my head in my hands, seeking a pathway lost. The music in my earbuds died a very long time ago. OK, listen closely: there is no magic button. There is no escape, so why not turn off your machine? Just disconnect. Power down. Why not? But remember: beyond that darkness – soothing, languorous and weirdly welcoming – there is only the further dark.

Stand up. Walk to the window. Lift the blind and gaze out, across and down at the street. Observe the back of your hand reflected in the glass; why does it look like it belongs to somebody else? Go into the bathroom but you don't seem to need to pee. Splash water on your face. Avoid the mirror. Decide to sprawl on the comfy couch and stick your feet on the coffee table. There's a hole in one of your socks but no big deal. You wonder how many times the hands of your clock have gone round since you last looked. You flip through the pages of a book. Nothing makes sense. Don't think about the screen on the desk your emails the blank messages. You could close your eyes. Is there light outside? Ticktock. It's morning. It's evening. And you glance at your phone over there not ringing never ringing.

Or you could go out to the cafe just one hundred steps down the road, or the public house, maybe, just across the street. The Rose and Crown. Maria and your other friends will be there, chatting away as though nothing at all has ever happened. You take a pew. A drink appears on the table in front of you. You nod thanks. You are fine, thanks. The conversation turns away from you as you evidently don't feel much like talking today. But all you want, all you are waiting for, really, is for just one of them to ask you: What happened, mate? When you pressed the button? Did you press the button? Will they will they will they will they will they ever ask?

But no. They barely look at you. No one asks. You've got that floaty feeling. Reach for the table edge. Hold on tight. Now your friends are all laughing at a joke and you make a huge effort to join in but your laugh is mistimed. They don't notice. So study your nails. Then your fingertips: are these loops whorls arches the same as they ever were? You've had enough. No point excusing yourself. Just head for the toilets where you find yourself waiting waiting waiting for the tap to stop rinsing soap off your hands. Dare the mirror at last and see your features your eyes your lips your hair start to fade to fade to fade. Blink. Then look away. No second glance. Keep on walking, touching and holding each object as you reach it. The dryer, the wall, the door jamb, Maria's hand . . .

SAME SAME BUT DIFFERENT

SHE WAS STAYING in a part of Bangkok choked by a tangle of overhead power cables. The nearer we got to her place, the stealthier she became. She was acting like a burglar. Halfway down a deserted side-street crawling with cats and stinking of sewage, she came to an abrupt halt in front of a three-storey building that had bars on the ground-floor windows and a front door made from a combination of wood and corrugated iron. As if she were being watched, she slowly pushed the door open and we entered a gloomy, low-ceilinged hallway with a wooden staircase just about visible in the distance. She started towards it but stopped when I asked, 'No light?'

'Keep your voice down!' she snapped. 'It's late. People are asleep. The bulb's blown.'

Earlier that evening, in the bar, she had been very attentive towards me, occasionally touching my knee and making sexual innuendos; now she didn't seem bothered. There was an air of officiousness about her, she had a job to do and was keen to get on with it. At the top of the stairs she flicked a switch and one of two overhead strip bulbs flickered into life.

A tiled landing ran off to our right with doors on either side. Creeping along, we passed a picture on the wall of the bespectacled king whose image seemed to adorn every public space in the city. There was even one in my room back at The Grace. The picture was hanging askew in a cheap, gold-painted frame that did nothing for the regality of the subject.

The bulb was blown in her room too. Through a narrow, frosted window a shaft of street light fell diagonally across the floor, strong enough for me to see the room was sizeable but bare: a single mattress on the floor covered by a crumpled white sheet, an enormous rucksack leaning against the wall with several items of clothing spilling from the top and a few others in a pile on the floor. Hot and stuffy, the room could have done with an airing and the tiled floor clearly hadn't been swept in a while, judging by the grit that crunched under our feet as we came in. Kicking off her flip-flops, she padded over to the bed and started to arrange it, even though there was nothing to arrange. I hung back. All evening I had been feeling aroused, but now sex was the last thing on my mind. I thought about Miriam and could almost hear her telling me to 'just go for it'.

She finished smoothing the sheet and started heading for the door.

'Where're you going?' I asked, trying to disguise my anxiety.

'Bathroom,' she replied. 'You gonna stand there all night?'

I moved into the room proper and she slipped past me out the door. I dragged my feet over to the bed and crouched down, beginning to inspect the sheet. Up close, it didn't seem as dirty as I had imagined, so I sat on the edge of the mattress and removed my trainers. Moments later I heard the unmistakable sound of someone urinating into a toilet bowl. I swung my legs up onto the mattress, rested my head and back against the flimsy partition wall, and listened for a while.

I began to review the changes I had made to my life in the last few weeks, in the process of which I experienced the old familiar panic: had I done the right thing? Anna hadn't thought so, and yet she hadn't made much effort to try to stop me. If I was determined to ruin what we had, the life we were building together, she wasn't going to stand in my way. The funny thing was, at no point had I mentioned splitting up. I had simply said that I was thinking of quitting my job to go travelling for a while, and maybe hook up with Miriam in Thailand, but for Anna that was another way of saying I wanted out. She would brook none of my attempts to make her think otherwise. 'You're obviously searching for something, but I don't see why you have to smash up our lives to go looking for it.'

She was right. I *was* looking for something, had been for years, but I could never put my finger on what it was or where I might find it. Be it at work or at play, nothing had ever sustained me beyond the initial burst of interest. Not that anyone could tell. I could feign it with the best of them, I could put on the face of a contented, successful careerist and pass myself off as someone to look up to and admire, but inside I felt like the only person doing backstroke in a pool full of front-crawlers. The day I cracked and spoke to Miriam about it she said, 'Sounds like you're having an EC.' When I looked at her askance she said, 'Existential crisis' and advised therapy. I laughed. I was as likely to start seeing a shrink as I was to drink paint. When it came to such matters I was, and had always been, a confirmed sceptic, more inclined towards self-help than psychiatric, and yet a belief in my own abilities hadn't brought me any closer to discovering the source of my angst. Perhaps I would never discover it. As I sat there in that dismal room, feeling a long way from home, waiting to have sex with a person who clearly had as much feeling for me as a dog for a fence-post, the walls seemed to be closing in.

It was the first night of my first trip to Bangkok and, so far, the city had been a huge disappointment. I had expected the noise, the pollution and the overcrowding, but was surprised by the squalor and the crumbling buildings dotted with rusting air-conditioning machines. I'd been in a grumpy mood since landing at the airport. Needing a room for the night before heading to Koh Samui to meet up with Miriam, I had spent a long time at the hotel reservations desk in the arrival lounge leafing through glossy brochures that featured page after page of sky-scraper hotels. To my inexperienced eyes, they all looked the same. I couldn't choose between them and regretted that I hadn't thought to book something back in the UK. More from impatience than a desire to help me decide, the young woman at the desk had tapped her French-polished nail on the page and said, 'Very good this one. Central, cheap, have pool,' but for some reason she failed to mention that The Grace was also a knocking shop. Later, when I walked into its faded, high-ceilinged lobby and saw the amount of middle-aged Arab men lounging around with young Thai girls draped across their fat bellies, I was repulsed. I was no prude, and this was Thailand after all, but there was something so off-putting about the scene I almost cancelled my reservation. I only didn't because I couldn't face traipsing about the city in the mid-afternoon sun searching for an alternative. Not on the back of a non-stop, fourteen-hour flight from Manchester.

Later that evening, after a revitalising sleep, I left The Grace to find something to eat. In a nearby food hall I had an extremely tasty dish of deep-fried fish in sweet chilli sauce, accompanied by a steaming-hot bowl of egg-fried rice: all for the princely sum of five pounds. Things were looking up. My fellow diners consisted almost entirely of Western men and their Thai 'girlfriends'. One guy, wearing an England football shirt and clearly stoned, had been eyeing me from the moment I arrived. He was one of the few men sitting by himself and after a while he got up from his table and came and sat on the bench next to me. I resisted the urge to move to another table as I didn't want to draw attention. I was feeling conspicuous enough. He introduced himself as Pete, Pete from Peckham, and within minutes was telling me, in a very loud voice, about all the countries he'd visited and what he'd got up to and where he was planning on going next. In this way I learned that he'd been on the road for almost a year, crisscrossing south-east Asia on a seemingly endless quest to, as he put it, 'have it large'. He made me think of Miriam, who'd been travelling for a similar amount of time, in the same part of the world, making me jealous with all her Insta posts. She seemed to be having the time of her life. Travelling seemed to agree with her, but the same could not be said for Peckham Pete. Gaunt enough to be skeletal, he had dirty, broken fingernails, crusty, sun-bleached dreads and a long, wispy, unkempt beard that put me in mind of a wizard. If he had left the UK with any light in his eyes, not a trace remained. On and on he prattled. At one point, just for something to say, I told him I was off to Koh Samui first thing in the morning and he started bombarding me with tips. 'Stay away from Lamai

Beach. Boring as fuck. Fulla tofu eaters and yoga freaks. Head for Chaweng. That's where it's all 'appening. Cheap booze, drugs. You name it!'

After an hour or so in the food hall I felt a headache coming on, caused by a combination of listening to Pete and the glare from the blinding strip lighting. I had to get some air, stretch my legs. As I stood up Pete said, 'You off, then?' I nodded and he added, 'Nice meeting you.' His disappointment was all too apparent. I smiled and walked over to the counter to pay my bill. While I was settling up, I could feel Pete's lecherous eyes on me. I couldn't wait to get away.

I spent the next or hour or so meandering around a set of narrow, deserted back streets that put me slightly on edge. At one point I fetched up in what amounted to an African quarter. I was so surprised to find such a high concentration of black people in such an improbable location that I was momentarily confounded. My overriding feeling, however, was one of relief. No-one seemed especially interested in me. For the first time since arriving in the city I wasn't being gawped at.

When my feet began to ache - Converse trainers are not ideal for pounding pavements - I popped into a bar. A narrow hole in the wall with a few stools jammed up against a counter, the place was deserted. In the cramped area behind the counter sat two dark-skinned Thai women with long black hair and more attitude than I was prepared for. They didn't so much as nod, let alone try to serve me. I stood at the counter and waited for one to approach, but instead they averted their eyes and started speaking in Thai. I was baffled. They had clearly seen me, and it was obvious that I was waiting to be served, so what the hell were they playing at? So much, I thought, for the famed Thai hospitality. I cleared my throat and, trying to disguise my anger, said, 'Excuse me, would it be possible to get a bit of service, please?' No sooner had I finished than an old white guy with a copper-tan face and a grey, walrus moustache emerged from a room behind the counter through a beaded curtain. Though quite bald on top, he was sporting a grey pony-tail and was dressed in a black sleeveless T-shirt that showed off his flabby tattooed arms, and a pair of washed-out denim shorts. I pegged him for a retired biker seeing out his days in the tropics. He came straight over and said, 'Where you from?' His accent was North American and, judging by the way the girls stiffened in his presence, either owned the place or ran it. When I told him I was from London, he visibly relaxed.

'Well that explains a lot.' He stared at me before continuing, 'Listen, no offence, but as a rule we don't usually serve your type in here. Gotta bunch o' Nigerians round the way who were using the place to peddle dope. Had to bar 'em, see? But you're all right. And just to show there's no hard feelings, have a drink on me. What's your poison?' I couldn't believe my ears.

'I'm good,' I said, then turned and walked.

I spent the next few minutes ambling along a busy main road, trying not to think about how much I missed Anna, becoming increasingly annoyed at having to negotiate the narrow, overcrowded pavements. Several times I was forced to walk in the street. At other times I had to press myself against a wall or a shop front to allow people to go by. All the while I kept getting stared at. During our last WhatsApp chat, Miriam had encouraged me to make a trip to the famous

Khao San Road. She'd called it 'the spot' and said it was full of 'hot chicks'. It didn't sound like my kind of place, but it was either that or head back to my hotel room to watch TV.

The tuk-tuk ride got me to Khao San Road in about twenty minutes. On the way, the narrow maze of streets became clogged with vehicles and the air increasingly polluted. Several times I had to cover my nose and mouth to avoid inhaling the cloying stench of petrol fumes, and such was the humidity that even in an open-sided tuk-tuk I was sweating all over. Toy, my poker-faced driver, deposited me at what he said was the quieter end of Khao San Road. Thick with backpackers, it didn't seem quiet to me. Toy and I haggled good-humouredly over the fare before I relented and paid him what he originally asked for. Wearing nothing but a pair of faded Hawaiian shorts and some worn-down flip-flops, he kissed the back of my hand theatrically, started the engine of his tuk-tuk, turned it down a side-street and was gone. Moments later I was surrounded by a trio of small Thai boys. They seemed to appear out of nowhere and must have been waiting for the right moment to pounce. None looked older than twelve. Tugging at my arm and fighting with each other for my attention, they shoved their wares into my face with barely controlled aggression. One had a forearm full of leather bracelets, another was clutching a fistful of fake gold jewellery, while the third specialised in what looked to me like satin scarves. Everything was available at a 'special price'. Politely but firmly, I told them I wasn't interested and to emphasise the point wriggled free of their clutches and strode purposefully away. Long after I'd gone I heard them calling, but I didn't look back. I didn't dare.

There was no other way to get down Khao San Road except

to stroll. At every turn someone was blocking my path. With a mounting sense of frustration, it eventually dawned on me that I was in a rush to go nowhere and that I would have a far better time of it if I did like everyone else and slowed down. It was all too easy to see why the road attracted so many backpackers. It had an aroma of vice almost as pungent as the roadside food stalls. Miriam had described the area as vibrant, which was beginning to seem like a euphemism for noisy. Techno blared from open-fronted, neon-lit bars and each bar had its attendant knot of silver-tongued, English-speaking touts shouting at the passersby and shoving laminated drinks menus into their faces. 'Happy Hour cocktail. Beer cheap cheap.' For a while I managed to avoid making eye contact with them, but eventually a dark-skinned middle-aged man in a pair of denim shorts caught my attention and shouted, 'Hellooooo!' When I smiled, he patted his arm, said, 'Same same, but different!', cackling at the top of his voice. I was so embarrassed I put my head down and hurried away as fast as the crowd permitted, the sound of the man's laughter, and those of his co-workers ringing in my ears. Feeling conspicuous again, I took cover in a nearby Irish pub.

Soft lighting. Stained wood panelling. Unvarnished wooden tables and chairs. Upholstered booths. Framed olde worlde posters advertising whisky and Guinness and Irish coffee and other famous beverages from the Emerald Isle. Gaelic background music. Shannon's Pub was striving hard for authenticity, but as someone who'd visited Ireland a few times, I could say with certainty that the overall effect was more Oxford Street than Dublin. At a glance, the clientele seemed to be a relaxed co-mingling of Thais and Westerners, most sitting towards the rear of the pub below a mounted wide-screen TV, watching a re-run match between Man United and Everton. Among them I noticed several United strips, worn by Thais and westerners alike. For several minutes I stood near the deserted bar watching the game ebb and flow until I heard a male voice say, somewhat tetchily, 'I can help you?'

I turned to see a Thai barman staring at me. He was young, pasty-faced and bony, with close-cropped dark hair and a couple of silver hoops dangling from his right ear lobe. His leather bracelets, tattooed fingers and crushed white t-shirt with a picture of a snarling Joe Strummer screamed *I might be a local, but I'm worldly, so don't even think about patronising me.*

'Pint of Guinness, please.' It felt strange ordering Guinness in Bangkok, but I figured I'd try it if only as a way to compare and contrast.

'You must be rich.'

A female voice this time, English, home counties. Turning to my left, I saw a young, elfin-faced white woman standing at the bar beside me. She had braided, strawberry-blonde hair and wore a white, half-cut blouse with an elasticated bottom that clung to her visible rib-cage. In the gap between her blouse and what I later came to know as Thai fisherman's trousers – a loose-fitting kind of skirt-trousers held together by straps – I noticed she had a sunken stomach and that the top of her black knickers was showing slightly.

'Were you talking to me?'

The barman turned away to watch the game. He seemed grateful for the opportunity. The woman stepped closer to me, cupped her hand over my ear – a surprisingly intimate gesture that gave me a jolt – and whispered, 'The Guinness is over a tenner a pint.'

I must have reacted with shock because she stepped back

and started nodding her head. Before I could say anything, she leaned in again and whispered, 'I'd recommend the local rum. You can buy a bucket of it with Coke for about a fiver and it lasts a lot longer than a pint of Guinness. We could share it. That way you won't have to buy me a drink.' She stepped back again and stretched out her hand, which struck me as oddly formal after her earlier behaviour, and said, 'Kelly.'

Slightly bemused, I shook her clammy hand and said, 'Afia.'

We took our bucket of rum and Coke, served with ice-cubes and two straws, and went and sat at a pavement table near the entrance. The heat was a welcome relief from the chill of the pub's air-conditioned interior and I took it as a sign that I was already beginning to acclimatise. As soon as we were seated Kelly said, 'Know why they serve it with straws?' I shook my head. 'Apparently, you get less oxygen drinking through a straw, which means you get mashed a lot quicker.'

I gave her a quizzical look. 'Isn't that a myth?'

She shrugged and replied, 'Who the hell cares?'

Using both hands, she lifted the plastic bucket to her head, sucked long and hard on her straw and handed me the bucket as though we were smoking a peace pipe. I took a sip and almost had to spit. 'Damn, that's strong!'

Kelly laughed. 'That's how they serve it here. You get used to it.' She patted my forearm. 'Diddums. Don't worry. The ice'll dilute it.'

The condescension didn't make me warm to her but I definitely fancied her. She was pretty, no doubt, with a confidence, even arrogance, that belied her slight frame and softly spoken voice. She had the look of someone who'd seen it all and bought the commemorative mug. Under the street light, her tan was more visible and deep enough to suggest she'd been away a long time. I was grateful that she wasn't covered in mosquito bites. She had the odd one here and there, on her forearms and ankles, but nothing like some of the women I'd seen. She didn't look like she had the pox.

'I hope you're not expecting small talk,' she said, suddenly. 'I don't do it. Can't. Too boring.' She bent forward, sucked on her straw, straightened up again and said, 'You've probably got all these questions you want to ask me, but I make a habit of telling girls my life story after I've slept with 'em, not before. That way I don't scare 'em off.'

Leaning back in my chair, I made a deliberate show of appraising her. I was hoping she might keep talking, as I was enjoying her forced attempts to appear interesting, but she simply looked at me, a half smile on her face, a teasing smile.

'Drink up.' Using one hand this time, she lifted the bucket and held it in front of my face. I took a sip, pulled away, but she kept the bucket in place. 'C'mon, get it down you.'

I swallowed hard and went back for seconds, taking several long gulps through the straw. 'That's the "spirit",' she said, and winked. When I could take no more I shoved the bucket away, almost spilling the contents. She laughed, lifting the bucket to her face and sucking on her straw till she became hollow-cheeked. When she finished she was flushed red and clearly out of breath, though she tried to hide it. She set the bucket down, smacked her lips a few times and said, 'Might be cheap that stuff, but it certainly does the job.'

I was already feeling tipsy. 'You trying to get me drunk?'

Kelly smiled and said, 'And I thought I was being subtle.'

I couldn't work out how long I had been asleep, but it must have been a good few hours because when I opened my eyes dawn had broken, the light penetrating the room and throwing its scuzzy décor into even sharper relief. Kelly was nowhere to be seen and I immediately knew she had gone. The fact that all her things were missing confirmed my suspicions. I stood up, swooned, had to sit down again. I felt dreadful. My head was pounding. My neck and back were stiff from resting against the wall for so long. My throat was parched. Desperately, I swallowed some saliva, but it had little effect. With considerable effort, I started hauling on my trainers and just then I heard movement in the bathroom next door, followed by the sound of running water. Kelly?

I laboured to my feet and shuffled to the door to check, but when I opened it I saw a short, fat Thai man come out of the bathroom with a towel wrapped around his waist, his dimpled gut hanging over the top. He hadn't seen me, so I pulled my head back into the room, closed the door quietly and tip-toed back to the bed. For some reason I felt safer on that side of the room. For a while I just stood there looking around, as if I couldn't quite believe Kelly had gone. I walked over to the chest of drawers and opened them one by one. Empty. What was I hoping to find? Feeling sorry for myself, I realised it was time to leave. I didn't have a clue what part of the city I was in, so I decided I would hail the first taxi I saw and get it to take me to The Grace, no matter the cost. As soon as I thought that my heart sank. I didn't need to check my bumbag to know Kelly had stolen my money.

The taxi driver clearly didn't believe my story. When we got to The Grace and I asked him to wait outside while I went in and got some money from the safe in my room, he insisted on coming into the hotel with me. I was offended by his mistrust, but I didn't have the energy to argue. At the reception desk, he satisfied himself that I was a guest then waited in the lobby while I went up to my room on the sixteenth floor to get his fare. When I entered the room, I resisted the urge to throw myself on the bed. It looked so inviting, so luxurious. My anger at being robbed was already beginning to subside, mostly through exhaustion, but also because, having had the chance to think about it, I realised it could have been a lot worse. I had lost about two hundred pounds worth of Thai baht, but my credit card, passport and the rest of my cash were tucked away in the hotel safe. Still, I decided that I would report Kelly to the police. I knew she would never be caught. Her description would probably fit dozens of women in the city and I doubted whether Kelly was even her real name, but it was the principle of the thing.

Back downstairs I paid the driver, tipped him for waiting, and told my story to a smiley receptionist whose face was caked in skin-whitener. She listened patiently then got on the phone. Within minutes a young policeman arrived, wearing a brown, skin-tight uniform with his shirt tucked into his trousers. He was from the tourist division and just happened to be in the area. Sitting next to me in the bustling lobby, near a large bay window with tinted windows, he used a small notepad and pencil to take down the particulars of the theft. When he'd finished, he scolded me for not taking Kelly back to the hotel. He said that all guests, even casual visitors, had to register with reception and must give a valid form of ID. His advice made my hairs stand on end. Before leaving the bar, I had suggested to Kelly that we go back to my hotel but she had refused, saying she would feel more relaxed at her place. That may well have been true, but she obviously wanted to avoid detection. The policeman confirmed that it was unlikely she would be caught but commended me for re-porting her. He said it would help when it came to compiling criminal statistics and that it gave the local authorities useful anecdotal evidence of what he called 'inter-tourist crime'. Apparently, it was quite common.

After I'd given my statement, I went into one of several massage parlours that operated in the hotel lobby and treated myself to a rejuvenating back, neck and shoulder rub. Throughout the treatment, I thought of Anna. It had only been a few weeks since we'd split and there'd been no contact at her insistence. I yearned to hear from her, and actually got out my mobile with the intention of sending her a WhatsApp, but thought better. She was unlikely to reply and a snub was the last thing I wanted. After the massage, I went to a nearby travel agent and booked a flight to Koh Samui, scheduled to leave in three hours. I also reserved a bungalow in a beach-side resort called Tiki-Tiki. It had been recommended by Miriam. She'd stayed there once and enjoyed it so much she'd posted a favourable review on TripAdvisor. The plan was to meet her there when she arrived from Vietnam later in the week.

On my way back, I felt hungry and stopped in at an open-fronted cafe that had an A-board on the pavement outside advertising English, American and Continental breakfasts. The place was deserted except for an elderly white couple sitting side-by-side at a small table, poring over a map. When I walked in they shot me a glance then quickly looked away and began to fidget self-consciously. The day before, fresh off the plane, I'd have bristled, but at that moment I felt sorry for them. They seemed so uncomfortable.

At the counter, I ordered a couple of croissants and an Americano from a cheerless old Thai man, then went and sat at a table near the entrance. I had to put on my sunglasses to combat the glare reflecting off the tinted windows of the skyscraper building opposite. For the next few minutes, waiting for my breakfast to arrive, I watched the traffic go by, both vehicular and pedestrian, trying in vain to ignore the smell of petrol and exhaust fumes. At one point a tuk-tuk raced by, the engine droning like a swarm of bees. A scrap of paper went flying into the air then came fluttering down again, blown this way and that by competing currents. Just as it was about to settle, it got caught on another current and went soaring upwards again. After a few seconds it blew down a side-street and out of view and I found myself hoping that it was still airborne, flitting about the city like a butterfly.

BACKBONE

MY FATHER LONG ago said – about something I had found tough, really tough, almost too tough, for me, almost too much – that the thing was to find your way to letting it shift from being a big thing to being a small thing.

This I thought sage. This I thought helpful. This I remembered.

Easier to remember, perhaps, than to actuate.

My partner and I would always joke about my having had back surgery. My partner at the time. The joke was about the fact – true or imagined – that I was the kind of person who would walk into a room always in the company of my surgery. With, as it were, my surgery on my arm: May I have the pleasure of making you acquainted with my back surgery?

Or – we'd be out on the street, in the city, and someone would, say, jostle just that bit too hard on their way past, and my partner – whose comic timing I have to say was better than mine – would wait just a beat and then call out, Hey, don't you know she's just had back surgery? And then my partner would turn to me po-faced and say, I don't think they appreciate that it was *major* back surgery.

Anyway, that was the joke. It served purposes.

❧

So. This is the way a friend of mine used to start his stories. So.

So – I needed some backbone. I signed a form. I had the strangest feeling that the anaesthetist was laughing at me as I went under. Five. Four. Three.

Anaesthetic is the strangest thing. The strangest thing. Complete surrender. How can such complete surrender be acceptable? That degree of trust.

I woke up. And I'll be honest. I woke up happy. I knew there was something solid in me now, something fixed.

Though I could not imagine what had gone on inside my body. If I'd been asked to describe what it looked like in there now, I couldn't have said.

A visitor. My mother. She stood at my bedside and she smiled and she wept. I found this lovely and I found it also unnerving. And then I was alone, because she left.

I lay there. I lay there a while – I had to lie there a few days in fact, for the backbone to take.

Here are some of the things I began to notice as I lay there (I gave them numbers as I lay there to create some kind of order in my mind):

1. I could wiggle my toes. I was grateful. I'd been worried beforehand that this facility might be gone. (Though my toes – afterwards – hard to explain – but they felt disconnected.)

2. Flat on my back I did not know how to move. There were people who came and went. They adjusted things attached to me – wires and tubes. But this critical matter of how

to move was not something anyone seemed compelled to address. I myself, in the state I was in, shelved the issue for later.

3.   I had not been told I would no longer know the difference between what I saw, eyes shut and eyes open. This confused me. It all looked the same. I'd open my eyes and see the beds lined up opposite, the rows of bedside lights on the wall behind – and then I'd close my eyes and see the exact same thing. It was alarming. I found it distressing. Even to think of it now. The implications were – hard to grasp. How was I to proceed with any confidence when I no longer knew if I was awake or asleep?

Something else.

A woman arrived. One of the beds on the opposite wall. She was beforehand – her procedure. She was beforehand. I was afterwards. It was night. The lights were dim. She blessed the nurse who accompanied her in. She wished her a good life. She seemed to go through some kind of ritual placement of objects. This seemed important, though I struggled to grasp what she was doing or why. I myself had done nothing like it. I had arrived and unzipped my boots and slipped off my clothes. I hadn't blinked. I'd signed my form. I hadn't blessed anyone. And then the anaesthetic. Six. Five. Four.

She had arrived with bags. A lot of them. These bags were plastic. Blue. She clutched them in her fists like a wild array of blue balloons. I was flat on my back, but with my head slightly raised I saw. And I heard the rustling as she took things out of them.

She had arrived with her husband – I assumed him to be.

He stood and watched close by. I remember his head was – tilted to one side.

She was rustling all the time. It made me smile.

He watched and I watched as she set things out. Cloth – a length of cloth – on top of the side table. Small items – great care – on top of this. On the the . . . shelf, table, table-top over the bed – that swivelled over the bed – perhaps it was a basin. I don't know. Perhaps there was a towel. The last thing she did though – she rolled out a rug. A small rug. Great care. And then she turned to the man, to her husband, asked for help. I think perhaps what she wanted was alignment – the the the the the the side table, the edge of the rug, the bed . . .

He raised both hands. He said something to her. Perhaps he said . . . you know, I can't be sure. His voice was gentle, hard to hear. I can't be sure what it was he said.

When he'd gone – the man – and then when she'd gone – the woman – when she'd gone for the procedure, her procedure, a man in green appeared – snorted – a sound like laughter – said, You're kidding me – cleared her things away. It took no time at all.

Having seen the effort she had gone to, I found this troubling. I felt – great concern. I had . . . how can I describe it? I was becoming increasingly anxious that the woman might not return.

I did not want to think of it. Watching her I'd forgotten where we were. But when they came for her she'd been upset. Nil by mouth. Weak and distressed.

Now she was gone and all her blue bags.

It was night time quiet. The lights were low. A storm was

flickering in my cranium. I put one hand on top of my head to try to calm things down. Something was shifting, rising, teeming – something . . . microbial. My eyes were open or shut. Explosions of colour gave way to soft fur. A studio theatre with inky drapes felt familiar and benign but then it fell apart and was a vast and funnelling black hole.

Later on she was crying. I couldn't see her. It was dark. Later still I would wonder if she was even real – I couldn't know. When I'd seen her, had my eyes been open or shut?

Open, shut, I cried with her. Afterwards I slept.

I would think of her again much later, but at the time I had things on my mind. For one, I could not seem to get up. My hands, my arms, my legs, moved fairly freely – yes. My head up off the pillow – just a bit, not for long. For the rest, it felt like I'd been stapled lengthways through the middle and the giant staple had attached me to the bed.

The pain was tremendous.

My toes remained oddly detached. Long afterwards they seemed to try to move for the rest of me.

When a nurse showed me the mechanism that could tilt my bed, I pressed the button. My head was raised, my upper body too, the ward came more fully into view. It seemed stable.

Don't get me wrong. When I left, I left sleek and slender and upright – a new and improved version of myself full of screws and rods and other things besides. A vague concern I might be struck by lightning. But I had backbone. I was spineless no more.

I could give you some associations of spinelessness – what it means to be without backbone at all. First up: a man attempting to crawl, flat out, face down in the dirt. This image perhaps comes from a film.

The dressings came off. There were large staples too. These had held the wounds together. The doctor used pliers. It was hard not to notice how she flinched.

The scars. The scars were livid. They ran in very straight lines beside the spine. There were rows of tiny legs where the staples had been. These tiny legs looked like they were running and running.

I'd not processed, somehow, that afterwards – after the procedure – I'd not be able to move, ever again, the way I'd moved before. I had not understood that it would seem to affect every small articulation.

I would envy the bodies of dancers, and gymnasts. It would seem not impossible, not far-fetched – another version, another me, who might have done just that . . . that bend, right there.

In my shoes my toes moved with longing.

Movement – it was so awkward. There was a way to get in and out of bed. No twisting. Roll. Roll to get up. Roll like a bug to get up.

Interest in the words exoskeleton, endoskeleton.

Imagine the tools – the tools they would use – the force it would take – to leave a person rigid – to leave a person full of rods and screws.

❦

I wanted a reversal. I had a dream where I banged and banged on the door and I begged, Take it out! There is no way back, they said. The whole thing would crumble. It's part of you now.

Time passed. Time passed. What had happened to my body was unspoken. Part of me.

So.

So time passed. It was much later. I met the translator. Everything she said was provisional. Subject to change. You might think it would be annoying – but I found that I liked it. I hadn't expected this. If you'd asked me before I would have thought it preposterous for anyone to want to spend their time with someone who would seem never to get to the point. She would say things like, I think . . . What I mean to say . . . I have a notion . . .

The first time I saw her – an event in a bookstore. The kind of thing where the event is happening but even so the store is open for people to browse the shelves. She was the event. A man asking questions. I'd stopped in after work to look for a book.

It was the trailing off that caught my attention. I thought perhaps something was wrong with the microphone. I became aware of these – silences, in the conversation.

When I met the translator, I'd not thought much about the procedure in years. I'd thought of it a lot, at the start. It was hard not to. Then time passed. The scars were no longer livid. Those running legs faded and faded and then they were gone.

Perhaps it was now a small thing, a smaller thing. A big thing, but not as big a thing as it had been before.

There was no pain now. I felt nothing.

The way she spoke. The way even . . . if I could describe it. The way even *she sat on her chair*. Who would have thought that could be so . . .

I sat at the back of the store to wait for the end. I spent half the time pretending to read but I was really in a panic staring at my hands.

Adjustments, refinements, rearrangements. She clutched them in her fists like a wild array of balloons. Pauses in between as she took time to think. Nothing taken for granted. Nothing allowed - not for long - to be fixed.

And I saw it. I saw this thing running through me. Running me through. Its grip.

Sometimes she'll look at me, and I'll think . . . I think she looks at me with pity? And I think perhaps that I should tell her, about what happened to me. Though I'm not sure I'd be clear, that I'd know what to say, that it would make sense. Where would I start?

She's seen the scars on my back - but that's not it, that's not, that's . . . that's not what I'm talking about.

WHALE WATCHING

SHE WAS STANDING on the headland when the whale came into view. Dishrag white, a floating giant barnacle. The man was spread cross-like on its flank, caught in a cat's cradle of harpoon hemp. There was no-one else to see it, only her. She had started running as soon as it left the harbour; she knew the way. The creature turned towards her, watching her from its one pig-eye; the man looked, too. And then it turned again, facing the open sea.

The man waved to her, as they disappeared into the mist, towards Ireland.

'Goodbye,' she said, waving back.

When she told, toothless gums nah-nahed at her, hands came together and trapped her in a corner of the school-yard. Names boxed her ears.

'Thicko!'

'Fibber!'

'Twpsin!'

'Liar, liar . . .'

And yes, next day, at the harbour, the whale was there again, and the waving man was walking about, talking to the crowd.

'There!' her teacher told her. 'You mustn't make things up! That's what films are for!'

'Miss' spent her Saturdays at the Palace in the big town. 'We must visit the *set* as often as we can,' she told the school. 'It will be an educational experience.' She brought *movie* magazines into class, and showed them pictures of the *stars*. One day, she brought the book, which had the same name as the film. 'It's too old for all of you, but I shall read you some.'

'Call me Ishmael,' she began. It was enough.

She told them how brave the whale-hunters were, how many useful things came from whales.

They lived in Wales, didn't they? The children scratched their heads.

'Margarine. So much better than butter, so much easier for cooking! Oil. Potions for your mothers' lotions and make-up. Where would we be without them?'

They made models out of newspaper, water and flour. The boys put them in puddles and watched them sink.

Whenever they visited Lower Town, where the filming took place, teacher's legs grew longer and shinier. Her lips were red against pale, pillowed cheeks, beneath coils of hair, stacked like lobster-pots. She edged the children towards the *stars*, careless of the water, the *lens* of the camera. The *director* motioned them away, the teacher's cheeks reddened, even through their whale-oil glaze. Yet they still went back the next day.

Weeks later, after the film *crew* had gone, and the coast was quiet once more, she climbed to the headland again. Far below, pieces of rotting carcass were washed along the shore, caught amongst the jagged outcrops, floating in the rock pools, along with a pink hair-slide. Later still, she saw a group of seals playing with scraps of white flesh, passing them from nose to nose, smiling.

And there was blood, she was certain there was blood . . . spreading strands like dulse seaweed – on the seals, on the rocks. How could there be blood if it wasn't real?

She knew what she had seen, and if she had seen it, it must be true.

Soon, the people of the town forgot, going back to their fishing and farming, waiting for holiday-makers who never came. In time, another film came along, with new actors. Brighter stars in even bigger cars, who stayed longer; who were Welsh, like them, and drank in the pub, rather than the big hotel; drank in the pub again and again. Other things were different, too. Cameras taking photos of cameras, televisions in every house, some of them in colour. (Marriage.) Phones in every house, to make gossiping easier; cars in every drive, making the world smaller. (Children.) Soon the old film was forgotten. Only she remembered. Remembering, as she dredged nappies through bleach-water, her hands as wizened as the whale. As her husband snored beside her. As she wrote her name in the dust on the shelf, where the book lay. She had bought it she didn't know when . . . or perhaps when the librarian told her one too many times, 'You've borrowed this before!'

A heavy book, as heavy as the creature, full of weighty words that she couldn't understand, meanings she could never fathom. The Whale meant something. The Hunt meant something. But what? And the teacher had lied when she said it began with 'Call me Ishmael'. Page after page must be got through before that, lines, paragraphs speaking of Leviathans, and Spermacetti, and Rights and Orks. How they killed, or were killed. Of their bones and teeth decorating the land.

There was no Great White, the white came later, in the story proper. She drew the book out, from where it stood, amongst thinner, lighter tales of nurses and doctors in love, or Cowboys fighting Indians. She wanted to read it, but the alien words floundered in her head, 'hypos/Manhattoes/circumambulate' flailing against the children's crying and squabbling, and her husband's complaining. She put it back in its place.

And soon it didn't matter that she couldn't read it. The film came back to her, in a little plastic box she must post beneath the television. She could watch it again and again, while the family yakked and pulled and grew around her. All she had to do was press a button, and rewind.

When the famous actor died, the local paper printed his picture, writing about his visit to their little town. Scrunching her eyes over her glasses, the points of her scissors laboured around the article, with her thickened knuckles, her stiff thumb. She put the piece in her special box, with all her other cuttings, yellowed by the years.

'I met him,' she told anyone who would listen. 'He put his hand on my head, tangling my hair.' She was afraid for her new pink slide. Her mother had rowed with her for losing the old one on the cliffs. The day she had seen the whale.

'Call me Ahab,' he said, his voice dragging his words, low. There was something wrong about that . . . If he was Ahab, there would be only one long black pleated leg facing her. There would be a white line cloven down his face. He wouldn't smile, which he did, before moving back through the crowd.

Later, he appeared on the step of the trailer, his cheek forked like lightning. His wooden leg caught between the treads. She was glad. It made sense again.

'The whale bit it off at the knee,' someone in the crowd whispered. 'It's not wood,' another voice added. 'It's the bone of a whale.'

'It's not bone . . . it's . . .'

Whatever it was, *he* was as he should be . . . if he was Ahab. Until he smiled at her again.

Her teacher shot slit-eyes at her and pulled her away.

'I know, now, that it was jealousy. I didn't understand then.' Perhaps she should have left her story there. But no, the words spilled out of her mouth, bubbling up, as she told how she had seen the whale, far out to sea, with the actor strapped to its side.

There was no name-calling any more, but faces turned away, hands lifted to stop sniggering breath. People in the market, her children. Not her husband; he, too, was dead by then.

'You're muddling what you think you saw with the ending of the film,' Mari, her daughter, told her.

How did *she* know? She hadn't been born then; she herself was only a child, a small child. Had she ever seen the film? 'Only a million times, when we were growing up!'

'Look!' she said to no-one in particular: Mari, who had already walked away, her dead husband, an empty room, showing them another photo from her box, one she had cut from a film magazine, when her fingers moved more easily. 'There! That's me!'

And it was, a girl, of about five, with her fringe pulled back by a slide; pink, it would be, if there was colour. A girl with a Peter Pan collar, and Mary Jane shoes. A pleated skirt, with a pin in it. She was standing at the front of the crowd, on the edge of the quay. That was the first day of filming, before the visits with school.

Her fisherman grandfather had gone there early, hearing they may want him – or his boat – and he had taken her. So she was there, at the very beginning, when the big, shiny cars arrived, when the ship with its three tall masts pulled into the harbour, when the hammering, shouting, dragging, lifting started, to make towers of wood for the cameras, to hide fronts of houses, to make new ones, which were old.

'See,' her grandfather said. 'Those ships are just the kind that would have berthed here last century. See, that car . . . you'll never see a tidier one round here.' Time chopped and churned with the tide, in front of her eyes.

'I went every day after that. Early, before school. Late, after. And then there were our visits with the teacher. That's how I'm in the photo. I was there so much, always near the front.'

That's how she was so quick to spot the whale heading out to sea. Why she was the first to run. Why only she saw it.

Time was like that now, rewinding, fast-forwarding like her video tapes. Soon, there were grandchildren to tell, to show the yellow pages. When they were small, they nodded and smiled, and said, 'Yes, how wonderful, Nain.' She hugged them and their words close. She put them in a different box. But they grew, too.

'Tell us about Taid, Nain,' they would say. 'Shall we look at some photos of him?' Perhaps there were some, somewhere, but she didn't know where, and her film box was always at hand.

One of them, his name just beyond reach, took the faded picture from her, looked at it near his eyes.

'This isn't here, Nain. It's in Ireland. See the signs in the street behind? And our harbour has the cliff rising above it. That can't be you.'

She looked at the picture again. The boy didn't know how the film men could change things, how they could change young men into old, and back again, legs into ivory stumps, rubbish bins into barrels, how they could paint a cliff in, or take one away.

It *was* her. She had been there.

The grandchildren came with the summer, sent for sun and fresh sea air. Yet they spent their days staring at screens, and flicked their thumbs up and down. They said you could find the whole world in a phone.

Still, if she asked, they would take her to the harbour. There was colour, now. Blue, red, yellow painted houses. An ice-cream van. Rainbow sun-shades.

'Much better,' people said.

The film people had taken the colour away – what little there was back then. They didn't want it. Not here. They wanted drab stone, moulding wood, grimed window-panes. Cobbles. They could magic all these, as they had done with the cliff, and the signs. But it had been many years before the colour came, following the tourists, who had finally discovered the town, along with their ice-creams and crab sandwiches and boat-trips. Yes, they did that now, sleek, fast boats, out into the bay, bird-watching, dolphin-spotting, paying good money. 'No sightings guaranteed . . .' When they came back, she would hear their wonder. 'I saw a fin!'

'It jumped out of the water!' 'They followed us for ages!'
A whale, sometimes, a small affair, and yet they made such
a fuss.

What was so special about this, she asked herself? Dark
curves, that could hardly be glimpsed, except through a glass.
Camouflaged by the black troughs of the sea, except for those
showy jumps.

Her whale moved on top of the water.

It was white, and huge.

'I've seen a whale,' she wanted to say, the words coming
close to her mouth.

'I've seen a whale,' she said. 'Here, just here, and then . . .'

The children, or children's children, hurried her away.

On her good days, they would take her to the cliffs, where the
farm had been.

'I was born here, it was my home,' she would tell them,
waving towards the buildings behind her. Holiday cottages,
now, 'sought after, in sight of the sea.' Yes, it was what she
woke up to, every day. It was part of her. They had said the
same about the story; the sea was part of it, too. The sea
meant something, like those other things that were supposed
to mean something.

This place, high up, looking both ways, was one of her
favourites. The water did everything here, on different days,
at different times. And it was where she had seen the whale
disappear.

'I ran, as soon as the mooring broke free. I knew which way
it would go; I knew the currents. They - the film people - followed only the marked tracks, and stumbled at each outcrop.
Have I told you this before?'

She followed the beast along the coast, running from cove to cove, over the cliff tops.

'My pink hair-slide broke free and skittered down the cliff. I couldn't see above the height of the gorse, but I knew where I was going – home. I was the one who got here first. I was the one to see the whale rounding the corner. I was the one to see it disappear, with the famous actor tied to the side.'

They always shuffled glances then, in time with their feet; their thumbs would start that fidgeting again, and they would say, 'No, no!' 'It wasn't like that at all.' 'Look, it says here . . .'

They showed her things she didn't want to see – a picture of a white cylinder, with wires and cogs behind, a man pulling levers inside.

'Look!' They were fond of that word. And she lowered her eyes to whatever was on the little screen. But she saw nothing, she didn't have to see, unless she wanted to.

They told her things she didn't want to hear.

There was no whole whale. Just bits – a tail, a head, sections that they moved around on a barge, putting them in the water when needed. Or . . . there were three models, but none of them whole . . .

Sixty feet, eighty-five feet, one whale, three. No whales, parts of whales, a model in a tank, a picture on a studio wall. Rubber, steel.

'An internal engine to pump the spouting water!'

'Dye in the latex skin, so that it could "bleed"!'

'A publicity stunt, Nain! Just imagine the press coverage such a story would get. "Hollywood star nearly drowns, swept out to sea on the back of a whale!"'

'A myth,' another announced. 'Built from half-truths, a muddle of events. Look, a section broke free; the actor nearly drowned being dunked in a tank in the studio. Then they all said different things. The coastguard sailed to the rescue! The RAF was called! But none of it happened! The camera guy says this . . . the director says that . . . Gregory Peck something else entirely! But they all seem to settle on "No whale!"'

'No,' she said. 'They must have forgotten. They had so much to do. They moved on quickly.'

They moved on to another film, another story. It became nothing to them.

The children leave with the summer. She is glad.

Soon, everything they've said is gone again. All the 'looks' bundled away, along with their forgotten names. And the whale drifts out of the harbour, great, white, whole, with the famous actor trapped in a web of twine. She runs along the cliff, her pink slide falls, and there it is again.

Soon, she sees the sea every day, just as in her childhood, in this place they've put her in, calling it 'home'. Home again, sea again.

And there are new people who listen to her story, and say 'How interesting!' Or, 'Good!' no matter how many times she tells it. She cannot see the film any more - her eyes are too dim. Besides, none of the other 'residents' want to watch it. But the nice girls will read to her from the book, if she asks, when they have the time.

It is the ending she wants to hear. How Ahab raises his hand from the flank of the whale, beckoning his crew to carry on with the kill.

'I saw it,' she tells them. 'I saw the whale disappear into the mist, with the famous actor tied to its side. He waved at me, so I said, "Goodbye."'

'No,' the girl who is reading to her that day tells her, a girl who pays attention to the words on the page. 'Ahab gets pulled into the water. It's the Parsee who is caught on the whale. And he doesn't wave. They changed it for the film. They changed the whole ending. It's what they do, for dramatic effect.'

After the girl has gone, she puts the book in the bin.

And the whale turns towards the open sea, and the man raises his hand to her.

'Goodbye.'

DAVID ROSE

GREETINGS FROM THE
FAT MAN IN POSTCARDS

THIS COULD BE, if Bognor had a cathedral, a tale of two cities, twin poles in the life of Wilson Thomas.

– I'm going as far as Guildford. Any good to you?

The shortest distance between two points, there being no motorway, is a meander, in this case the A285, A283 and A3100. It is on these procrastinating curves that Wilson Thomas has come to rely for his mental health, his life.

– You can put that nightie on the back seat.

There is another, identical, locked in the boot.

– Little gift for my wife. Well, I say my wife. Always take them something when I go home. Was it a holiday in Bognor, or business? Personally I live there. Not easy to own up to. I mean, what does anyone know about Bognor except George the whatsit's dying words? Bugger Bognor. (*Map of Britain. Bognor marked in red. Caption: Welcome to Bognor, Backdoor of Britain.*) Its only claim to fame. Almost Joycean. Irishman goes for a job on a building site. Foreman asks him, sort of proficiency test, 'What's the difference between a joist and a girder?' Quick as a flash on a frosty night he comes back, 'One wrote *Ulysses*, the other wrote *Faust*.' Not a literary man, then? Visit the pier? (*Two explorers silhouetted in a tent. Night time. Caption: 'Where's my pith helmet?'*) Met my wife on the pier. Donald McGill exhibition. Working visit for me. Professional card-man. I like to say that. Shades of green shades, sleazy glamour. Actually more prosaic. Belle Vue Cards. I rep for them. Plus a little creative work. My wife helps me with that. Amateur cartoonist.

It was love at first sight. They were both peering at the same framed card. He noticed the dimple in her cheek matching the one between her shoulders. She looked up. Eyes of postcard-sky blue. He raised his cap. Her dimples deepened. The sea glittered, like the glass beads on his mother's throat, his earliest recollection, tickling his eyes.

'I've an original McGill of my own if you'd care to see it?'

He drove her to his digs.

'Not many on the market these days. Difficult to come by unless you have contacts. Gives you a little *frisson* knowing it's the actual paper he worked on. Speaking of *frissons*, I've another McGill in here.' He dropped his trousers. Embroidered mothers-in-law all over his shorts.

He had the McGill framed and gave it to her. The un-nuanced figures of Curate and Vamp, secure in their ink outline against the washes of colour, brought afresh the first rapture of childhood as they opened it together.

Her first present to him was a pair of musical shorts. They played 'I Do Like to Be Beside the Seaside' at the touch of a microchip. He put them on to propose. 'I don't know your name yet.' 'Er, Thomas, Wilson.' 'Yes, Thomas Wilson, I will.'

– She did a little sketch of me. Caricature. At least, I hope it's a caricature. I had it copied, printed up. Send them to her on my longer tours of duty, captioned 'Greetings from the Fat Man in Postcards'. Funny, women go for the fuller figure. Thin men don't realise. Look at HG Wells. Never short of female admirers. Used to call him Treacle Wells. One of his women was asked why she found him so attractive. Said, Because his skin smelt of honey. Extraordinary. 'Stands the Clock at Ten to Three?' I told my wife about that once. She said, Sounds fun, let's try. Anointed me with a pot of Gales. Every so often, one of us will say, Let's have an HG Wells night. Only we moved on to Lemon Curd. Did a Midlands tour a few months ago, sent her a jar, with a boxed chipolata and a note, 'The shape of things to come.' Duncton. Making good time. Another trip, I phoned her anonymously, did the old heavy breathing. She just said, cool as you like, 'If you want the asthma clinic you've got the wrong number,' and hung up. You'd like my wife. Ever been to America?

This will peter out beyond Petworth.

– Petworth Park. Sounds like a municipal tryst for lovers. As I was saying, we do all right, we larger men. Takes women unawares. I grant you a novel called *The Fat Man* wouldn't have the same ring, but that's only prejudice. I usually stop about here, have a breather, stretch my legs.

At exactly here. Mid-point of his journey, zenith of his weekly trajectory. Marked on the Ordnance Survey as Ball's Cross. Here he is poised between two worlds. He will drive into a lane, walk up and down, lean on a gate. His tongue searches his teeth, seeks out the small molar cavity. Into its rough protective burr his soul nestles. He will be here for several minutes while the magnetic field reverses.

He will drive up the narrow road, turn left, then on to join the A283.

– The quilted fields of England. I love this countryside.

Even the names resonate. Chiddingfold. Could be Old English for 'cemetery', conjures up the cosiness of village graveyards. All safely gathered in. Hambledon, Bramley. English as autumn mists. Pictures of this sort of landscape – maybe a shire horse in the middle distance, church spire far distance – still work their magic, guarantee the sales. Anything rural or ecclesiastical or both. Even quite modern buildings can do it. Know Guildford Cathedral? Only finished in 1961. Still a popular card. That's how I met my wife. She was sketching it. Naturally I took a professional interest. Suggested she did a watercolour, maybe soften the cathedral, age it a little, submit it to my art director for a greetings card. She did, he went for the idea, I went for her.

It was love at first sight. He had leaned over her shoulder, watched the pastel smudge the deep-grained paper. Her long hair matched the quaking grass, ruffled by the same breeze. Her chin set in concentration, a soft furrow echoing a distant field. He retreated until she was packing up, handed her his card.

They drove into town, had coffee and scones with a view of the Guildhall, then drove through darkening Surrey lanes.

This was the pattern of their Sundays for a month.

On the Sunday of Michaelmas, after their coffee, he parked in sight of the cathedral, wound down the window. 'You'd make a perfect Mrs Wilson Thomas. You might even enjoy it.' 'Will I, Wilson Thomas? Yes.'

– She became very interested in colour-washed pen and ink. We both love the work of Thomas Rowlandson, his chromatic delicacy against the robust penwork, the feathery foliage. I got her to do a series of views in that style, tried to get the firm to accept them as a set of upmarket postcards. Came to nothing. I had a few printed up, send them to her when I'm on the road, with a little poem on the back, something out of Clare or Herrick or William Blake. Blake is her idol. The watercolours, the woodcuts - she loves them. Did you know he lived near Bognor? Felpham, few miles along the coast. She wanted to visit it, soak up the atmosphere. Tricky. Had to head her off on that. Suggested a little project of my own - trace the locales of Wilson Steer's works. Personal interest - he was a distant relative on my grandmother's side. I'm named after him, in fact. So whenever I have a few days' leave, we've been trundling round the country, Suffolk, Yorkshire, Stroud Valley, tracking down the footprints of his easel, so to speak. She copies the paintings, I photograph the scene. 'Then and now' sort of thing. Surprising how much of the country is still unspoiled. Turn down a lane, find a stile, follow a path between furrowed fields. Smell of wet earth. Leafmould in the hedgerows. Like generations of wisdom, sifting into the soil. She'll put her arm through mine, say, Breathe it in. I know just what she means. You'd like my wife. See that programme on cancer on the box?

Wilson is much possessed by death, and sees the skull beneath the skin. For if one of them should die? Or leave? Easier to face the knock upon the door.

Wilson is not, has never been, a political man, but he has watched, appalled, the bi-polarity of the world crumble. He is unnerved. The world now reminds him of a pre-Columbus globe in reverse. He sometimes feels the axis tilt, feels the slide and scramble. Each stop at Ball's Cross becomes a little longer.

Wilson has read somewhere of a scientist who requested his ashes be made into a firework, who ended his earthly intactness in the starshower of a score of rockets.

He thinks of him now, thinks of himself, sees his wives and assembled guests, with their sausages on sticks, gazing at the flare and burst, thinks of his soul ricocheting off the stars.

THE WHITE CAT

LINDA HAD SPENT most of June trying to kill the white cat. For her first attempt, she used a simple method: three tablespoons of rat poison in a saucer of milk. She left the saucer next to the sliding doors of the villa. A few days later, she found two dead birds in the garden and one in the swimming pool, the grey feathers mangled in the gutter. Linda collected the birds in a shoebox and buried them beneath the bougainvillaea.

After that, she bought a BB gun from the hunting store in the mall. But when she tried to practise she couldn't pull the trigger. She said it brought back memories of her grandpa's suicide.

'Would you believe me if I told you I'm an animal person?' Linda said, leaning against the kitchen island where I was eating my cereal. She wore denim cut-offs, a faded pink T-shirt and a plastic golf visor. Her skin was aged from too much sun and the split ends of her blonde ponytail fluttered in the breeze of the AC.

'You are?'

'Of course I am, honey. I've had plenty of pets. I ride horses. I would never kill an animal except in self-defence.'

Linda didn't want to kill the white cat, she explained. The

cat had terrorised her. It left decapitated lizards on the door-step. It stared at her while she swam. Plus it was ugly. A tiny head and a long thin body covered in pink sores and clumps of white fur. A missing eye.

'Have you ever seen a cat with one eye? It's gross. The skin on the socket is all pink and clenched, like an asshole,' she said, and puckered her lips and laughed.

I assumed Linda was exaggerating about the white cat. Since I'd moved into the villa, she'd sent constant emails about the black bugs taking over the kitchen, advising me to scrub down the kitchen counters with rubbing alcohol and a paper towel, even though I'd never seen a black bug. I'd never seen a white cat either.

Cute Room and Pool View, the ad had said. The villa was a bargain for the price. Located in a compound next to the beach, the villa had a perfect swimming pool, shaped like a kidney and surrounded by trailing plants and palm trees. The blue and green tiles scrambled together and turned gold in the midday sun, like a Byzantine mosaic. Linda lived inside the villa and had decided to rent out the pool house in the garden.

'There's something super cute about this place,' Linda had said when she'd opened the pool house's door. 'I'd live in it myself if it wasn't for the villa.'

The interior was basic. A metal bed frame stood on top of the grey lino flooring. There was an old desk with a broken drawer and a shower drilled into the wall above a drain. Access to the villa's kitchen and the swimming pool were included in the price. I moved in the next day.

Linda said she worked for an insurance company but during my first week in the villa she never left the house. She rose at 6am every morning and watered the garden in her denim cut-offs. When she heard me enter the kitchen for breakfast, she would follow me and launch into one of her monologues.

The only positive thing she ever had to say was about her childhood in Hawaii. She'd named the house 'Villa Aloha' in honour of her homeland. Fridge magnets of seashells and surfers clung to the kitchen's magnetic surfaces. In the living room, the only sign of life among the white carpet and white leather sofas was a doll of a hula girl with frizzy hair, a rainbow-coloured lei and sun-faded skin, which sat on top of the drinks cabinet. During her tour of the villa, Linda clicked a switch on the doll and we stood there and watched the disturbing whirl of its hips.

On the day Linda told me about the white cat I spent the rest of the afternoon in my room. I tried to fill out job applications but I struggled to concentrate. At sunset I took a break and went to the supermarket. It was dark by the time I got home and I had to climb over the wall of the villa to get back in. I reached my foot onto the brick wall and lifted myself over the iron railings. Linda had promised to get an extra clicker to open the front gate but never did.

The moon was huge that night. I got changed into a bikini and went for a swim. I laid on my back and bobbed around on the water, like a leaf. The pool water was warm, like chicken soup. The smell of chlorine relaxed me. I closed my eyes.

Then I heard a splash. Something had entered the pool behind me. I thought it must be Linda, but when I turned she wasn't there. Nothing was there. I grabbed my towel, went back to the pool house and locked the door. The AC was on full blast and goose pimples spread across my body. I climbed under the covers to get warm.

The next morning I woke up later than usual. I didn't get

out of bed for breakfast. My muscles felt tired and I had a fever. Around 11 am, Linda knocked at my door.

'Everything OK in there? I want to show you something.'

'Oh yeah?'

'Yeah, look at what I picked up from the store.'

A small harpoon appeared from behind her back and she presented it to me like a present.

'Is that another gun?'

'Something for the white cat. Will you help me, honey? I know you like to stay up late so we could take it in shifts. By the way, did you see that son of a bitch last night? It was drinking the pool water.'

I told her I had some work to do and shut the door.

For the next few days I avoided Linda as much as possible. Instead of eating breakfast in the kitchen, I kept bread and peanut butter in a plastic bag underneath my bed. I didn't have a knife so I smeared the peanut butter on with my finger, tearing holes in the bread.

Each day grew hotter and more humid. I started to notice all the faults in the villa. Mould gathered on the ceiling. Door handles came off in my hand. Every afternoon, the smell of sewage cut through the scent of Linda's jasmine and hibiscus. When I laid on a sun lounger, I was bothered by flies or red ants swarming in the grass. The palm tree by the pool had a rare disease and the fronds had withered and browned.

I was surprised to receive an email asking if I was available for work. I dressed in a blue shirt and pencil skirt and took a taxi to the company's headquarters. Most of the desks were deserted and there were cardboard boxes full of papers on the floor. The managing director gave me a tour of the office and sat me at a desk next to a guy named Bill.

'Bill can show you the ropes – just ignore him if he asks to borrow any money,' the managing director joked and then left.

Bill wore blue jeans and a tie-dyed T-shirt. He was chubby with a large mop of curly hair. His arms were a battlefield of eczema. I noticed a large tub of E45 behind a tower of takeaway coffee cups on his desk.

It didn't take long for Bill to set up my computer. There were a lot of emails to answer. For the rest of the week I worked late every night in the office. When I got home from work, I climbed over the wall and went for a midnight swim in the dark. I didn't switch on the pool lights because I didn't want Linda to know I'd come home. I only said hi to her on my way out in the morning. 'Go get 'em, tiger,' she would say and continue to water the plants.

By the end of the week I was exhausted. I left the office at 7 pm and stood in a long queue for a bus. The sun was setting and the humidity made me feel feverish and dizzy. Bill's car pulled up and he offered me a ride. I said yes.

Instead of driving home, we went to a bar. I asked Bill a few questions about his life, out of politeness. He asked about my living situation and I described the villa to him.

'So it's just you two in the house, you and Linda?' Bill asked. His chubby fingers wrapped around his beer bottle like a paw.

'Well, technically Linda is in the villa and I'm in the pool house.'

'What does Linda do?'

'Insurance, I think. She rarely leaves the house.'

'She must be divorced.'

'Why do you say that?'

'There's no way she could afford to have a villa on that compound. Someone must have given it to her.'

'I don't know. I think she's just sick of life.'

When Bill drove me home, he parked outside the front gate and I asked if he wanted to come inside and see the villa. No guests were allowed onto the property without permission, Linda had said, but it was late and I decided to take the risk.

'You'll have to climb over the wall though.'

'What?'

'Linda hasn't given me a clicker yet. For the front gate. Don't worry it's fun – we can pretend we're burglars.'

Bill struggled to swing his leg over the railings on the top of the wall. He listened to my step-by-step instructions and landed softly on the grass. He looked cute, like a racoon. I showed him the swimming pool and the garden, which shone nicely in the moonlight, and opened the door of the poolhouse.

'Oh,' he said.

'It's small, I know.'

His eyes scanned the metal bed frame and the lino floor. 'How much do you pay her for this?'

'It's cheap.'

'You know it's the maid's room, right?'

I heard the door click behind me.

Bill must have seen the look in my eye. 'Families in these villas always make their maids sleep in an outhouse,' he said. 'You've made it nice though.'

A lizard ran up the wall and I jumped. Bill put his arm around me to calm me down and then kissed me. The sex was clumsy even though it felt rehearsed. Afterwards, he snored and I couldn't sleep. Around 4 am he started to grind his teeth.

I woke up to the sound of the front gate and Linda's SUV

pulling out of the driveway. She liked to spend a few hours in the mall at the weekend. I pushed Bill's fat arm to wake him. His eyes opened and he smiled at me. I regretted hating him so much while he was asleep.

'Do you want to go for a swim? Linda won't be back for a few hours.'

The sun was bright and the pool water was hot against our skin. We swam and then we kissed some more.

'You know, I'm happy they hired you,' he said and pulled his face away from mine. It was a surprise.'

'A surprise?'

'Have you decided what you'll do when the office closes? You can't stay here.' He studied my face the same way he had studied the room. 'Oh, you didn't know.'

The company was on its last legs, Bill explained. Most of the staff had been made redundant before I arrived. He was hanging around for some extra money before he went travelling.

Bill left before midday. I guessed Linda would return around 1 pm and she did.

'Hello stranger,' she said. I was lying on the sun lounger, drenched in sweat. 'Would you mind helping me unload the trunk? I struck gold at the garden store.'

'Sure.' I was glad to see her.

The trunk was full of strips of bamboo, different types of rope and a lever mechanism. Linda passed a bundle to me, then I carried the bundle inside the villa. Once the job was done, we stood in the kitchen and drank lemonade.

'I'm making a cage.'

'You're what?'

'A cage. For the white cat. It won't know what hit it.'

She planned to build the cage by weaving the bamboo together like a basket. I helped her cut the wood into identical lengths and collected some of the dead fronds from the palm trees to camouflage it. She screwed the lever mechanism onto the outside of the villa, next to the swimming pool.

'All you've got to do is lie on a sun lounger. Put one hand on the rope, the other hand on a glass of Sauvignon Blanc, and wait for the cat to fall into the trap,' she said and demonstrated the technique.

'Wow, it works.'

'Of course it does.'

Linda manned the cage for a few hours each day. When I came home late from work, she would leave potato chips and a can of beer for me to take over on the lounger. It was relaxing to sit by the pool and rest.

I considered telling Bill about the cage but I knew he wouldn't understand. We went for lunch together a couple of times after he stayed over. He talked a lot about his upcoming travels.

One night, Linda waited for me by the pool until I got home. She was wearing a large sun hat and looked happy.

'We did it!' She jumped up and handed me a glass of wine.

I looked up to where the cage should have been hanging from its rope, but the cage was gone.

'We did it?'

'Yes, ma'am. That nasty son of a bitch kept wriggling and hissing but I took care of it.'

She hadn't been able to shoot it with the harpoon. Instead she put the cat in a potato sack and fastened it with a seat belt on the passenger seat. She drove for an hour along the highway and into the desert. When there were no more buildings in sight, she threw the potato sack out of the door and drove away as fast as she could.

'See, I am an animal person,' she said. Deep red scratches covered her arms and legs. Her whole body smelt of antiseptic and sun cream.

'Yes, you are.'

My last day in the office was uneventful. The managing director walked past my desk a few times and counted the computers, desks and chairs. I had no reason to say goodbye to Bill so I snuck out while he was at lunch and took a bus home.

There was a note on the door of the pool house: *Gone away for a week. Eggs in the fridge, feel free to eat them or they'll go bad. Clicker on the breakfast bar. Enjoy! Linda x*

I wondered where she might have gone. I tried to imagine her in an airport, wheeling her suitcase through the departure hall in her denim cut-offs. Or sitting on a plane, eating a bag of nuts.

A girl who worked as cabin crew once told me they keep a special blanket on board every flight, in case someone dies. The body is covered by the blanket and left buckled in its seat, so passengers won't be disturbed by the sight of a dead man or woman being carried down the aisle.

I hoped Linda wouldn't die on her flight. Villa Aloha felt strange without her. I went to the kitchen and ate some eggs. Then I took one of her beers out to the pool and waited until dark to swim.

The worst of the summer temperatures were over now. The heat had started to break. As I swam, a breeze floated across the garden and the shadows of the palm tree fronds twinkled across the water, like fingers on a piano.

That's when I saw it. Its pink sores shone under the moonlight. It had a missing eye and a missing ear too. Its white fur looked wet.

I swam towards it and let out a miaow, but it didn't miaow back. It looked tired. The cat laid down on the grass next to the pool and seemed to fall asleep. As if it had walked for miles across the desert, to rest its legs, to swim.

MAXINE

IN THE YEAR of Asbestos, country of Endland (sic), Maxine gets a job to read words to a blind man called Casper, what lives alone outside the peripheral ring-road, in a district beyond all forces of yuppification.

Maxine don't know too much bout 'geo-demographic dynamics' etc that is talked about on TV but she knows very well that a powerful permanent hex-ring of dog shit, broke glass and partly crushed up Strongbow cans is keeping the Stasis in that neighbourhood.

On her journey that morning by olde tram she chews gum forever, her jaw a machinery, eyes bright. Kids in prams nearby look from M to their mothers what have 'long since forgotten how to cry' ©. Tram passes through the city (S_____). Getting off at the stop right near Casper's place M. takes the gum out + sticks it to a poster for some new Bangla movie, kneading residue deep in the pixelated faces of stars, their transfigured appearance what she hopes will be an omen for the day. Something has to change.

Casper's place, a shithole on 33rd floor.

As a startup for reading he asks Maxine to take 3 chapters from a closed-down airport novel called A *Romance of Sadie.*

The book is just a turgid paste of words that knots up in her brain and mouth and M. finds it boring, wishing there was something less predictable – a story about robots and consciousness, a story about a new kind of sunlight – anything but reading porn to old blokes.

When the reading is all done Casper pays her (£4.50 the hour) and she goes home.

Other jobs of Maxine involve reading to:
- hyperactive children
- persons/animals in a coma
- voice recognition software
- dying persons/animals
- prisoners
- the dead
etc

One night there is a bombing in centre of town. Front of shops are hanging all off again and main entrance of the shopping mall is a cliché debris of twisted metal, filthy trashed consumer items and limbs/body parts all motherfuckered into dust. Pundits arrive and set up to start filming segments, rearranging debris and other aspects of the carnage. All around taxis and private cars double-up as improvised ambulances, every single bystander a temporary trauma nurse, every driver an unqualified maniac of urgency, every victim screaming blood out all over upholstery and no one knows what's on the radio.

On the pavement near the bomb scene, a spray paint graffiti makes a promise or prediction that nobody reads:
THE THOUGHTS OF THE LIVING REPLACED WITH THOSE OF THE DEAD.

Rescue workers are going back and forth w the wounded, shaking their heads at the dead deceased that lie carelessly anywhere. All the while sniffer dogs and assorted looters emboldened by breakdown of lawlessness freely walk the rubble, attentive to strange vibrations from down below fallen masonry and looking for stuff to 'purloin'.

The air in all directions is 'alive with distant sirens' when Maxine gets there to scene of explosion – reporting for reading duties. A Doctor on all day and all night shift sends her Immediately to the commandeered Gymnasium of a nearby school what has been turned into a temporary hospital/morgue. The whole place is stuffed with the wounded/ dead pulled out and then carried from their wannabe graves under the waste-scape that used to be Primark or possibly Lidl, no one seems to remember or care.

Later, in the Hillsborough classroom with a frieze done by kids depicting the naïve evolution of quadrupeds, Maxine cleans wounds with Amateur knowledge and bulk-buy disinfectant, comforting persons in distress and isolating those in danger to others or themselves. When electric power predictably fails she wanders in the Great Hall and reads in whispers by candlelight to those wounded still capable of listening.

She reads from her favourite stories like *Kick-Boxer* by Andrej Rublev and *Corrosive Surface of a Pessimist Malefactor* by Samira Shapiro Sustenance. She reads from *A History of Starvation* and *Advent Adventures of the Anal Adventurers #5*. She reads from *Soil Stealers* and *Full Power Harry Goes Back Underwater in London & Paris*. She reads from *Long Tuesday* and *A Manual for the Strict Correction of Boys (Revised Edition)*.

In half-light of the hall people are dying, wounds bleeding out all about, as the poets say, and 'ketchup all over the screen' ©. Some of the dying have real faces, others just faces from AI. M. tries her best to focus on real ones but sometimes gets confused. Over time the AI gets easier to spot cos those figures in particular seem to lose interest in her reading the more it goes on – their composite faces a mesh of glitch inattention, eyes wandering, artefacting earnestness, then wandering again.

As the night wears down further to the bones M. finds herself with a small group of badly injured schoolgirls, their bodies hidden deep down under swaddling of bandages. She reads from *All New Nature Boy*, *Sally Knew Best*, *Blunt Instrument* and *Peter Leper Jones*. She reads from *Hirashima!*, *Forgotten Moments* and *Gogolo Ultima Gogolo Poveraa*. She reads and reads until the dawn light is creeping in around her unannounced and all the wounded and all the dead and all the murals what the schoolkids have drawn up there on the wall and everything is all touched by the very 1st and very fine and very golden rays of early mourning sun.

After the episode with the bombing there is a global slowdown and in accordance all around Endland (sic) things get slower and slower. Cars go slow on the roads, people shuffle slow and then slower on pavements and everyone – human and animal – takes a long time to make decisions about anything or do anything at all.

Scientists of Endland mount a huge competition to see what the cause and solution to the slowdown is, with New Universities and olden think-tanks etc competing to demonstrate they profound understanding and business acumen. But on the day comes to announce winner of the competition it is rapidly uncovered that there has been a terrible fraud and the 'Prise Money' stolen slowly cent by cent and siphoned/sent off to the Canary Islands in a unreachable Offshore Account.

For reasons that make no sense Maxine is selected to investigate the fraud. She has to journey to another city where she is given lodging in a squatted shop unit with some guys that speak only English and who are apparently running a startup sweatshop to assemble illegal umbrellas. Maxine takes a mattress in the disconnecting corridor but can't sleep after work at the Fraud Squad cos the constant hammering, bending of metal and sweating of fabric. At intervals above the din come squeals of delight by the children (of the guys), who are from time to time sent outside for random testing of the umbrellas in the test-rain that falls from a hose-pipe, each test session a metaphysical whirlwind of childish unruly footwork, splashing and twirling in all directionz and all of it is watched by Maxine as she peeps out of a spy hole in her 'living space' while the kids, unaware of any audience, move across the concrete of the forecourt like a cut-price 3rd-rate Gene Kelly routine badly motion-captured by drunks.

Maxine's investigation gets off badly after very shaky start. She interviews key suspects who will not let her into their apartment or apartments and only talk to her thru a keyhole. Her head is filled more and more with lies, disinformation, false information, counter-intelligence and generalised nonsense.

Months pass. Investigation founders (sic) and the globalised slowdown continues. War comes along also, long rumoured but always anyway 'something of a surprise' and the Agency that Maxine works for – providing 'professional services in vicinity of reading' – goes bust cos most of their workers in Endland are swiftly conscripted on a precarious contract and shipped off to the front line of wherever. Even that army needs people that can read.

Not wanting to be any part of the war and sacked from her incompetent investigation into the corrupt competition as already mentioned Maxine doesn't know what to do. She loses faith in the free market, then loses faith in religion and patriarchy but not necessarily in that order. Before long she ends up down on her luck and on her knees, alienated and sleeping in a bed made with unhappy vibes down the Food Bank along with rest of the scruffs and n'er do wells of that era and area, hungry, and indeed just like totally demoralised.

There is a long complicated induction process where M. is explained the methods of checking food in and out of Food Bank, application of Compound Interest etc, system of E-Numbers and Additives and fines for overdue returns etc. After that she gets to work chatting w disgruntled other paupers and also roped into helping people w their increasingly lunatic Tax forms, Psych Assessments and curse of Pharaoh's Nightclub. The work is hard and morale all set to general low, also not helped by the slowdown which is still substantive in effect or daily operation.

One day when she hits rock bottom eating a cold re-heated tinned soup and starving to her own bones, Maxine resolves to leave town alone, setting off w/out appropriate clothing or footwear.

Outside City Limits she pass first through a rocky wilderness, then through a green pasture, then through another rocky wilderness etc in which (i.e. the latter, second wilderness, after the pasture) she gets total lost. Without water and without a map or workable sense of direction M. becomes dehydrated and in deep trouble of her life.

Come night fall, in the thrall of her starvation delirium Maxine finds wreckage of a vehicle from a convoy that was probably burned up very long time back. On the bonnet or windscreen dirt and/or dust someone has written the words DIE FOREIGN DIE and below it in another hand, PAY ATTENTION MOTHERFUCKERS. She crawls inside to shelter the night and soon listens to howl of wolves from darkness beyond. At night when the temperature drops below zero (o) and there is no functional WiFi, Maxine is hallucinating, shivering and experience what the pessimist scientists call signs of upcoming extinction.

She hears

- more sound of animals outside
- echo song from childhood
- shimmering 'eye movement sound'
- unsettled nautical skin hallucination of radio waves

Sometime she think she is really ~~gonna die~~ dead hidden in the ~~bus~~ vehicle in the deep of ~~somewhere in~~ the cold night when she feels a ghost hand on her shoulder. That ghost is ghost of Casper, a so-called ex-Boxer ex-Para and part-time ex-'Jazz' Promoter, the self-same dead man who in first part of story she was reading to when he actually went and died. Casper (ghost) takes her by shoulder and beckons her towards him, leading her out of the wreckaged ~~bus~~ vehicle and down the embankment of ~~earth~~ sand, across the ~~field~~ desert to an oasis.

⚘

Time passes.

In the Oasis (actually a Premier Inn) Maxine recuperates strength and orientation. Ghost Casper lingers in the room also while she is sleeping, listening to audiodescribed movies on demand to while away the time. When Maxine wakes up she reads him some of the books left in room by previous incumbent.

She reads him *AtomKraft* by Jon Slither, *Solitary Confinement Dancer* by Maisie Wahacha, *A Ray of Light* by Ash Diameter, *The Rat Catcher's Racist Rollodex* by Riannon Gruel-Hindenberg (?) and *Perspex Advantage* by Claustrophobia Shanti.

When it comes time to leave they skip reception, go out the firescape down into the car park behind the building and off into the night without paying the bill.

Arriving back in S_____ large parts of the city is now burning and on fire, initially as part of a simulation possibly for television but possibly for the firebrigade training video. The value of the money they have reduces daily because shifts in the currency exchange. Most days are taken up trailing round the city looking for advantageous currency transactions, searching 'a different rate' etc or arguing with blokes that have problematic Cholesterol count or unhealthy body mass index in pubs that look like the Jubilee is probably still happening.

M. plays the fruit machines and ghost Casper stands with her, invisible to other customers, watching the internal workings of the machine and trying to help M. to win big cash payouts. The plan doesn't work. There are no lines of three Apples. Only lines of hand grenades, lines of transplant organs, lines of bottled tears. No Win.

In the rage of the ongoing fire and lacking any other place to shelter the make they way back to Casper apartment on 33rd floor. They sit together in silents at the UPVC window that will not open more than a crack for health and safety reasons and the blind man listens to the faint sound of distant asbestos removal and wild fires 'beyond' meanwhile Maxine vapes furiously, blowing scented exaggerated fumes from out of the window crack and out to the city, watching the starlings flocking and watching the cars moving on the road down below them wide and white eyed sea monsters in the fog and watching the drones hovering invisible above them in the smoke fumes etc and dream of escape.

In the year of Carpark.

Bereft of income and purpose Maxine hitchhikes in another direction city of Endland (9 letters beginning with B) but before she can even get there the cops pick her up, give her a warning, look at her papers, beat her black and blue, give her another warning then tell her to go back on her way in a reversed direction, pointing back down the M1. If they ever catch her around there again they will confiscate her shoes etc.

She gets back to S_____ in the middle of night and retreats to a flat she was squatting before. Some other folks have moved in – family with kids in one room and another with some guys that are trying to get into movies playing Jihadists. All night they are practising prayers and making strange moves in front of a broken mirror in the hallway. One morning car pulls up outside

In the year of Dark Matter. Maxine gives up on living in the squat again, gets drunk in a Micro-pub what used to be an abattoir (Crown and Whippet) and the bar fills up w soldiers psychologically scarred and damaged goods from previous war as mentioned and grotesque undercover cops.

Another war starts. There is a blackout.

In the year of Erasure.

Maxine reads to Casper (ghost) a book about a Liar crucified all lol lo-fi DIY on rollershutter door for his part in a gangland rivalry. She reads him about a Sandwich Maker's apprentice who was incorrectly exiled by the Home Office. She reads him about a child or someone older working in a Children's Prison it is not exactly clear. She reads about Windrush brain drain, new Gun Laws and military chic. She reads Curse of Brexit, armed struggle and Shameful Secrets of Past. About trees felled by Securicor. About cash injection to subliminal brain. About girls making out under OfficeMax surveillance cameras to earn extra £££ from guys on night-shift security. About Bonus for Boners in Dachshund Fashion Trousers. About a rave in a shit field long years ago, about rain and arrival of dawn, Ecstasy and rusted cars or rusted smiles. About a nightclub called Sudden Fall. About deliberate vandals strung up on the chain link fencing, about deep scars and closed pits and minefield on new build community football pitch. About Internet search history of a destitute bachelor. Special Offer Nine for the Actual Price of Five. About rewiring electrics of Juvenile Delinquents and electrification of train wrecks. About train delayed by morning suicides. About drones that haunt the Emerald forest. About liars in uniforms and polyester slacks. About reskilled ex-offenders in onesies and telesales. About council kickbacks and late night kickabouts on wastegrounds the way to the match. About stairwell or stairwells to heaven. About kids that tagged shelters along the way into Pitsmoor with cursive *LAYABOUT* or block capital UNHEIMLICH and GAYDAR ROBOTNICK. About shit-talking videos on your Whatsapp group and about a dream of a new alternative to Whatsapp called Mishapp. About shame. About UKIP idiots topped off with razor wire and Gazza on bail again. About Twin Blondes in single Fat Suit. About The Savile will come back and get you. About home-neutered cats and Dangerous Dogs act. Bad standup in Student Union. Cineplex firealarm and firearm and Nachos microwaved in kitchen-joke with fake sauce of spermicide. Quality Metrics of a Desolate State. Lone drunk nites in A&E. Corbynista cabaret. Tommy fucking Robinson. Punching underwater and punch-drunk pillocks in privatised taxi rank tell jokes that punch down. Force-fed red faces with German Meat in Xmas Market chatting crusty fuckers sure to be or soon to be Undercover cops. Immigrant narrative you strove to forget. Playing hard to regret. Tourist Branding Car Park under parliament. Unlock King-corpse in Multistory Hidden Zones. About nightly shitting in underpass by terrible light and Angry on Internet Megabyte Rage. Crisis kids all drowning in lorries all stuffed inside boats all trapped inside trains then stuffed down blind and endless tunnels. Closed shoppes and Chemotherapy. Chemtrail conspiracies. Rental cars. Lost Souls argue in Nail Salon of Year. Frozen landscapes. Diaspora. Third generation. Stolen election w Heavy Metal soundscape. Cardi B Looks Depressed While Out With Her Dog After Controversial Breakup. Investment or Missed Opportunity. Emotherapy. Dogging in car parks all over at midnight. £500 ASOS shell suits and planking at night before cinnamon challenge. Drink your mental age in pints. YouTube clips that only last 8 seconds. YouTube clips that will not load. Last gasp of Endland (sic). Rapeseed virgins. Asbestos. Strewn contents of diaper waste. Spewed fog. Dogs set loose in elaborate traffic. Last Exit from Narrative. Class System and Life Expectancy. Dream of paralysis and dream of ruins or the dream that you run into ruin of Shopping Mall Foodcourt. Reggae version of that old song Nightmare Faces. Living Large. The Vape Escape. About Bowie dead and the dead dead blue between channels that some people say is haunted by no voice. Buildings clusterfucked with satellite dishes. L.S. Lowry postcard with captions in Arabic. Your dad. Dementia. People yelling about gender wars. A glittering whirlpool of insults boasts and falsehoods. The Spread of M.E. or imaginary Parkinsons. Hotspot Cancer. Sound of Epic Laughter from flat downstairs. Last gig you saw M.E.S. he was more or less hiding behind the speakers. Encore WHITE LIGHT-NING as crowd exits the room. Hate speech and hate crime. Viral ads for Vans Chequered Pumps. Vitamin Supplements. School exclusions to keep the audit clean. How to Develop the Habits of Successful, Happy People. Empty shops w water features closed now tho still illuminated. Anti-Vaxxers with Terminal Whooping Cough. Hand-me-down handbags from Coats De Rohan. Fake-ass fake ass implants and spray tan kids teeth rotten with bad debt. Uber to your surgical appointments. Content will not load in your country. Vault the fence and jump the ditch and vault the low wall and jump the rusted stream, walk up filth hill, the low rise getting steeper to the treeline and clamber over barbed wire and walk on deep and into the forest where the trees are older than time itself.

Medley of old hits from any era no matter who or no matter why.

Take a look at what you missed.

Take time and Take it to the Max.

The last pub closes when the money runs out.

History Will Not Be Kind to You.

Last words she reads to him are these.

Last song on the JukeBox is *Goodbye Felicia*.

ADRIAN SLATCHER

DREAMS ARE CONTAGIOUS

'I AM ON Air Force One, and Donald Trump has invited me to sit next to him. He calls over for one of his aides and a few minutes later we are delivered a platter of New York pastrami on rye. He insists I try them first, and I ask him if it's because he thinks the food is going to poison him, and he laughs, and says something about "ladies first", and somehow the sandwich is just something which we can both talk about so that I'm at ease with the President of the United States. I'm constantly thinking, this is strange, I don't know why I'm here, and then the plane sort of jolts as if it's hit an air pocket – well, I hope it's hit an air pocket and it's not a missile attack or something – and Donald Trump is white as a sheet and suddenly looks like the old man he is, and I pat him on the hand and reassure him and I think, that's why I'm here, to make sure he gets down all right. I tell him I am a Jehovah's Witness so that if anything happens I'm okay with it, that my place in heaven is secure, and that if he wants I can pray for him and that seems to relax him. And then the plane starts to nose-dive . . .'

'Carol . . . ?' I prompt, after the pause continues for a few seconds.

'. . . and then I wake up.'

I sit back, creating a bit of distance between us. My chair is straight-backed, uncomfortable enough to keep me from falling asleep even during the most repetitive of testimonies, whilst Carol's chair – the client's chair – is shorter, rounder, and more comfortable, the sort of chair in which you might feel comfortable enough to talk about your dreams.

There are the usual signifiers. I explain that dreams are the unconscious speaking to us, and that not everything in a dream is significant, that much of the detail of the story is the random detritus we pick up during the daytime and doesn't actually mean anything in itself. Perhaps there had been a news article about Donald Trump? Had she seen a late-night film showing a plane crash? I told her what I thought, and she nodded, taking it in, and asked a few questions, and then talked a little bit about her life. She didn't mention her faith again, and I didn't want to be the one to bring it up, but it seemed important.

She looked pretty normal, well dressed, carefully made up, with an expensive haircut, the kind of woman who you would speak to if you were buying perfume for your girlfriend or your mother. Only as she left did I notice that she wore the most solid, sensible shoes I'd ever seen.

'That's the fifth one this week,' I told Zuzanna from the other room. 'They are all having dreams about Donald Trump. I wouldn't mind, but why now? I thought we'd have got used to him by now. Did British people dream of Obama? Of Clinton? Of Dubya?'

'Dreams are contagious,' she said, 'you know that.'

And I did know that. I had told her everything I knew about dreams whilst she worked on her algorithm.

'Maybe it's a sign that you should stop,' she said, 'and, by the way, I have finished the beta.' And she pronounced it to rhyme with feta not with metre. I loved how she said the word.

'That's great news,' I said. But I have appointments booked in all week . . .'

'Stop now,' she said, 'before you catch the contagion.'

Her logic was impeccable.

That night in bed we made love and as I moved on top of her, finding my rhythm, I pleaded with her to 'say it'.

'Beta,' she said, 'beta, beta, beta, beta, be-ta . . .'

Zuzanna was a software engineer originally from Katowice who I had met via an online forum but who happened to live in the same city as me. Soon we were dating, and before I knew it she had moved in. My dream-consultation business had been going for over a year and had turned into something of a success. People were looking for something in their lives.

I had gone online to see if there were any dream apps that I might be able to recommend, and that's when I'd found Zuzanna. She was marshalling a team of programmers across Eastern Europe and South East Asia to develop an AI bot that would make me redundant. The demand for dream consultation meant that the business would never develop with just one person doing it. Zuzanna had great plans for her software to go global. She paid her programmers in a cryptocurrency that was powered by the amount of new dreams appearing in the world. Every time someone wrote about their dream on social media, Zuzanna's bots scraped the information and fed it into a database. In the early days new dreams appeared every few hours, but now, with a substantial database, new dreams were becoming as rare as mathematical primes.

The next morning I woke early. Zuzanna was already at work taking advantage of her programmers being in different time zones. I returned to my booth in the labyrinth of short-let offices in Carmichael Street and carefully attached a sign to the door.

DREAM CONSULTATIONS
ARE NOW ONLINE

Because of unprecedented demand all dream consultations will now take place virtually.
Our team of operators will respond instantly – day or night – to your latest dreams and for a fraction of the cost of an individual consultation.
Sign up here.

And as well as the URL that Zuzanna had given me there was a QR code that people could scan.

I spent the next hour cancelling appointments. I emptied the kettle and unplugged it, cleaned up the small kitchen area and took the memory card from the server linked to the CCTV camera that looked over the entrance hall.

I walked home rather than getting the bus. At each major junction was a group of Jehovah's Witnesses, quietly and unobtrusively going about their business. There were more women then men, though I noticed that there were never any single-sex groupings. They stood next to a sandwich board and handed out literature, but mostly they just talked amongst themselves. I noticed that the women all wore very sensible shoes, like the ones Carol had on, and suddenly it made sense – they were standing up all day. I remembered where I'd seen other Jehovah's Witnesses and went around town until I'd been to every location, but Carol was not with any of them.

Over the next few weeks, I no longer had any reason to be at home. The dream-consultation software was running like a dream. The AI bots were sophisticated enough to not need manual tweaking. Zuzanna was mainly dealing with the associated problems that came with having a software platform going viral. Our joint bank account went in the red at one point as she bought more server space, more cloud hosting. We'd not considered the difficulty of scaling up. The free trial had brought people in, but was costing us a fortune. She sold some of her cryptocurrency via one of the new exchanges, and I cashed in an ISA I'd had for over a decade.

By the end of the second week, things were stable, but Zuzanna had been asked to fly to San Francisco to meet some venture capitalists who were interested in investing. I could have gone over with her, but she didn't need me there, and I have always hated long-haul flights.

Our last night together we didn't even want to make love, it was enough to just lie beside each other in a kind of mutually exclusive silence punctuated by occasional small reminiscences.

'Maybe you will have dreams when I'm away,' she said finally.

'I don't think so,' I said sadly.

Over a year earlier, several months before Zuzanna moved in with me, there were a group of us from work in the pub. It was a happy-sombre occasion. There had been a large number of redundancies. I'd somehow managed to hang on, but most of my friends had taken the money. Jack started by saying 'I had the strangest dream last night'. Everyone groaned. 'We don't want to hear it,' Lindsey said. 'No, I do,' I interrupted suddenly. 'Tell me.' I listened to what Jack had to say, and, without being asked, gave my interpretation. The others then told their dreams, so there was only me and Lindsey left. 'Oh, go on then,' she said, and hers was the strangest and saddest of the lot.

'Now your turn,' she said.

My brow furrowed. I couldn't remember what I'd dreamt last night. Nor the night before. Nor, I realised, for endless nights before that.

'I don't dream,' I said, finally.

'You must have - you just don't remember them.'

I went quiet, and they didn't push me on it. A week later I put in a request for redundancy and it was accepted.

Experiments monitoring brain activity during sleep have indicated that even non-dreamers do dream, they just don't remember them. I recall having dreamt as a child, but at some point I must have stopped remembering them.

That was when I'd set up the dream-consultation business. I realised it was partially vicarious, as I pored over the recollections of other people's dreams, yet never had my own to share. Perhaps this immersion would help me; but after over a year of doing this, I still didn't dream.

With Zuzanna away, I was free to spend my time as I wished. I copied the memory card from the CCTV onto my computer, and watched again the footage of my last client climbing the stairs and ringing the bell, and then coming in for her consultation. I had a phone number and email address for her, but as she'd not booked another consultation I didn't really know how to use them without worrying her.

I had identified five regular spots where the Jehovah's Witnesses assembled, and there were at least three there every day, usually a man and two women. That meant fifteen people in town every day, and I never saw the same ones twice at the same spot, which meant that, assuming they took Sundays off, there would need to be 4,500 over the course of a year. It couldn't be possible that there were so many in a single town. I would just need to keep looking and eventually I would bump into Carol again, as if by accident.

What did I want to say to her?

I wanted to know if she'd continued to have the dream about Donald Trump after seeing me, or if I'd somehow cured her.

The communications with Zuzanna had become more haphazard. I always knew how to find her, of course. There were a number of geek channels that she had set up for discussing the software, and then again, there were the forums devoted to cryptocurrency. But non-work communications had almost ceased. I realised I hardly knew her. I even created an account under another name with the dream-consultation bot. Without dreams of my own, I recycled some of the many that had been told to me over the year. The bot was good. The explanations were plausible. I recognised my own contributions to the algorithm, but after a few days of this, I realised the bot was responding in a way that I never could have. Whereas I would hear twenty dreams a week, this software was hearing twenty thousand. And, just as Zuzanna had predicted, genuinely new dreams were rare.

By this point nearly everyone was having dreams about Donald Trump.

☙

I only intermittently checked my bank account, so it was a surprise when the ATM ate my payment card. I went online as soon as I could get to a computer.

Zuzanna had withdrawn the last of our funds. How could I have been so stupid as to trust her?

But there was a message from her on one of the secure channels.

'I've had to protect our investment,' she said, 'and here's the key.'

She had sent me a link to an online wallet for her crypto-currency. I used the credentials she had provided me with and there it was – my money had all been transformed into something virtual and, rather than stealing from me, Zuzanna had made me a multi-millionaire. But without Zuzanna around to explain how, I couldn't easily transform this into any currency I could actually spend.

With my need for some petty cash, and having started biking around town all day to speed up my watch of the Jehovah's Witnesses, I signed up to be a courier for one of the new gig-economy delivery firms.

It was a week after I started that I took the order for pizza. My bike was idling on the strip where the restaurant was, but the delivery was out of town, at the edge of our normal delivery zone. I worked out that I could make this my last of the day, and head back via a different route to where I lived. Zuzanna had asked for a face-to-face via video conference that evening. I picked up the delivery from the pizza restaurant and packed the boxes carefully before hoisting the backpack over my arms.

Although I knew the area I wasn't sure of the actual address, as it seemed to be a side road on a quiet estate. I had to ease up when I got onto the estate to work out which road it was on. It was called the Orchard estate and so there was an Apple Drive, a Pear Tree Avenue and, tucked away, a Blossom Close. I jumped off the bike, but I wasn't in a particular hurry, other than to get back for Zuzanna.

I found number five, a tidy, nondescript maisonette, with a sharp message on the glass of the porch: 'No Flyers. No Hawkers.'

The door was opened after a couple of rings by a boy around twelve years old.

'Hi. Pizza,' I said, smiling.

'Mum!' he shouted.

There was a shuffling behind him and he just stood there. Given that payment was on the app I could just hand it over to him, but I thought I should wait for an adult.

A woman came to the door. It was Carol, my last client. With my cap on, advertising the delivery firm I worked for, and her focus on the pile of pizza boxes in front of me, she didn't notice me at first.

'Hi, it's Carol, isn't it?'

She looked up. There was recognition but puzzlement.

'You came for a consultation. A dream consultation.'

She smiled.

'This is funny, meeting you here,' I said, but wasn't sure what was funny about it.

'I live here,' she said.

'Of course. I gave up the business,' I said. 'It wasn't working out for me.'

'Oh, that's a shame,' she said. 'You were very helpful.'

'Was I?' I said. 'It's hard to tell. Most people don't come back, so I never got much feedback. But there's an app now you can use any time you want and it lets you give a rating on how helpful the service was.'

'An app?'

'Yes, for interpreting dreams. You can download it to your phone. There's always someone there when you want to discuss them.' I didn't want to tell her that it was a bot rather than a person. I should probably have brought a flyer. But, of course, I never expected to bump into one of my ex-clients doing this job.

'Do you still dream of Donald Trump?' I asked.

I thought she was going to close the door on me.

'Doesn't everyone?' she asked, genuinely surprised.

'I don't,' I said, truthfully.

'You're lucky,' she said.

There was a voice from inside. A man's voice.

'It's the pizza delivery guy,' she shouted back.

'I shouldn't have come,' she whispered. 'Alan doesn't know.'

'Oh,' I said, 'well, I'm glad you did. You were my last client.'

'Really?'

'The app,' I said.

'Oh yes.'

We stood there, more awkwardly than before. I wanted to say something.

'I liked your shoes,' I said, stupidly. 'They seemed very sensible.'

We both looked down at her feet. She was wearing bunny-rabbit slippers.

'Thank you,' she said, amused.

The solid brogues were neatly lined up on a shoe rack just inside the porch door.

'Enjoy your pizza.'

'I hope it all works out for you,' she said.

'Oh, this is only temporary.'

'I have to go.'

'Your pizza will be getting cold.'

'Yes, my pizza will be getting cold.' She was about to close the door, then she hesitated.

'They don't stop,' she said, 'the dreams. Once they start, I mean. Every night. It scares me, I don't know what to believe in any more.'

'It's all right,' I said, 'dreams don't really mean anything. I'm sorry if I gave you the impression that they did. People want them to mean something, but they're just . . .'

'Random detritus?' she said.

'Yes, random detritus.'

She closed the door behind me and I wheeled the bike off the estate.

When I got home it was time for my call with Zuzanna. It was early afternoon in the States. The connection wasn't that great. She kept fading in and out. At the end of it, I realised she wouldn't be coming back. I stayed up as late as I possibly could before my tired eyes got the better of me and I lurched over to the cold, empty bed.

In a second I had fallen asleep.

That night I dreamt I was on Air Force One having a New York pastrami sandwich with Donald Trump.

WEANING

SHE WAS LOSING the names of places. Every time she dropped a feed, let the milk in her breasts come then lessen, another part of the city disappeared. Someone once said Sheffield was a dirty picture in a golden frame. She was forgetting both, the town and the gritstone encircling it. One bright Sunday, she walked out past The Norfolk Arms and the black clutch of the plantation. The baby sat upright in the heather with his chubby legs splayed, shoving strawberries into his mouth and letting the juice trickle down his chin. She ate nothing, tried to count the green tower blocks in her line of vision. Gleadless. She said it out loud so she would not forget. Her husband phoned, his voice steady with concern.

'Where are you?'

'We've gone for a walk.'

'Where?'

'The place where I climb. The big rocks. Beside the car park.'

Later, she learned that it was Burbage. They had a map in the house, inherited from her father-in-law and she circled it in biro, marked a neat X.

As the weeks passed, the map became a maze of noughts and crosses. Attercliffe. Meersbrook. Norton. She pinned it to the wall of the bedroom with blu-tack and when the baby slept she could run her palm flat over it, feel the indentations of the pen, trace an inventory of her loss. Other names were stubbornly recalled. Meadowhall. Don Valley. Owlerton. When she was a teenager, she used to kill time thumbing through the records in Rare and Racy on Devonshire Green even though her parents owned no record player. On the wall was a framed map of Sheffield bomb-sites. The black circles looked like bullet holes. The map seemed to have more dots than spaces. Her grid of the city was starting to feel like that. The shop was gone now and she wondered what had happened to all the records.

One morning, she woke up with the word Heeley on her tongue. She had been dreaming of the City Farm, the sturdy legs of the goats that crowded by the fence and lunged for scraps, alert and noisy, the smell of wet straw and new rain, the farmyard cat who stalked between the pens. By lunchtime, Heeley had gone and she was forced to find the road on the map, the place she knew the farm was. The Health Visitor called round while she was unloading bags of shopping from the car.

'Is this a good time?'

They drank lukewarm tea from mugs decorated with pictures of biscuits. The Health Visitor's said I *Know How To Party* underneath a drawing of a pink frosted party ring. The Health Visitor asked her about the crying spells and how long they lasted, whether she was getting enough sleep. The Health Visitor did not ask about the place names and their slow vanishing. The Health Visitor nodded earnestly and kept her hands folded in her lap.

'The way you feel is nothing to do with weaning, with breastfeeding,' she said. 'You're looking for something to blame.'

The Health Visitor left her with the address of an Australian website offering Cognitive Behavioural Therapy. A gym for moods. You had to pay. Then you had to answer a series of questions. They were called Initial Questions. She scrolled through them on her phone at night but none of them seemed relevant. The only important question now was *where am I?*

She had taken to falling asleep holding her son's snowsuit. It was maroon-coloured with a fur trim and it had only fitted him for a short time when he was newborn and his head still flopped. Now, at night, she clutched it and imagined him older in the snow, pictured him toddling through all the white-covered, quiet places of the city, the parks now nameless to her. She thought of his footprints in the woods by the side of the stream. There were crossing places, rough stones that dogs scampered over, low overhanging branches. There was a memorial to a plane that came down here decades ago, crashing into the bank. There were climbing frames and silver slides and swings where children squealed to be pushed higher. There were places for sliding, families dragging sledges obediently up the slopes. How could she keep her son safe and near if she did not know where he was walking? She took the map down and shone the light of her phone on it, haloing the script, the roads and boundaries. Endcliffe Park. Bingham Park. Whiteley Woods. She circled every one obediently.

When he fed from the bottle, her baby was meek as a small

lamb or a piglet, swallowing quietly, the formula milk running down his chin. She sat him in the crook of her arm and kissed the top of his head as she tilted the teat towards his mouth. The tablets were making her wake at 2 am, 3 am. Her heart skittered. Outside, foxes made their low, catastrophic noises, ran along the tops of fences, skirted over walls and vanished into the last secret places of suburbia.

She read articles: 'The Hardest Eight Weeks of My Life' and 'What Nobody Told Me About Oxytocin'. She scrolled through advice on stopping breastfeeding, found only support to continue. But mostly, she read the map, running her finger from left to right and from top to bottom, following the course of the A57 out through Broomhill and Crosspool, skirting Rivelin and curving towards Strines. She could remember driving out to Ladybower, misjudging the bends and taking them too quickly, watching the wire hair and rust of the moors easing into view.

Standing before the full-length mirror, she found her breasts had disappeared altogether. For the last six months, they had been swollen with milk, pale blue veins standing out under her skin. Now, her profile had flattened. Her nipples were the colour of freckles. She dropped her t-shirt to the floor and ran a hand down from her collarbone to her navel the way she touched the map. Her body was Sheffield. She would have to learn it again.

From the top of their road she could see the south side of town. In Sheffield you could always get a view of somewhere else, always get up high enough to look across the rooftops. Still, she sought out elevated places. The Greystones pub with its tarmac, makeshift beer garden. The Brothers Arms. The high point of the General Cemetery. Each of her journeys was charted, noted on the map with a faint line lest she forget it. At home, her phone buzzed with messages.

You should breastfeed again. He's still so tiny.

You should stop gradually.

You should stop quickly if you're going to do it. Like pulling off a plaster.

It's hormones.

It's sleep deprivation.

It's emotional.

You're grieving for your child.

She deleted the mood gym. She stopped texting friends back. When that wasn't enough, she drove down Abbeydale Road South, out through Totley to Owler Bar and then across to Barbrook. She left the car in the lay-by and walked the deep groove of the track out to the little reservoir. There were aimless ducks and the remnants of disposable barbecues, patches of blackened grass. A lone swimmer was making pitiful progress through the weed and peaty sludge, his face set with determination. She crouched by the side of the bank and cupped her hands around her phone and released it into the water as if she were returning a frog to the wild. It slipped easily into the darkness and was gone. On the way back, she visited the stone circle. A flattened ring of twelve squat stones, angled towards each other, their conversation long since interrupted. She consulted her map to know what surrounded her. Ramsley Moor and Big Moor. Then the unnamed things, the indifferent sky and the slow planes.

She began to enjoy the way her son handled food, his

detachment and curiosity. He would lift raspberries into the air and repeatedly scrunch them between his fingers, only putting them towards his mouth as an afterthought. When she gave him strips of bread, he sometimes chewed on them but just as often raised them and let them drop ceremoniously. Crusts gathered on the kitchen floor. Then he would grin his toothless smile and grunt. There was joy in the letting go. He loved to throw squiggles of pasta, to flatten his hands in peanut butter. She took him to cafes in the city centre where he flung the mango and avocado she'd so carefully sliced and packed in a plastic tub on the ground to be squashed and trodden, oozing juice into the reclaimed boards. Nobody ever minded. Everybody smiled at his smeared face, the blobs of food on his nose and forehead.

On the last day of the eighth week, she bundled her baby into a sling and set off from Lady's Bridge, checking the map as she went, not for directions but for place names. There was a spidery footbridge, metal and tall. The Cobweb Bridge. Her footsteps echoed on it. The walls were pink and green with graffiti. She could follow the Five Weirs Walk all the way past the industrial estates and then walk back along the canal to the basin. It was a grey, humid morning and she was sweating already. There were diversions and footpath closures and the route sent her past old foundries and sleepy sandwich shops with chalkboards outside. The could hear welding, men shouting over the din. Somehow, just when it seemed she would never rejoin the water it would appear, rushing constant on her left. Attercliffe, a proud bridge, the weir running silver. By the shopping precinct, she took her baby out of the carrier and leaned him forwards towards the sound. A heron appeared to their right, stepping thoughtfully from depth to shallows. Her son squealed and flapped his arm, bird-like and sudden. There were shopping trolleys and tyres, lengths of orange rope. Life was everywhere around them, endless and derelict and broken. It did not matter, she thought, what any of this was called. It was all pure river.

PURITY

EDWARD AND MARCIA had got into the habit of walking along the cliff-top at dusk. What, here on Auskerry, Edward was tempted to call *the gloaming*. The sultry day was much cooler now and, indeed, would soon be cold. At this latitude the summer sky was still pale, but the first stars could already be made out. Marcia had something she wanted to tell Edward and Edward did not want to hear it.

They ambled hand in hand towards the remains of the chapel, not really intending to reach them. Marcia said she would show him the whirlpool she had been observing that afternoon, a new and especially large one. Her red hair looked almost purple in this light. She was lustrous, thought Edward. She was certainly pregnant, he could tell that, and she knew it, and she was very happy. Despite everything, Marcia had always wanted a child.

She couldn't leave her telescope unattended on the cliff, but Edward had his binoculars and he stood and looked out at the whirlpool while Marcia sat on a rock, brushed the small stones out of her sandals and explained it to him. She had noted it a week before, but it must be much older, unless it had grown unusually quickly. It was as though the water were being slowly stirred by the invisible spoon of a giant cook. Marcia would film it if they could charge the battery for the camera. Edward nodded. If she liked. The seals were gone from the beach. Luckily, there were no pups at this time of the year.

Edward wondered who the father of his wife's child might be. He could not be absolutely sure that it was not himself, but he was almost so. That was what Marcia did not know. The extent to which Edward was sterile. He had kept that from her. She thought that they had just been unlucky so far.

- There's a chance we will see a meteor tonight. It is the Perseid season. It will be easier after midnight, when it gets really dark, he said.

He knew they wouldn't be out so late.

So, who was the father? He couldn't believe it was that old goat Jack, let alone Denny, and there was literally no one else on the island. It could have been one of the visitors. There had been none for months now and he couldn't recall any of their faces. None of them had ever spent a night on Auskerry. That would have been quick work even by Marcia's standards. Maybe Edward had got lucky, if that was the word for it. Of course, from the gene-spreading point of view, a random tourist could be a good idea, setting aside the barbarity of it.

Marcia started to talk about what fun it might have been to be on an island like this when you were a child and she might have told him then, but they were both stopped by Monboddo's stentorian roar. A sound they had heard many times. The eeriest sound they had ever heard certainly and not alarming, nor unexpected, even, but every time they heard it it moved them. It could not be heard without emotion.

Monboddo was the leader, at the moment, of the orangutan clan that had taken control of the chapel ruins and the area around the lighthouse. The roar was not directed at the humans, or probably not. The ape might have been moved by the churning whirlpool, or he might have seen a comet.

Edward and Marcia saw a group of the apes now a few hundred yards ahead of them, sitting, relaxed, chins on chests, like so many boulders or standing stones. The husband and wife knew these particular animals and could have approached them, but they had no wish to disturb and so turned around and began to walk slowly back towards the compound.

- *Apes of idleness* is Shakespeare, you know, said Marcia. I read that today.

- Apes and monkeys are known for mischief, cheek and lust.

Edward pointed out the late blossom on the brambles. There were still buttercups in spring and blackberries in autumn. That made the island seem normal, although normal, he supposed, was just what you got used to.

Behind them, Monboddo raised his long arm and pointed far into the galaxy.

Edward wandered around the compound to see about the fences. It was nonsense of course to build fences to keep out orangutans, but he felt it provided some kind of discouragement, although it could prevent no determined animal. There was an ape on the roof now. He thought he recognised the young male, Conrad, who had learned to spin a teetotum and who had then exhausted his interest in that, or his understanding of it, and could not be persuaded to pick it up again. But Edward couldn't be sure it was Conrad at all. The light was against him.

His interest in the fencing was motivated by the fact that someone or something was breaking it regularly. The staples were pulled out of the posts and wires prised apart. It would take some strength, but who was doing it? Jack and Denny Norton, the stockmen, did not bother fencing their own house and they viewed Edward's arrangements with some disdain, but he did not think that they would take the trouble to break his fence.

Jack had said that the fence made it look as though Edward and Marcia were in a cage while the apes roamed free. *Beasts*, Jack called them.

When he went inside, Edward was careful to shut the door properly behind him. Conrad could stay on the roof if he wanted to. There was an ape skull on the shelf where Edward threw his hat. That had never met with any attention. There had been a stuffed orangutan, on which coats had been hung, in the hall, but he had had that burned as soon as they had moved in.

The distressing gurgling in the pipes meant Marcia was in the shower. He hoped she had bolted the door. The orangutans loved being squirted with the shower hose. Unless the bolt was thrown, they always, at least one of them, appeared in the doorway for a spray. Then they would run away grunting indignantly and happily, their faces puckered with delight, only to reappear within a minute for another go.

Udo was sitting in the armchair listening to music. Or at least he was wearing the headphones, which he liked to do. He was leafing through the photograph album, another favourite pastime, and he ignored Edward. Udo turned over the cardboard pages of the book with that meticulousness and apparent hauteur that animals have. This kind of behaviour was an indulgence that Edward was barely prepared to allow. Was he being ignored? Was it appropriate to say that of an ape? Well, when he and Udo sat in this room together and

Marcia came in, the ape did not ignore her, he could tell you that. Edward took the album from Udo and looked at the page. A much younger Marcia in a bathing costume. He wondered if Udo could recognise her. What did an animal, who lived so much in the present, make of a photograph? He closed the album and replaced it on the shelf. These were not scientific questions. Udo removed the headphones and folded his hands across his great belly.

– Very well, he seemed to be saying, I am listening. What is it you want?

Udo had picked up some kind of stress injury to his right arm. They had seen him favouring it. He allowed Edward to examine him now. Some swelling, but healing was in progress.

As soon as the door from the bedroom clicked open and Marcia walked in, Udo broke away from Edward and waddled over to the woman. The apes walked awkwardly on the ground like great damaged spiders, appearing to have longer and more limbs than they do. Marcia kissed and tickled the ape, while Udo feigned, or felt, hilarity. She gave Udo the jug of pens and he scuttled off to find paper as if eager to please her.

– If apes are capable of nostalgia, said Edward, does that mean it is a mistake to say that animals never feel that, or should we say that the apes are no longer animals?

Now Marcia ignored him. Edward was annoyed with her for meddling with his experiments, muddling their purity, and she could tell that. Udo should really be in a cage outside with the other subjects Jack and Denny brought in for weighing, measuring and blood-testing.

– You shouldn't kiss the apes, you know. We had one go blind last month and we don't know why.

Edward had finally agreed to let Jack shoot the blind

orangutan, an elderly female, but the creature had gone missing before Jack could catch up with her.

– I think you're jealous, Edward.

Marcia now tried to kiss Edward, but he shied away, not wanting to put his lips where Udo's had been.

Jack Norton walked in, followed by his son, Denny, having no more notion of knocking on the door than an ape, perhaps hoping to surprise Edward and Marcia in just such a situation.

Old Jack's stone face spoke a one-word vocabulary: scorn. His son was simple-minded and therefore friendlier looking. Nonetheless, they were clearly father and son.

– What's he listening to? asked Denny.

Udo had the headphones on again.

– Benjamin Britten, said Edward.

– I'd rather listen to a blackbird, said Denny.

– Oh, Denny, said Marcia, smiling.

– Shut up, Denny, said his father.

Jack thought Edward and Marcia, equally, were too soft with the apes, too intimate with them and at the same time too squeamish. Jack would not give the apes names, though Denny would. Edward looked at Denny's filthy T-shirt, which he wore almost all of the time that he wasn't bare-chested. It had the words *Spit Car* printed on it, which he supposed was a band, or had been once.

Edward was not surprised, but he was dismayed, to see that the Nortons had a brace of rabbits almost certainly intended as a gift for them, but actually a torment. Neither Edward nor Marcia could skin and gut a rabbit. When they had first been given such a gift, they should have confessed this, but Edward, at least, had been too ashamed and now, many rabbits later, it was too late. They would have appreciated the fresh meat. Edward had buried the gifts behind the compound and had had to bury them deep in case an ape dug them up and humiliated him. There was a rabbit cemetery back there now. Sometimes they were given a haunch of seal meat, strictly speaking, contraband. That was vile. Either they didn't know how to cook it, or it was always vile.

Edward looked at Jack and Denny with helpless disgust. They were very hairy men, with hairy wrists even, while Edward was fair and balding. Even Udo was going a little thin on top. The apes were slowly becoming Scottish people while the stockmen devolved. There were always males hanging around this house, hanging around Marcia really.

Marcia gave their guests a small glass of wine each and Edward took the rabbits without thanking. Jack would leave his wine untasted somewhere discreetly before he left while Denny tossed his back and made an extraordinary face at what he found to be the appalling sourness of the drink. Marcia stood close to Denny during this performance, partly because she found it so amusing and also because it prevented Denny from staring so candidly at her breasts, which he would otherwise do throughout the visit. Denny's potential excitement at the chance of overlooking Marcia's sunbathing antics was easily imagined by Edward.

Udo wanted a glass of wine, but Edward would not allow that. Jack snorted. Edward felt closer to Udo than he did to Jack or Denny.

A small female orangutan, Grace, now appeared from the bedroom, where she had been rummaging absolutely without permission, wearing Marcia's bra on her head, in imitation of Udo's headphones. Denny was overjoyed, pointed at Marcia's chest and choked on the dregs of his wine. Edward blushed, somewhat to his own amazement.

After the stockmen had left, Edward asked Marcia if she was all right. She was surprised and guessed that he wanted to be asked the same question, but she wouldn't ask it.

– Denny, he said.

– Well, naturally, I do feel very slightly eaten alive.

He put his arm around her shoulders and smoothed the palm of his hand proprietorially across her breasts. Udo stared and Marcia gave a soft chuckle which could have meant any-thing, Edward thought.

At the quay where the tourists used to disembark, there was a signboard giving the history of the Auskerry experiment in some detail. No one ever read it. It had been erected in the wrong place so that you had to shuffle past it too quickly, to get out of the way of the people behind you. Besides, everyone already knew what it said and most of the visitors were more interested in the birds, or even the plants.

The signboard reminded everyone of Lord Monboddo's famous declaration, *the orangutan is an animal of human form, inside as well as outside . . . the dispositions and affection of his mind, gentle and humane, are sufficient to demonstrate him a man*. He had also said that the orangutan is like a man because he can feel shame, but that was not on the board. Strange man Monboddo, after whom, by tradition, an or-angutan was always named; he was important in the history of nudism, being a champion of what he called the *air bath*, which he practised in the privacy of his bedroom.

None of the orangutans now on this island had ever been to Borneo or Sumatra. It had been some generations since those places had become no longer habitable by apes and some ten years now since the last human had left, so far as anyone knew. The Laird of Auskerry, coincidentally, Marcia's great-great-grandfather, had paid for the capture and transport to Orkney of as many of Indonesia's orangutans as was practicable. The cost had been extraordinary, but far from crippling for a man of such wealth.

The project had attracted some criticism. Some thought that these funds might have been more sensibly expended in aid of the many millions of humans displaced at that time. Others suggested that Orkney was a wholly unsuitable habitat for orangutans. These people simply failed to understand the nature of the experiment, thought Edward.

The apes had taken time to even begin to get used to the new environment. Some of them, dominant males, had become unduly aggressive, exhibiting signs of what it would not be wrong to call mental illness. A number had been destroyed. Jack would have loved that. A few young apes had been born with egregious deformities and these creatures had also been destroyed. The first births of healthy orangutans had been greeted with joyful excitement. Since then there had been more than one instance of twins, unheard of in south-east Asia.

The climate of Orkney had been a challenge to the apes, an inspiration to their renowned intelligence. Of course the island was now warmer and much more humid than it had once been. That suited the apes better. Air quality had deteriorated in some respects. Humans often suffered asthma-like symptoms, which had yet to be observed in the orangutan. Edward had once found an asthmatic ape, but further investigation had shown that the animal had been imitating the symptoms, perhaps mocking a sufferer, and was perfectly free from respiratory difficulties.

It could not be denied that the Auskerry experiment was compromised. It was not being conducted according to the purest principles. The two species of orangutan had been intermingled unavoidably, for a start. The world was stricken and this was the best that could be managed. No one was pretending that this was a really good idea; the world was out of really good ideas. Much of the southern hemisphere was inarguably in crisis and Scotland was fortunate to enjoy even this level of normality.

The apes were now prospering. Predictions were being confounded. Truth to tell, there were perhaps already too many orangutans on Auskerry. It was yet to become clear how such a dense population, in itself a success, would affect the apes, and what the man in charge of the experiment, effectively Edward, would do about it, if anything.

Edward considered that the apes represented something very old and something new, a starting again. How would human beings adapt to a world of ecological disaster? They might need to become less civilised in order to survive. Which was the most endangered species on Auskerry?

What Edward thought that he had observed among the island's inhabitants was the development of a system of segregation, even Apartheid.

The arrival of a boat was always good news, but Jack complained about the unloading, although it was definitely one of his jobs.

- I'll have arms like a fucking orangutan if I have to do this much longer.

Edward made a note to speak to Jack about his agricultural language in front of the tourists, and Marcia. He had never got round to that and he didn't need to now, because there had been no tourists and very little contact with the mainland for some months.

When there had been visitors, Edward had done his best to intercept them before they could ask Jack and Denny any questions about the apes. They were both actually quite knowledgeable about birds.

– What do the apes eat?

– What I give them, Jack generally said, as though he was used to feeding them gravel.

– Hungry enough, they'll eat it.

If they asked Denny, he would reply, cheerfully,

– Same as me.

That was close to being true, but as Denny was often eating a choc-ice, and spreading a great deal of it over his face, when he offered this answer, it did not give a good impression of the project. Although it was a fact that Grace would crawl through fire for a lick of Denny's choc-ice.

Edward evaded the other favourite question, which was how many apes were there. He did not know. How was he meant to carry out a census with only Jack and Denny to help him and Jack more or less refusing to do it?

The apes ought to have been an attraction to tourists, but their behaviour was problematical. Certainly, Edward did not believe that the disappearance of the tourists could be attributed to anything the apes had done.

The orangutans had taken to occupying the stone structures on the island and they could be territorial about them. The visitors had to be warned off. But then the apes were curious about the tourists and were inclined to imitate them, following them about, looking at birds, pointing at seals, crowding round to listen to Marcia's flirtatious conversation.

When he saw the apes pretending to be human, Edward sometimes wondered whether they were only pretending to be apes.

They could be embarrassing. Occasionally, some of the young male orangutans became very interested in the sheep. Denny drew everyone's attention to this whenever possible. Edward wondered what the apes thought about Jack killing the sheep. The young males would also masturbate in front of the visitors, and that was not something that anyone wanted to see on their holidays. Edward had once seen an ape hunched over in fervid concentration as he guided a party past the outskirts of the chambered cairn and had quickly ushered the group towards the cliff-top. In the poor light, Edward had not been sure that the figure had not been Denny. Denny learned from the apes.

Edward tried to keep the Nortons busy with rat extermination. This was a difficult task as the poison was a temptation to the animals. And he got the stockmen to show visitors the various plants that may have been brought over with the orangutans and which had made their own desperate adaptation to the changing Orcadian climate. Jack liked plants and was usefully succinct in the telling of his careful observation. Denny was good at finding the plants and sometimes at remembering where he had found them.

The truly disturbing thing had been the time when the visitor had been attacked. Against all advice, indeed instruction, she had stepped away from the main party near the chapel, what was now unwisely referred to as the ape village, and she had been knocked down from behind. Clothing had been torn and a bag taken, which, it turned out, had contained only sandwiches. She had been badly rattled and threatened to make a fuss back on the mainland, but she hadn't, or, at least, if she had, no one had taken any notice. Edward had got that group off the island as quickly as he could. The assailant must have been one of the apes. Orangutans had once been famous for their gentleness, but they were animals and would behave instinctively under the right stimulus. Even so, Edward could not dismiss the suggestion, also not dismissed by Marcia, that the assailant had been Denny.

That had not been the last party of visitors, but one of the last. No tourists for a while now. No tourists and no supplies. If the food ran low there were the sheep, the rabbits, the seals, fish. Edward and Marcia would need Jack and Denny for that. No point in making enemies of them. It was not clear that they could easily leave the island. They had no seaworthy boat. Those were the arrangements.

Edward warned himself against paranoia. He had told Marcia how he had stepped out of the compound and seen two apes with their heads together and how they had pulled apart when they saw him, as though they had been talking about him. Marcia had laughed. She was too carelessly brave, Edward thought.

The four people were trapped on the island as though the subject of an experiment conducted by an unknown hand.

The summer heat was sweltering, but their thick-walled old stone house was quite cool. Edward did not think that it was necessary for Marcia to wear so little.

– What if Denny comes in? You know he never knocks. Or Jack?

– Oh, fuck Jack and Denny. I'm not living my life to suit them. It's bad enough being trapped on this island at all.

She pulled Edward towards her by his orange tie, which he

wore, loosened, despite the heat. She let it run through her hand. Grace and Charity pulled his tie too.

Once or twice, Edward and Marcia had made love outside, outside of the compound, like animals, when they had been almost certain that the Nortons were busy with their poison on the other coast of the island.

Edward's opinion of Marcia as a scientist, as an oceanographer of a sort, was that she was bold, unpredictable and unorthodox. Sporadic in her efforts and that perhaps because she was suffering from a depression. What he most wished to speak to her about right now was sunbathing. Edward did not really know this, but he thought, indeed he feared, that Marcia was sunbathing naked or almost so, on the beach. He very much wanted to tell her not to do this.

– The Nortons might see you. Denny might, and the apes.

– What does it really matter if it is only them?

– I think it would matter very much to Denny. To the apes, not so much. Then there's the visitors.

– I don't sunbathe anywhere where anyone might see me. And I think you underestimate the Nortons. Even Denny.

– I don't know how you can be so naïve.

Marcia did not answer him.

– They'll see you, he said.

– The apes and seals are always naked.

While Marcia was out, Edward went into the bedroom and found the photograph album upset on the floor. The snaps were everywhere. He did not look very hard, but he did not see that photograph of the youthful Marcia in her bathing costume.

Marcia was by no means inclined to obey Edward, but along with her towel she took her telescope and folder. She made her way not to the beach near where the seals lay, but to the cliff-top above it. She wanted to look at the whirlpool in this tide and to sketch it. Such an old-fashioned technique, but the only way with whirlpools. Some of her watercolours were quite beautiful and they fascinated Denny. He even tore his eyes away from her chest to look at them. She might give him a sketch. It was hard to tell what was kindest: to *encourage* him, as Edward put it, or not. Marcia was well aware that the island was a lonely place, a place of longing and that she was the only woman on it.

Sometimes a handful of orangutans would sit on the cliff-top and, apparently, watch the seals. They were not there today. She set up her equipment, which involved taking a number of light readings, a procedure which required some precision. She scanned through the seals with the telescope. She counted them. She admired the great variety of shades and leprous speckles. The animals themselves were a whole beach of colours. It was here that she had found Denny's dog, the one that had bitten the young orangutan. It must have fallen off the cliff, the edge of which was treacherously friable, although Jack would not believe that. They were lovely. All of the animals were so beautiful. She knew that she and Edward lied to themselves all of the time and to one another now and then, but the animals were always themselves, unless they could learn to deceive.

She was distracted from the seals and from the whirlpool by three orangutans, all females, on the beach where she most usually sunbathed. That large flat stone where she luxuriated like a seal. She thought she recognised Grace and Charity, but the other ape she did not know. She watched them making their spidery progress over the rocky beach. They stirred pools with their long arms and scampered in that four-legged way from the sudden surf. It was a while before she could make up her mind that she knew what they were doing, but she could see them quite clearly through the telescope. They were gathering shellfish. They were eating as they gathered, as all gatherers do, and they also made a little pile of mussels and cockles to take away with them, Marcia supposed. She was sure that Edward had never noted this behaviour and she was pleased to have such a thing to tell him. Would they make themselves sick? Shellfish could be difficult for anyone.

Edward was wondering about the interest that the apes had in Marcia. They could become obviously sexually excited in the house, something that Denny invariably pointed out with glee. He had the mad idea that the sparring orangutan clans might compete for Marcia. He did not even know for sure that the clans were a real thing.

When Marcia told Edward what she had seen Grace and Charity doing, he clearly doubted her, even if he did not say as much. Marcia was upset and Edward did not bring up the sunbathing again. But he did notice that when she undressed, she did so in the dark so that he could not see if she had been wearing her costume, as he had intended.

Edward thought he might go for a swim. Not in the sea, which made him nervous, but in that stretch of peat-dark water they called a tarn, without really knowing what a tarn was. He wanted to walk and to have a think. He felt he had plenty to think about.

He had been watching the apes groom. He had been amused at the way Grace would graze her own forearm, nibbling at the midges and flies caught in the web of her long red hairs. The apes loved to groom one another and sometimes tried to demand this attention of Marcia and himself. Of course, Marcia gave in to them. He had watched her grooming Charity, and whenever she found a fly, a flea or a grub, she had popped it into the orangutan's mouth, very much as it was expected she should. Then Charity groomed Marcia, running her gentle leathery fingers through the woman's auburn hair and feeling through the folds and creases of her clothes. Charity found something and offered it to Marcia to eat and after only a moment's hesitation, Marcia had eaten it. This had disgusted Edward and he had said so. Marcia had told him that it was only a seed, but he did not believe her. He knew that she lied.

He walked over a rise and the little group of tarpans cantered away from him. He had ambitions to ride one of them one day. He knew that Marcia and Jack did too. The people competed for expertise in these things.

He thought the apes were consciously copying the humans. He had also noted that the animals to whom he had given names, who visited the compound most often and got talked to, were behaving differently to those wilder creatures, identified by codes if at all, who had to be captured to be brought in for measuring and tests.

Edward was afraid he was being ganged up on. His paranoia again. Jack and Denny seemed to have a stronger bond than him and Marcia, and he could no longer be sure of his wife's loyalty. He could command these people, push them around, but he had no faith in his own superiority, less than they had probably.

He looked around him. The sky was so blue and the new heather gave a sheen to the world. Marcia's colour, almost, he thought. This island could be an Eden were it not for Jack and Denny. Or should that be, were it not for Edward?

He reached the tarn and started to undress and fold his clothes neatly on the dry sand. He had brought his swimming trunks, the badge of his Fall, he noted, wryly. He felt a rock, smooth and hard like a large pebble, with his toes. This was not the place for pebbles. He dug at it with his toe and then his fingers, almost sure that it would be that common thing, the shallow brain pan of a sheep. But it was too round and clever for that. He pulled out the skull of a man from the reluctant sand but then weighed the lichen-stained head of an ape in his relieved palm.

He recalled a dream, one he had not recalled before. He had been cleaning the bath, spraying it with the shower attachment and the drain had been gathering hair, in a hirsute maelstrom. Hair is disgusting when you see it like that. The dirty soapy water being sucked thirstily, chokingly through all of that hair. More and more hair. Long red hair and then that metallic red which was Marcia's in the heather light, and he had a vision of Marcia and a powerful ape in the bath together, soaping one another with cheerful erotic abandon. Marcia ran her fingers through the thick pelt of Monboddo's muscular back and Edward knew it was not Monboddo but Denny even though he always remained an orangutan. Then he woke up.

Edward pulled up his trunks and stood with the brown water round his ankles. He could tell that the presence behind him was not a dream. For all of their caution he had detected their quiet bestial breathing. He could hear the coarse fluctuation of the cheek flaps of a large ape. He had conjured Monboddo from his dream. He did not know what to do.

Perhaps he ought to face the apes, the little group that he was sure waited behind him, but he could not summon his courage. They would throw him from the cliff like Denny's dog. He did not think that they would follow him into the water. He trod forward carefully, feeling his feet sink into the soft sand. He tried not to disturb the water as though that were the consciousness of the apes.

They did not follow him as he had supposed they would not. Nor did they begin to skirt the shore of the tarn as he had feared they would. He risked a glance behind him. The apes were picking through his clothes and draping them about themselves. His shirt was thrown into the water where it sank hopelessly.

To his left, just for a moment, he saw a figure he thought was Denny slip below the hill. He had raised a hand, but the figure was gone. Surely Denny would have helped him.

Edward walked slowly across the tarn. It was never necessary to swim, but he stroked the water aside with his arms as he waded up to his chest. Monboddo and his apes had not moved. Edward continued to look behind him, almost defiantly now, as he reached the further shore. This was why he did not see the second group of apes awaiting him there and which suddenly rose to meet his white dripping nakedness as he stepped into the air again. There were several apes here, all females. An elderly creature he did not know shuffled over to him, standing as upright as a man, and reached out her hand with its crooked wrist to touch his pale face. He dashed this away before she reached him and ran through the apes, painfully, breathlessly among the spiky heather in his silly swimming trunks. A shameful bleat might have escaped him. Again he was not followed, not even by a call.

Jack said it was Denny's birthday. Would they like to go over for a drink and some stew? Such an invitation was not turndownable. What might they say? They were busy? They had been asked elsewhere? The promise of stew was delightful. Edward put on a dark jacket and Marcia a tight but high-necked protective jumper. She had decided to give Denny a whirlpool sketch as a birthday gift.

Obviously, Denny's party was going to take place outside of the Nortons' house, inside which neither Edward nor Marcia had ever been. It was a barbecue, but with stew. There was music, loud and barbaric. There were many apes, some of which were more or less always there as though they regarded Jack and Denny's house as their own and some of which perhaps had been invited to the party. Much drink had already been taken. Also by the orangutans. Both Jack and Denny had taken off their shirts. Jack looked younger the more naked he was. Edward felt frail beside him.

The Dayaks have a story which says that the gods made the orangutan the day after they made men, but they had been celebrating and were still drunk. Some of the apes seemed to be playing with a ball. Others had umbrellas. They loved umbrellas. Denny was thrilled with his picture and took it immediately into the house. He went in to have a look at it several times during the party. Marcia, of course, could not be flattered and had half an idea that she should regret the gift.

Denny wanted to dance with Marcia and they did dance in a manner of speaking. But the music was horrible, and Denny did not know how to dance and was already a little too drunk. He reached out his hands in the hope that Marcia would take them, but she did not. His fingers wove the air like a magician's.

Jack and Edward looked on at them unhappily. Edward thought, for the first time, that he knew why Jack did not like him. It was because Edward was the purveyor of this useless and dangerous knowledge, this science. It was Edward's fault what had happened to Denny and to the world, and yet for all his cleverness he could not catch a fish, gut a rabbit nor even make a fire with that miraculous ease that Denny could manage.

Denny had stopped dancing and was now showing Marcia how he was trying to teach the apes to make a fire, in which they did seem to be very interested, but at which they had evidently made no progress. The apes might have done better if they were not drunk. Jack found their drunkenness funny. Edward thought the Nortons both too intimate with the apes and too brutal towards them. Jack called them *beasts*, but he drank from the same cup as them.

He went over to look at Jack's generator, powered by petrol. They had little enough of that left, but little enough use for it. Jack's contraption was ingenious. He wondered where he had learned of such things. He didn't really know anything about him. A young ape came over, sent by Denny, for some of the bundle of newspapers, to help light the fire. Then he became curious about the papers and began sorting through them, turning the pages and getting frustrated by how difficult it was for him to do that without tearing them. Various advertising inserts fell out promoting impossible goods and services. Among these Edward found the photograph of Marcia in the bathing costume. He gave it to the ape to put on the fire.

From his corner by the stinking machine, conscious that he was already a little tipsy himself, he had his vantage. Edward and Marcia thought the apes essentially beautiful. Jack and

Denny took it for granted that they were very ugly. Looking like an ape meant being ugly. Edward told himself he must not hate people and must not say that he did to Marcia. He no longer knew what counted as normal behaviour, for apes or humans. The answer was changing.

Jack was teasing Conrad, offering him a cup and then snatching it away from him, splashing him with the hot stew and flicking at his youthful cheek flaps as though in mockery. Jack had had too much. Edward could have stepped over and distracted Conrad, or Jack, but he decided to watch. The ape must finally have lost its temper, but in a way that Edward had not seen before. He reached out for Jack's hand and quietly crushed it, not brutally, not breaking anything, but from the new expression on Jack's face, very painfully. Then he let him go and Jack got up and left Conrad to sip punch and stew straight from the cauldrons.

That had seemed a very human punishment to Edward. That was not how the apes were with one another. He wondered if he would ever get off this island, over the abysmal sea.

Edward woke the next morning and found himself thinking about Denny. He felt he had to go to see him, to talk to him about Marcia. He wanted to punish Denny but did not know that he would be able to do that. Jack had been down at the quay all that morning and Edward knew that he would find Denny alone at his house, if he could find him at all. He made his way across the heather with empty hands.

In the ape world, to have three men competing for one woman would be a disaster. Who would win that competition if it were allowed to run its course? Who would Marcia choose if she were allowed to choose? A huge beetle zoomed past his ear.

Would it be a good thing if Denny were cleverer? More like Jack and less like the apes. The difference between himself and Denny was not a matter of education. It was more to do with language, or education made clear through language. It was not what Edward knew, because Denny knew a lot. But both Denny and Jack had a predictable lack of mental agility. If Denny were the father of Marcia's child, then it might be born an idiot.

He noted the tarn over to the left and became more aware of his surroundings. He was surprised he had not seen more orangutans. There were so many now it was unusual to see none on even a short walk and Edward had initially been on his guard against a large group. Jack had once joked, if it was a joke, that they might invite hunters to the island, as a way of raising revenue they did not need. He saw the smoke from the Nortons' fire. You could smell it even from here in this clear air. He might get a plate of stew before he had to speak harshly to this hairy boy.

He could see things were not right before he could see clearly how wrong they were. He had never known Denny the worse for drink except at his party and only a very drunk man would lie like that, and he was too close to the fire. The fire smelled bad. There were no apes around at all.

Denny was dead and his shoulder and one side of his face were burned or at least blistered. On the way to being meat. One arm was twisted under him unnaturally. He had been thrown or dragged there. He had not fallen like that. Where was Jack? Where were the apes? Edward could see Denny's rifle propped by the door. He got the boy out of the fire. One side of him smouldered but the other side of his face was largely undamaged by the flames. The fire had not been fierce.

Denny's body must have put it out. The unburned profile was the wrong colour. Red, even purple, but not because of the fire. He might have been poisoned, Edward thought.

Edward knew Jack was down by the quay, but he felt sure he would never see him again. This part of the island was for the apes now.

Edward had been running as best he could until his legs would not carry him through the heather any farther. He had fallen more than once and his face stung with the cuts from the unforgiving woody stems. He had wanted to get to the quay but did not really know the best way from Jack's house and he had not wanted to go via the compound because that was too far and perhaps for fear of what he might find there. Marcia had gone to the cliff-top or the seal beach.

He stumbled again. When he raised his head, that old female orangutan was looking into his watery eyes or off to the side of him as though she were blind. Her averted gaze allowed him to stare at her. She was beautiful. It was natural to love the apes, because they were beautiful. If this creature would come back to the compound with him, he would give her a nun's name as he had with Grace and Charity and others. What would that be? This is what was happening, so he knew that it was what was meant to happen, what had been hoped for. He reached for her face, the moustacheless chin beard a little grey. He stroked the beautiful muzzle. He hoped he had been forgiven for slapping at her hand after his swim in the tarn. She touched his sharp cuts with the tips of her tough fingers, tenderly.

CONTRIBUTORS'
BIOGRAPHIES

RICHARD LAWRENCE BENNETT is a writer and psychogeographer based in Arundel, West Sussex. His work has been published in *Ambit* and in the *Lounge Companion*. He is seeking representation for his debut novel *The Ramayana of Croydon* about mysticism in south London. You can find out more about him at www.richardlawrencebennett.com.

LUKE BROWN is the author of the novels *My Biggest Lie* (2014) and *Theft* (2020). He grew up on the coast of Lancashire and works as an editor in London as well as teaching at the University of Manchester. 'Beyond Criticism' was shortlisted and commended for Best Original Fiction in the Stack Awards 2019.

DAVID CONSTANTINE has published several volumes of poetry and a novel, *The Life-Writer*, as well as four short story collections: *Under the Dam* (2005), *The Shieling* (2009), *Tea at the Midland* (2012) and *The Dressing-Up Box* (2019). With his wife Helen he edited *Modern Poetry in Translation*. In addition, he has translated the work of Hölderlin, Brecht, Goethe, Kleist, Michaux and Jaccottet. Born in Salford, he lives in Oxford.

TIM ETCHELLS is an artist and writer based in Sheffield and London. His work shifts between performance, visual art and fiction. As well as being Professor of Performance and Writing at Lancaster University, he works in a wide variety of contexts, notably as the leader of Sheffield performance group Forced Entertainment. His 2019 collection *Endland* (And Other Stories) was a reprise (plus new stories) of his 1999 collection *Endland Stories* (Pulp Books). He was the winner of the 2019 Manchester Fiction Prize.

NICOLA FREEMAN started out in arts journalism and publishing and has since worked as a curator, writer and editor in museums and galleries. She is a Jerwood/Arvon mentee (fiction) 2019/20. 'Halloween' is her first published short story.

AMANTHI HARRIS was born in Sri Lanka and grew up in London. She studied Fine Art at Central St Martins and has degrees in Law and Chemistry from the University of Bristol. Her novel, *Beautiful Place*, is published by Salt Publishing in the UK and Pan Macmillan India. *Lantern Evening*, a novella, won the Gatehouse Press New Fictions Prize 2016 and was published by Gatehouse Press. Her short stories have been published by Serpent's Tail and broadcast on BBC Radio 4. www.amanthiharris.com

ANDREW HOOK has had over a hundred and fifty short stories published, with several novels, novellas and collections also in print. 'The Girl With the Horizontal Walk' is part of a series of 'Hollywood celebrity death' stories, *Candescent Blooms*, currently seeking a publisher. Stories from the series have appeared in *Ambit* and *Great Jones Street*.

Forthcoming are a collection of mostly SF stories, *Frequencies of Existence*, and *O For Obscurity, Or, The Story of N*, a fictionalised biography of the Mysterious N Senada written in collaboration with the legendary San Francisco art collective The Residents.

SONIA HOPE's short fiction has appeared in magazines including *Ambit, Nottingham Review* and *Ellipsis Zine*. She is a Jerwood/Arvon Mentee (Fiction) 2019/20 and was shortlisted for the Guardian 4th Estate BAME Short Story Prize 2019. She is a Librarian and lives in London.

HANIF KUREISHI has published eight novels, including, most recently, *The Nothing*. His most recent book, *What Happened?*, a collection of stories and essays, was published in 2019. Born in Kent, he now lives in London.

HELEN MORT was born in Sheffield and grew up in Chesterfield. She has published two poetry collections, *Division Street* (2013), and *No Map Could Show Them* (2016), and one novel, *Black Car Burning* (2019). Her short story collection, *Exire*, was published by Wrecking Ball and she co-edited *One For the Road: Pubs and Poetry* (Smith-Doorstop) with Stuart Maconie. She teaches creative writing at Manchester Metropolitan University.

JEFF NOON is an award-winning novelist, short story writer and playwright, born in Manchester and now living in Brighton. His first novel, *Vurt* (1993), won the Arthur C Clark Award. His most recent novels are *Slow Motion Ghosts* (2019) and *Creeping Jenny* (2020).

IRENOSEN OKOJIE is a Nigerian British writer. Her debut novel, *Butterfly Fish*, won a Betty Trask award. Her work has been featured in the *New York Times*, *Observer*, *Guardian* and *Huffington Post* among other publications. Her short story collection *Speak Gigantular* (Jacaranda Books) was shortlisted for the Edge Hill Short Story Prize, the Jhalak Prize and the Saboteur Awards. She is a fellow of the Royal Society of Literature. Her latest collection of stories, *Nudibranch*, was longlisted for the Jhalak Prize and one story, 'Grace Jones', won the AKO Caine Prize For Fiction.

KJ ORR was born in London. *Light Box*, her first collection, was shortlisted for the Edge Hill Short Story Prize and the Republic of Consciousness Prize in 2017, and includes 'Disappearances', which won the BBC National Short Story Award 2016. Her stories have appeared in publications including the *Irish Times*, *Dublin Review* and *White Review*, and been broadcast on BBC Radio 4.

BRIDGET PENNEY was born in Edinburgh and is now based in Brighton. Her book publications are *Honeymoon with Death and Other Stories* (1991, Polygon), *Index* (2008, Book Works) and *Licorice* (2020, Book Works). Stories and non-fiction have appeared in print and online magazines, among them *Gorse*, *Snow lit rev* and *3:AM Magazine*. She is founder and co-editor of Invisible Books, publishing innovative poetry and prose through the 1990s with occasional manifestations since. Currently she is guest-editor for Book Works' new series, Intertices.

DIANA POWELL lives in the far west of Wales. Her short fiction has been published in journals and anthologies such as *The Lonely Crowd, Crannog* and *The Blue Nib.* 'Whale Watching' was the 2019 ChipLit Festival winner and was runner-up in this year's Society of Authors ALCS Tom-Gallon Trust Award. Her work has also featured in a number of other competitions, including the 2020 TSS Cambridge short story prize (third place), the 2016 Sean O'Faolain (long-listed), Over-the-Edge New Writer (short-listed), Cinnamon Press Prize (runner-up). Her novella *Esther Bligh* (Holland House Books) was published in 2018 and her short story collection *Trouble Crossing the Bridge* (Chaffinch Press) came out in July.

DAVID ROSE was born in 1949. After attending a local Grammar, he spent his working life in the Post Office. His debut story was published in the *Literary Review* in 1989, since when he has appeared in a wide variety of magazines and anthologies. He was co-owner and fiction editor of *Main Street Journal.* His first novel, *Vault,* was published in 2011, followed by a collection, *Posthumous Stories,* in 2013 (both Salt). His second novel, *Meridian,* appeared in 2015 from Unthank Books. He lives between Richmond and Windsor.

SARAH SCHOFIELD's stories have been published in *Lemistry, Bio-Punk, Thought X, Beta Life, Spindles* and *Conradology* (all Comma Press), *Spilling Ink Flash Fiction Anthology* and *Woman's Weekly* among others. She has been shortlisted for the Bridport and Guardian Travel Writing competitions and won the Orange New Voices Prize, Writer's Inc and the Calderdale Fiction Prize. She is an Associate Tutor of Creative Writing at Edge Hill University and runs writing courses and workshops in a variety of community settings. She is working on her debut short story collection.

ADRIAN SLATCHER was born in Walsall and lives in Manchester. He writes poetry, fiction and music, and co-edits the poetry magazine/press Some Roast Poet (someroastpoetry.wordpress.com). His short fiction has previously appeared in *Confingo*, *Unthology* and *Litro*, and in *Best British Short Stories 2018*. He is currently working on a novel.

NJ STALLARD is a short story writer and poet. Her work has been featured in publications including the *White Review, Tank* and *Ambit*. She was the winner of the Aleph Writing Prize 2018.

ROBERT STONE was born in Wolverhampton. He works in a press cuttings agency in London. Before that he was a teacher and then foreman of a London Underground station. He has two children and lives with his partner in Ipswich. He has had stories published in *Stand, Panurge, The Write Launch, Eclectica, Wraparound South* and *Confingo*. Micro-stories have been published by Palm-Sized Press, 5x5, *Star 82 Review* and *Clover & White*.

STEPHEN THOMPSON is a novelist, screenwriter and documentary filmmaker. His novels are *Toy Soldiers, Missing Joe, Meet Me Under the Westway* and *No More Heroes*. His feature-length TV drama, *Sitting in Limbo*, about the Windrush Scandal, was screened by the BBC in spring 2020. He is the editor and publisher of the online literary journal, *The Colverstone Review*.

ZAKIA UDDIN is a writer of fiction and non-fiction. She is currently working on a collection of short stories.

ACKNOWLEDGEMENTS

'Energy Thieves: 5 Dialogues', copyright © Richard Lawrence Bennett 2019, was first published in *Ambit* issue 235, and is reprinted by permission of the author.

'Beyond Criticism', copyright © Luke Brown 2019, was first published in *Mal* issue 4, and is reprinted by permission of the author.

'The Phone Call', copyright © David Constantine 2019, was first published in *The Dressing-Up Box and Other Stories* (Comma Press), and is reprinted by permission of the author.

'Maxine', copyright © Tim Etchells 2019, was first published in *Endland* (And Other Stories), and is reprinted by permission of the author.

'Halloween', copyright © Nicola Freeman 2019, was first published in *Halloween* (Nightjar Press), and is reprinted by permission of the author.

'In the Mountains', copyright © Amanthi Harris 2019, was first broadcast on BBC Radio 4 on 23 August 2019.

'The Girl With the Horizontal Walk', copyright © Andrew Hook 2019, was first published in *The Girl With the Horizontal Walk* (Salò Press), and is reprinted by permission of the author.

'Safely Gathered In', copyright © Sarah Schofield 2019, was first published in *Wall: Nine Stories From Edge Hill Writers* (Edge Hill University) edited by Ailsa Cox and Billy Cowan is reprinted by permission of the author.

'Dreams Are Contagious', copyright © Adrian Slatcher 2019, was first published online in *LitroUSA* and is reprinted by permission of the author.

'The White Cat', copyright © NJ Stallard 2019, was first published in *The White Cat* (The Aleph), and is reprinted by permission of the author.

'Purity', copyright © Robert Stone 2019, was first published online in *The Write Launch* and is reprinted by permission of the author.

'Same Same But Different', copyright © Stephen Thompson 2019, was first published in *The Good Journal* issue 3, and is reprinted by permission of the author.

'Vashri', copyright © Zakia Uddin 2019, was first published in *The White Review* issue 24, and is reprinted by permission of the author.

BEST BRITISH SHORT STORIES

Best British Short Stories 2011
(978-1-907773-12-9)

Best British Short Stories 2012
(978-1-907773-18-1)

Best British Short Stories 2013
(978-1-907773-47-1)

Best British Short Stories 2014
(978-1-907773-67-9)

Best British Short Stories 2015
(978-1-78463-027-0)

Best British Short Stories 2016
(978-1-78463-063-8)

Best British Short Stories 2017
(978-1-78463-112-3)

Best British Short Stories 2018
(978-1-78463-136-9)

Best British Short Stories 2019
(978-1-78463-185-7)

NEW FICTION FROM SALT

VESNA MAIN
Good Day? (978-1-78463-191-8)

SIMON OKOTIE
After Absalon (978-1-78463-166-6)

TREVOR MARK THOMAS
The Bothy (978-1-78463-160-4)

TIM VINE
The Electric Dwarf (978-1-78463-172-7)

MICHAEL WALTERS
The Complex (978-1-78463-162-8)

GUY WARE
The Faculty of Indifference (978-1-78463-176-5)

MEIKE ZIERVOGEL
Flotsam (978-1-78463-178-9)

This book has been typeset by
SALT PUBLISHING LIMITED
using Neacademia, a font designed by Sergei Egorov
for the Rosetta Type Foundry in the Czech Republic.
It is manufactured using Creamy 70gsm, a Forest
Stewardship Council™ certified paper from Stora Enso's
Anjala Mill in Finland. It was printed and bound by
Clays Limited in Bungay, Suffolk, Great Britain.

LONDON
GREAT BRITAIN
MMXX